Island Crossfire

A New Enemy Arises

Stephen L. Thompson

Island Crossfire

A quick trip to save lives on the island of Mindanao forces the Crossfire Team into war with a branch of the Abu Sayaf terrorists in the Philippine Islands. They discover a new threat in the Middle East that is about to be unleashed on the world through a powerful union of world terror organizations and Criminal Cartels. Each member of the team has to stand alone as the team races to prevent all-out devastation in the Western world.

- Stephen L. Thompson

Island Crossfire

Published by
Stephen L. Thompson
Facebook.com/CrossfireNovelSeries

ISBN- 978-1-943879-08-3

Published in the United States of America

Foreword

To my Christian readers –

The Crossfire series of action/adventure stories include depictions of violence which are unusual in Christian literature. It would be nice if there were no conflict or violence in our world. But we live in a time when evil is increasing instead of diminishing, when some men seem to be controlled by selfishness, madness, or evil forces. When the enemies of decent mankind are bent on subjugation of other men and women, righteous men and women must stand against evil. Please remember that the yoke of oppression is not lifted by prayer alone. God is our shepherd and we are his sheep. As long as there are wolves about, God will use some of us as sheep dogs to defend the rest of us. These stories are about people like that and the forces they fight against. The stories describe violence because it occurs in the real world and it is active in the lives of all people whether they recognize it or not.

To my non-Christian readers –

The Crossfire series include depictions of spiritual warfare and spiritual activity with which the non-Christian may not be familiar. These stories describe the realms and activities of both God and Satan because they are real and active in the lives of all people whether they recognize it or not.

Steve Thompson

CHAPTER ONE

The dream ended so suddenly, Andrea Mullins was jarred awake uncertain of anything, even where she was. It was pitch black around her and while the smell of the jungle was heavy with rotting vegetation, she had a moment of hope that everything that seemed to have happened recently was simply a nightmare from which she was now waking up. That small hope was dashed when she felt the thick, scratchy rope that bound her ankles together.

Memories of death, blood, and sacrifice flooded back into her mind. Moving her hand she found her husband's back in the dark. He was still asleep and she didn't disturb him. She would tell him about the dream when he woke up. Putting her hands together she prayed, "Oh Father, I'm sorry we can't do your work and your will. My flesh would see all of these men destroyed, but, I know that is not your way and I choose to live the life of Yahshua. Your will Father, not mine." Her prayer winged its way heavenward.

In normal circumstances, Andrea was an attractive, dark-blonde woman in her forties who was still lovely in appearance and demeanor. Normally, she didn't use much in the way of cosmetics and dressed for efficiency and comfort rather than to impress others. Right now though, she was about as bedraggled as a woman could be. Considering they had been forced to march through the jungle for two days, sleep in the dirt, and not allowed to clean the sweat and dirt off of their faces or bodies.

Andrea lay still and thought through the events leading up to their laying here on the jungle floor, tied with ropes and guarded by men who meant to kill them very soon.

Less than a week ago, her husband Frank and she had followed the Master's leading in returning for the fifth time to the Philippines to proclaim the good news of Yahshua and to minister to the lost.

They had travelled to a remote village in the southern part of the island of Mindanao. This was in response to a plea for spiritual help from a Philippine minister. Andrea

1

was impressed by the faith of the remote village whose members were desperate for the Word of the Father.

After reaching the village along with ten members of their home church, they gave them food and clothing which they had brought with them. This was followed by a fantastic first service despite the fact that there were only thirty people in attendance, Frank and Andrea had spoken about the Christian life and almost all of the people had come to the altar to give their lives to Yahshua. There were many sick and lame people in the audience and Frank asked them if they believed that Yahveh would heal them. They expressed their new faith and unanimously said, "Oo!" which is Philippine for "Yes". As the team members prayed for the sick, miracles happened and everyone who wanted to be healed was healed. The Master did many miracles that evening but the one that stood out in Andrea's memory was the elderly lady in a battered old wheel chair. She had cataracts in both eyes so bad that her eyes were white.

In the press of people seeking healing, Mrs. Majore was prayed for by one of the newest members in their team. His prayer was earnest for healing for the woman and the Master had touched her mightily. Tyler Monroe, the new member, said that he was thrilled when her eyes cleared up and became like brand-new brown eyes. But the best part was that the Father also restored her limbs which had been shriveled and useless for forty years. The joy in her eyes was mirrored in the rest of the people who had helped to support her as she stood up on straight legs and reached out with perfect arms and hands to hug Tyler Monroe. After that, the balloon went up. Everyone there ran out of the service to tell everyone else about the miracles.

The next night the second service was crowded by over three hundred souls. Frank had started to tell them about the Savior when he noticed that the people in the back of the tent had started melting into the dark and a nervous tension swept over the people. Many got up and left the tent.

There were still about fifty people there when the Crescent Dagger rebels entered the tent from the back and both sides.

Andrea remembered her briefing about the violent splinter group of the original militant Zultarian group. They were an off-shoot of one of several guerrilla organizations involved in a resurgence of violence in the Philippines during the past years.

This particularly nasty group of terrorists operated in the south of the country. The Crescent Dagger terrorists were conducting a religious war against anything Christian, or for that matter, anything not Zultarian fundamentalist. Hostage-taking was their latest trick.

The Philippine Government had informed the ministry team that the Zultarians had been trying to evict Christians from Basilan Island and then advised them not to go into that part of the country because they would not be able to help them if they were captured by the Zultarians. The Crescent Dagger faction was the latest and fastest growing group of terrorists that allied themselves with the principles of Zultar. They had gotten such a bad reputation in the last year that the majority of terrorists in the Zultarian movement disavowed any connection to them. Not that they were bothered by the kidnappings and killings, they did those things themselves. It wasn't the cruelty and inhuman disregard for life, even that of Zultarians that the Dagger evidenced in all their actions. It was so anti-life that it was demonic; these things didn't cause the rejection. The problem for the other terrorists was that the Crescent Dagger's highly publicized violence was so over-the-top that it was allowing the government to build wide support with the people against all of the Zultarians and making their cause disreputable. Andrea felt a cold touch of dread as she watched them move towards the ministry team.

Several of the new believers interposed themselves between the rebels and the platform where the Americans were. The rebel leader shot three of them dead where they stood and the others were shoved out of the way. His men then came up onto the platform and took both her and her husband hostage, tying their hands behind them.

As the rebels started to drag them off the platform, Tyler Monroe stepped in front of them and told them to release the pastor and his wife in the name of Jesus. One of the rebels on the stage had stepped forward and, with a

3

vicious swing of his large knife, beheaded the young man. Blood flew everywhere as Tyler's body followed his head off the platform to the ground. Everyone was shocked into silence. The rebels picked up both Frank and Andrea and carried them into the night.

CHAPTER TWO

Frank's head was feeling much better after the third day's forced march. He thought that he'd be so tired he couldn't function. But, he found himself capable of making it all through the day without help from his wife. As he woke up on the fourth morning of their capture he actually felt hopeful. He signaled their guard and went into the bushes to take care of his bathroom needs.

When he returned he sat down next to Andrea and gave her a smile. She smiled back and moved closer to him. Casually looking around and seeing no one within hearing distance she told him. "I had a vivid dream last night. I was sitting in the jungle and a glow approached me. The glow coalesced into a beautiful gold and white angel. She told me that the Master heard our prayers for deliverance and He is sending His sword to free us." She looked at him and didn't see the look of hope she expected. "Don't you think that is good news?"

Frank wondered if the punch he got to his head was interfering with his talking with the Father. "I would say that it is good news but I can't seem to hear from Yahveh or Yahshua right now and I really don't know what to say. I will tell you that I believe our Father in Heaven will deliver us and it will be very soon."

She cocked her head to one side, "How do you know it will be soon?"

He looked at her and wondered if he should tell her. Knowing the truth is always better, he said, "It has to be soon. My potty guard laughed at me and told me that tonight they will kill us."

Andrea blinked once and said, "Oh." Then she told him about the Krait.

That day they didn't march anywhere. They had a meager breakfast or lunch and watched the rebels as they talked and played cards. At six o'clock they got a fairly good dinner meal and some cheap wine to drink. It wasn't hard to figure out the symbology. This was to be their last meal.

Just as it started to get dark the rebels got agitated and moved around a great deal. When it was dark, there were whispered commands and a lot of rustling of uniforms. Things got still as the majority of the rebels walked out of the camp to the west. Obviously it would be a short walk since they left everything but their rifles. The darkness closed down over the camp and it was a chilly night unrelieved by moonlight or any city glow on the horizon.

The sudden flare of a bright light transfixed the two Americans and then drew closer. Three men walked up to them and stopped. The leader with the cruel face had a big flashlight in his left hand and a paper in his right hand. The other two men had large swords. The leader read the Mullin's condemnation for trying to spread a religion other than the one true Zultarian faith. For their crimes they were to be executed by beheading and the sentence was to be carried out immediately.

Trusting their faith in Yahveh and Yahshua, the Mullins simply prayed and calmly waited for their Heavenly Father to move.

The leader motioned the other two men to move forward and kill the two American Christians. Neither man moved. The leader was irritated and started to berate them when something like the fire of a welding torch was applied completely across his brain. The pain was so overwhelming he couldn't even utter a sound as he died. His face was contorted in a horrible mask of agony and suffering and it matched the faces of the two swordsmen.

Frank and Andrea didn't understand what was happening until all three of the men fell to the ground. Standing behind each one was a soldier with a bloody knife. The two swordsmen had been eliminated by large men in battle cosmetics and full combat gear. The leader had died at the hands of a similarly outfitted woman with dark hair. She reached down and switched off the flashlight.

Before they could ask anything, a lovely voice in English whispered right behind them. "Mr. and Mrs. Mullins, If you'll let me help you stand up I'll get rid of these ropes for you." They felt hands under their arms and one at a time they stood up and the ropes were cut away with what

6

had to be one very sharp knife. They hardly felt a pull and the tough ropes were severed.

The other three soldiers had lowered their night-vision goggles or NVGs into place and had been watching the area around the little scene. They now moved forward to help the two missionaries away from the camp. There were no words and very little noise. The soldiers, men and women alike, moved like shadows through the jungle.

After walking about three hundred yards they stopped and in the dark the two women helped Andrea to strap on a body-armor vest. The men helped Frank. As they finished, a fifth soldier appeared out of the dark and a faint light appeared. Frank and Andrea were shocked to see their peaceful and humble friend, Pastor Tim Carson, standing in front of them. He was dressed in body armor and was armed with a large rifle and a hand gun like the first four. He smiled a wan smile at them.

"Praise Yahveh we were in time. I'm so glad you're all right."

Frank smiled ruefully at his friend. "I'm happy the Savior sent you and your friends. Another minute and we would have actually lost our heads."

The six-foot, two-inch soldier who looked like the ideal U.S. Marine warrior said, "You would not have been touched. Yahshua sent us to save you and what He starts He finishes. We've been within rifle range watching you and the rebels for over four hours."

Andrea raised an eyebrow and coolly asked him, "Why did you wait until the last second?"

Mark Connelly didn't take umbrage at her comment; he took it literally and answered that way. "Traditionally, this group uses only a few members to be involved with their executions, something to do with their view on life and death. We only waited until the rest of the rebels left the camp. That way we only had to deal with three men while you were still their captives and it reduced the possibility of your getting hurt. Plus we are trying to avoid a direct confrontation with all of the terrorists until you two are safe."

Andrea's eyes opened considerably. "I take it then that you expect to "deal" with the rest of the group sooner or later."

The blonde woman that had cut their ropes was watching a dim but crystal-clear screen projected onto the left eyepiece of her battle glasses. "I hate to bother you but it is time to head for the LZ!" Tim looked at the Mullins and translated for them. "LZ means the evacuation landing zone."

Mark quickly led the way with the Mullins behind him and the rest of the team following them. Laura Malone continued to watch the screen and talk to Charlie Wu who was one third of the world away in the Crossfire Team's fortress back in Denver, Colorado in the United States. As they reached the evacuation zone which turned out to be a large clearing, she said, "I agree." and switched her battle microphone next to her chin to local communication. "The rebels are quickly tracking us and will be here before the evacuation chopper."

Mark shook his head. "I didn't want it to come to this." He keyed his microphone and said, "Red flight, vector three in four minutes, out." Then the whole group jogged out several hundred feet into the clearing and got down on the ground behind a small rise in the ground. The men and women, including Tim aimed their rifles to cover a wide swath of the jungle with the Mullins behind them.

Less than a minute later, several of the rebels came out of the jungle quickly moving in their direction. Tim asked Mark, "How can they track us so fast in the dark?"

Mark was timing out three events and whispered quietly, "They have infrared tracking gear. Our footprints stand out real well on the cool jungle floor." He made a decision. "Wait till I fire and then take out the scouts."

To the Mullins this came across as professional warfare, without emotion and without feelings.

Mark was sighting through his night scope on his M8 and picked up the lead scout. The other two were targeted by the others on the team. Mark carefully squeezed the trigger and the silenced round punched through the forehead of the lead rebel. He went down with a thud, followed almost immediately by the other two scouts.

As he lost contact with his forward scouts, the new leader of the rebels realized that they were up against troops with night vision gear and ordered the two klieg lights they were carrying to be lit up.

Unfortunately for him, they turned the lights on just when the two Apache helicopters arrived and unloaded on the rebel position. The lights died with the troops around them. The two helicopters flew over the target and their checked the terrorists backtrack, observing the area with their FLIR or forward-looking infrared systems. There had been no survivors.

Homing in on a signal from Mark's battle pack, a large evac chopper came over the jungle canopy out of the dark and settled into the grass near the team and the ex-hostages. Armed soldiers jumped out of the helicopters and kept guard while everyone boarded and the three helicopters left the clearing.

Andrea noticed that after the troops that had rescued them stood down in the relative safety of the helicopter that they all bowed their heads in prayer. Catching Frank's eye the two missionaries joined them.

Andrea looked their rescuers over after the prayer. She studied Mark, the military leader of the group. He was solid in his manner and his beliefs. His quiet manner belied his strength and power. She coolly appraised his solid good looks and rugged features as he scrubbed the battlefield cosmetics off of his face. Mark stood about six foot, two inches and probably weighted in around 200 pounds. Dark brown-black hair framed a face that one had to call 'honorable'. Andrea later found out that Mark's time in the United States Navy Seals had solidified his role as a protector of the innocent. He thrived on complicated situations and was a military strategist. The integrity he had in everything he did was like a giant rock foundation. He was a man you could count on to keep his word even if he had to die for it. He was a very detailed planner, but then if the situation went into the unknown he was just as quick to throw the plans out the window and go on instinct and training.

Mark's physique was what the average American thought of when they pictured an honor scout in a body like that of Arnold Schwarzenegger.

Jack and Laura Malone sitting together on the side of the helicopter made an attractive couple. Obviously they were both warriors and they too carried themselves with honor. Jack was a tall, good-looking young man with blonde hair and gray-green eyes. He quietly took charge of most situations and nobody, not even Mark, argued with him. He stood about six foot four inches and was, in his own way, just as muscularly solid as Mark was. His muscle mass was more fluid and compact and he didn't show the 'buffed' shape that Mark did.

Laura was a beautiful young woman with blonde hair and light green eyes. She obviously had a sharp mind and a big heart. She was at least six foot in height. In Laura there was a spiritual calmness and confidence that one seldom saw. Andrea's spirit had jumped when Laura had talked to them as she cut their ropes in the jungle. Her anointing was very strong and it was obvious that her walk with the Father was close and growing stronger daily.

Andrea then considered the female warrior, Sarah. Later she would find out that Sarah's mandatory military training in Israel had led to her recruitment by the premier intelligence service of her country, the Mossad. Her training and operational background had hardened her attitude but, so far, not her looks. She was a darker-haired version of Laura with a decidedly more aggressive attitude but she had an easy smile. She weighed about 130 pounds and stood right at five foot ten inches tall. Her confidence and the way she handled herself made Andrea glad that Sarah was on their side.

Frank found he could still hear from the Father in Heaven and he shouted to be heard over the rotor noise. "Yahveh wants me to explain some things to you when we get back."

CHAPTER THREE

They flew to Mati and transferred to the Crossfire's Citation X jet for the trip to Manila. During the flight Frank and Andrea had a chance to take a shower and clean up. In the capital city of the Philippines the missionary couple went to the American consulate and described their kidnapping and rescue. They were then accompanied by a State Department representative when they repeated the information to the Philippine government. The Philippine authorities had retrieved the bodies of the slain at the service site. The body of Tyler Monroe and the rest of their team were being guarded at a local hotel. The embassy sent word to them that the Mullins were alive and free.

There had been some press coverage of their kidnapping and the death of the four young men. They met the press briefly after completing their report to the local government. One of the reporters asked them how they escaped from the Crescent Dagger rebels. Frank took the question and answered for them both.

"The Savior provided a rescue team that got us away from the rebels last night."

The reporter took notes, "Will the Philippine government go after the group of rebels that kidnapped you and killed your team member?"

Frank shook his head. "No, they will not."

A woman reporter asked, "Why not?"

Frank looked at her for a second. "The local government had warned us that if we got in trouble with the Zultarians that there was nothing they could do to help us."

The reporter persisted, "What is going to be done to punish those murderous thugs?" Frank eyed the woman reporter and came back with, "There is nothing more that needs to be accomplished. Our Heavenly Father will judge them."

She sneered and shook her head. "That's fine in the next life, what about now? Do we just let them murder both American and Philippine citizens and leave their punishment up to the Father at some future time? What about the next killings they do?" Frank tired of debating it with her. "There will be no more killings by this group. None of them survived their encounter with the rescue team. That's all we have to say." He and Andrea stood up to leave.

The persistent reporter shouted, "The forty rebels were all killed? Who were the people that rescued you?"

The Mullins ignored her questions and left for their hotel.

That afternoon a heavy rain squall pelted the city and it was forecast to keep raining for the next several days. When it rains in the Philippines it is what most Americans would call a downpour. The Mullins travelled out of the city to a village that was normally a three hour drive. With the rain it took almost six hours with the vehicles sliding and slipping along the mud trails.

Running out of the rain and into the large corrugated steel building, Frank and Andrea were reunited with the rest of their team. After that they set up for the service they had scheduled to hold when they first came to the islands.

The crowd was exceptionally large for a rainy evening service because of the notoriety the Mullins had received during their kidnapping. As everyone got settled, Frank estimated that there were over six hundred people crowded into the building. Looking around he was surprised to see the people that had rescued he and his wife from the rebels standing to one side along with Pastor Tim.

After the praise and worship time which was shortened due to the noise of the rain on the metal roof, Frank spoke a message on holiness and held a salvation call. Over a hundred people came to the altar to give their lives to Yahshua. Afterward he asked if anyone wanted healing. Many in the audience came forward. Frank had them line up across the room and he and his team prayed for healing in the name of Yahshua. Many people were healed that evening also.

For the Crossfire Team this was exciting. There were several dozen healings that weren't just subjective illnesses. People with major diseases such as goiters, cancer, withered limbs, blind eyes, and other obvious problems walked away from the area of the platform completely healed and praising Yahveh. Jack Malone looked at the rest of the group and nodded his head.

Due to the torrential rains, the next two days of services were canceled. There was no way to get to the locations they would be praying at those evenings.

At five o'clock on Thursday, Frank answered the door to their suite and saw the Team and Pastor Tim waiting outside. He ushered them in and made them all comfortable. Frank was relieved that none of them had any weapons. He knew they were necessary against people of evil. He was glad that they weren't looking for a firefight today.

Jack asked him, "Your service was excellent last night and the healing service was very interesting. How can your team see that kind of response to your prayers when so many others don't?"

Frank sighed, "This will take some time in the telling. Honey, will you get some water for all of us?"

CHAPTER FOUR

Frank looked at the assembled group. "Understand that I am being obedient to the Father by explaining these things to you. Yesterday He told me to instruct your team as to this truth." Frank looked at each of them, one at a time. "First, you need to be walking closely with Yahshua. Close enough you can hear Him. Please understand what he wants more than anything is a submitted heart. If you're not in love with Him you need to know Him better and you will be."

Frank indicated his wife and himself. "We each spend at least two hours a day in uninterrupted prayer with Him, letting Him know that we love Him, He is our reason for living and seeking His direction for our lives that day."

"His relationship with you is only blocked by sin in your life or an indifferent attitude to Him and His Kingdom. If you have taken Yahshua as your Savior and believe in Him and His resurrection you will go to Heaven at the end of your life. If you learn to hear Him and do as He asks you to do things you will have the victory and the blessings here on Earth during your life. You say that Andrea and I have a major anointing. No, we don't. We have a close relationship with the Savior because we spend our time with Him. The "anointing" you feel is really just Him working through us in love."

"After you enter into that kind of close relationship with Him, He will know you are giving him your life to do with as He pleases. Remember that He sees your heart and not what you say. This means you have to get rid of any agenda of your own and lay down your life to do His will. This is what is called, "Walking in the Spirit". We don't do anything unless He directs us to do it. That way, we are doing His will and at that point, of course, He will respond to our obedience and petitions."

Sarah said, "So many healings. It was wonderful and I would like to be a part of something like that."

Andrea spoke up, "Sarah, Yahveh would like nothing better. He longs for you to serve the Kingdom like that."

Mark asked, "You're right, but, I really don't hear the Father very much. I hear from Him occasionally, but not all the time like you seem to do."

Frank looked at the younger man and smiled. "I understand your problem. You should ask the Father to show you anything that is hindering your relationship with Him. He will, Oh Yeah!, He will. But, He'll only show you one or two things He wants you to confess, repent of, and eliminate from your life. If you are obedient with those, He'll give you others until you're free from anything that gets between Him and you. Things like your agenda, selfishness, pride, lust, and all the other things that separate you from Him. As you progressively clear out the debris you will hear Him more clearly."

Frank smiled, "I can tell you this. Yahveh is extremely proud of you all. He is working through you in a way Andrea and I have never seen before. In some respects you are hearing from Him more clearly than we do. But, I believe that your personal walk can be improved upon. One thing I suggest is that you start using the true names of the Deity and His son. There is tremendous power in the true name of the Father and the Messiah. Lose the terms, God, Lord, LORD, and Jesus. The true name of the Father is Yahveh, pronounced yah- vey and the true name of the Son is Yahshua pronounced yah-shu-wa. Notice that the name of the Father, "Yah", is in the name of the Son as it says it is in the Scriptures. There are numerous scriptures where Yahveh says, "In my name" and to use His name. It is important that you do these things properly because Yahveh is a Holy God. Take the Lord's Prayer for example. The second line is printed as "Hollowed be His Name" It should read, "Sanctify His Name Yahveh."

The present names are part of Satan's plan to remove the name of Yahveh from the people. He did a pretty good job too. But, Yahveh is again revealing his name to the saints in these last days. We can cover this later and I will show you the Scriptures where the Father declares that the enemy will erase my name from mankind and in the last days it will be restored. To spark your interest, understand that the term *"vain"* as in *"You are not to take your God's name in vain"* means empty. Satan has been able to make the Elohim's name disappear, therefore it <u>has</u> become vain."

Laura asked, "Is there anything wrong with using those terms? And I notice you used the term "Elohim." Could you explain?"

Jack nodded, "It would really help,"

"Okay," Frank smiled again. "I suppose this is all kind of abrupt. I'm so used to using the Hebrew terms I sometimes forget how long it took me to change my own vocabulary. In a nutshell, 'Elohim' is the Hebrew word that is rendered as "God" in English. It means "Mightiest of mighty ones." The English word "God" is derived from the old European word "Gott" which is the name of the pagan sky god. It is equivalent to the Greek "Zeus", the Phoenician and Ammonite "Molec", and the name of the sky god of every other pagan culture, all of which I may add, originate from the ancient Babylonian worship of Nimrod."

"But the word "God" doesn't mean that to us today," interjected Mark. "So what's the problem?"

"What you are asking for is a seminar, and all I can give you is a brief picture. It is enough to say that I believe that the Christian Church today is full of Babylonian practices and terms, and even architecture that have been "Christianized" and "sanitized". But their origin is still of Babylon."

Frank took a sip of water. "Revelation chapter 18 speaks of Babylon. Verse 4 says, *Come out of her, my people, lest you share in her sins, and lest you receive of her plagues."* The "her" is Babylon, and Elohim is saying that his people, that is, the church, are in her. While it doesn't mean you are intentionally striving after Babylonian gods, it does mean that you are being deceived by Babylonian worship when you pray to the Father. He knows that you can only walk in what you've been taught and all that you know. But, I believe it is still offensive to Him. This scripture reference is to Jeremiah 51:45."

"The problem Judaism had at the time of Jeremiah, or "Yirmeyahu" to use his Hebrew name, is exactly the same problem in the church today. The Jews had the form of worshiping Yahveh Elohim, but they had mixed it with the worship of Ba'al, the pagan sun god. The people of Elohim refused to repent at Yirmeyahu's preaching, and so the Father judged them."

"Do you suppose Elohim likes having the name of a pagan god, albeit "christianized", ascribed to him? While this is something to think on, also understand that as a believer in both the Father and the Son you have been grafted into the tree of God's people, the Jews. Yahshua was a Jew his entire time on Earth and never wanted his children separated into groups that have been led not to trust, respect, or love each other. That is the work of the enemy. Study the Jewish roots of your Savior. I've got some literature for you that explain the feasts and festivals that Yahveh requires that true believers celebrate each year."

"Amazing." said Laura. "Is that the same with the other terms you mentioned? Are they also of Babylon?"

"Well," responded Frank, "let's start with the term "lord." It means nothing in American English, and it is a common title of nobility in England. But its origin also has to do with pagan deities. It is also the meaning of the word "Ba'al." "Master" would be a much better translation. But when you see "LORD" all in capital letters in the Scriptures, it is not even a translation. It is an outright substitution for "Yahveh", the name of Elohim. And then to add insult to injury, when referring to Yahveh in writing, people quote YHVH from the Old Testament and they don't even keep it all capitals."

"I see," said Laura. and "Jesus." Is it a pagan name, too? I'm getting convicted of this teaching as the truth and it is changing everything I thought I knew." Looking at the others of the team, it seemed like they were feeling as she did.

"There is debate on that. Some say yes, and give their reasons, and some say it is just a matter of transliteration, the Hebrew "Yahushua" being shortened to "Yeshua," then becoming "Iesous" in Greek, then "Iesus" in Latin, and finally "Jesus" in English, a name not even remotely resembling the original name given to our Savior, and also a name with no meaning in Hebrew. The name Yahveh gave his Son was Yahshua. Yahveh means "the self-existing one." His Son's name contains his name. It means

"Yahveh the Savior," or "Yahveh is Savior." Yahshua said he came in his Father's name.

"Well," he continued, "that's the bottom line. I'm not surprised if it is an overload. Pray about it. Try to use the Hebrew terms, even using "Messiah" instead of "Christ," such as "Master Yahshua Messiah" instead of "Lord Jesus Christ." In case you are wondering, there was a pagan deity named Christ long before Yahshua walked the Earth. You might sound strange to others, and even to yourself at first, but. I believe, in your spirit you might find a greater love and closeness to the Father, and also greater effectiveness in spiritual matters. Remember that Yahveh is love so you have to talk to people where they are at in love. They probably don't know the true names and will be confused or actively angry if you present this to them unless the Father leads you to talk to them about it. We still use the common terms as needed as we are led to by the Father."

"Another thing, the reason you need to learn about your Jewish roots is because Yahshua was a practicing Jew until the ruling Hebrew leaders had Him killed. He observed the Jewish Feasts, the high holy days, and all of the things Judaism held as holy. As he said in Matthew 5:17 *"Do not think that I have come to abolish the Law or the Prophets; I have not come to abolish them but to fulfill them.* Yahshua was completely a Jew and everything he thought, did, or said, was based on the Jewish viewpoint.

"My wife and I know that we have found that greater love and closeness as have many of those who have sat under these teachings. You are in spiritual warfare. The less of Babylon in you, no matter how familiar and traditional, the more love you will have for the Father, and, as Sha'ul (or Paul) says in Galatians 5:6, "Faith is effective through love." The more love, the more faith."

I am reluctant to mention an important requirement that is important to each believer for a reason most people don't know about. The reason I am reluctant is because it seems to me that your battle is not a scheduled event but more of an on-going conflict. The reason I bring it up is because I believe that even though governments are looking to place a computer chip in every citizen that is not the Mark of the Beast. I believe that the mark of the beast which at first will prevent people that don't agree with the coming one-world-government from buying and selling is their willingness to celebrate Shabbat every Friday night through Saturday night. This "marks" them as followers of Yahveh and Yahshua. It will be that a person that follows the Father's command to celebrate the proper Sabbath will not be able to work, own anything, buy anything, or have anything. If you think this isn't realistic just look at Germany and what Satan led the populace there to do to the Jews. But as one of the Ten Commandments it must be celebrated correctly to show your obedience to the Father. I believe that people that call themselves Christians don't see the importance of a "Jewish" rite or celebration. It is an easy "Mark" to notice since it requires a true believer celebrate it every week and do no work during the Shabbat. I don't know how you could do that.

Frank looked at his wife with a smile. "Pray to the Father in the name of Yahshua about all of this. Also, talk to Pastor Tim as you learn to walk the way the Father wants you to. Pray in the Spirit all the time and you will do greater things for Him."

CHAPTER FIVE

As the group sat there considering the ramifications of Frank's teachings, Laura got an urgent word of knowledge from God. Thrusting herself up and out of her chair she threw herself over the coffee table directly at Frank and Andrea who both looked at her alarmed. As she moved, she yelled "Incoming!" She gathered both of the missionaries in her arms and hauled the very surprised couple over backwards, along with their chairs, to the floor of the room.

Frank watched as the other team members went to the floor and drew handguns from somewhere. As they scattered across the room, a heavy hammering sound announced the arrival of decidedly unfriendly forces. A jagged row of holes opened up in the wall of the room that separated it from the hallway on that floor. Machine gun bullets whined through the air in the room above everyone, shredding the couches and chairs, turning the wood in the upturned coffee table into splinters and the cushions into exploding feather storms. There were at least three gunners in the hall firing through the wall when Mark, Sarah, Jack, Laura, and Tim started to return the enemy's fire. Following the training Mark had given them, each person fired ten rounds across the face of the wall spaced a few feet apart. The incoming fire stopped although one machine gun was still heard firing in the hall. Everyone quickly loaded a new clip into their handguns.

Mark was an expert in both the raiding and defense of a hotel room. He was pretty sure what the next step would be. He had drilled this routine into each of the team repetitively until they knew it too. As soon as the rounds stopped slamming into the furniture and outer wall, the team smoothly moved into action. Jack and Mark headed for the door of the room to the hall. Sarah went to one side of the back wall where she could cover the windows. She grabbed a piece of heavy furniture to use as a shield.

Laura and Tim holstered their sidearms and got Frank and Andrea to the far side of the room away from the punctured wall. Quickly tearing the beds apart they put both double-size mattresses over the missionary couple and then pulled furniture over so they could huddle behind it in front of the mattresses.

The door exploded into the room sending chunks of wood and long splinters everywhere. Then two grenades flew in and bounced off the side wall to land on the floor. One landed near Laura and she grabbed it and tossed it back out the door. Huddling down quickly she opened her mouth and covered her ears to disperse the pressure of the coming explosions. Both grenades exploded furiously. The one in the room sent razor-edged fragments in all directions. As soon as the whirling debris stopped flying, Mark and Jack surged up from behind the chairs they had crouched behind and went through the door with their guns up and hunting targets. There were five men still alive in the hall. Four of them had been injured by the grenade that Laura had sent back to them. The other one was still standing and trying to shake off the effects of the blast. Mark and Jack did not give them any chance of recovering. All five men joined the three other bodies on the floor. As he fell, the standing man pointed a finger at Jack and tried to say something but nothing came out that was intelligible.

Mark stepped back into the room and immediately ordered the next step. "Everyone out, NOW!"

Jack was watching the hall, the stairs, and the elevators for any more shooters as the others flooded out of the room with Sarah, still watching the windows, bringing up the rear. The entire group ran past the pools of blood and crumpled bodies and down the stairs for two flights. Suddenly there was a huge explosion above them that shook the entire building and made everyone hang onto something to stay upright. Laura and Tim fell to the stairs as the lights went out and dust and debris fell from the ceiling. After helping Laura to her feet, Sarah said, "Well, I think that took care of cleaning up our room!"

Mark found his flashlight and lit up the stairwell. Leading the others downward through the dusty air and fallen debris he held up his left hand and brought the group to a quick halt just outside the door at the bottom of the stairwell. He cautiously peered through the small window in the door. Then, opening the door slowly he stepped through and looked around. Motioning everyone out of the stairs he led them past shocked patrons and hotel staff. With all the weapons they had in view nobody seemed interested in stopping them. They went through the kitchen at a quick walk as the fire alarm belatedly went off and the kitchen staff started rushing towards the doors to the outside. The team and the Mullins had to circumvent piles of cooking utensils and food that had been knocked to the floor by the blast.

Mark gathered the troops just inside the dock service door. "Stay here until we get back with a vehicle." He nodded to Jack and they slipped out the door.

The fire alarm continued to ring and there was the sound of several sirens approaching the hotel from the outside. Andrea looked at Laura with wide eyes and asked, "What did you mean when you said that explosion cleaned up our room?"

Sarah shrugged her shoulders and calmly said, "The enemy probably used one or more rocket-propelled grenades or something larger. It felt like they blew the whole room out of the hotel."

Tim asked, "Why didn't they do that first and simply kill all of us?"

Sarah was still scanning inside and outside the hotel while she answered, "Because they are not that smart. They are on a constant Jihad where the glory goes to the individuals that were able to kill you. Frequently they don't understand that the goal is more important than the individual honor. This attitude was a blessing for us this time."

Frank had started to breathe properly again and was shaking the dust from his hair. His hearing was coming back after the grenade blast but everything looked blurred. Then he noticed his eyeglasses in his hand. Putting them on he looked around and asked Sarah, "Is this what your life is like all the time?"

Sarah smiled at him, "No, not really, we get holidays and every other weekend off." Seeing that the joke didn't register with the rattled missionary she just shook her head. "Sometime it's worse than this. It's like all wars, long periods of boredom interrupted by sudden violent episodes that occur in an eye blink. In our lives there tends to be less boredom and more action."

Hearing a horn honk outside, the group moved cautiously out the door. As they stepped out onto the dock a slim man in casual clothing jumped out from behind a large crate on the dock and grabbed Andrea by the arm and attempted to pull her away from the group. Sarah saw the move and stepped into the man and drove a palm heel strike to his jaw with her left hand. Stepping farther into him, she threw him off balance. Sarah's Jui Jitsu blow resulted from her constant practice with Jack. Driving off of her left leg she brought her hand up from her waist inverting her hand's position just as she struck the man's chin. She used the proper exhalation technique and shouted at the same time. Her blow lifted the man off his feet a good eighteen inches and broke his jaw in several places. The blow also scattered some of the man's teeth at the same time. The blow was so fast that Andrea never knew what happened. The man arched over backward and slammed to the concrete dock with a soggy "thud". Sarah took Andrea's arm and moved her away from the inert man.

There was a terrible odor and a demon stepped out of their dimension directly into the human one. The demon was unhappy his earthly minions had failed to kill the Pastor and his wife, so he took it on himself to complete his mission.

Laura's golden armor and the sword of the word exploded into being as she stepped forward to do battle. The Holy anger of God was on her face and she ran at the demon to prevent it from harming the couple.

Sarah drew her handgun and shot the demon five times. Every bullet blew large holes through the evil being and it stopped and looked at Sarah.

Laura reached the creature and cut it in half with her sword completing the extermination. Laura's armor faded from view just as Mark and Jack roared up to the dock.

Instead of their SUV they had "borrowed" a large, heavy Volvo truck and stopped just outside the dock. Jack ran around from the cab and waved them into the back of the vehicle. Climbing inside they found their M8s and body armor in the bags on the floor of the truck. Tim smiled, "Oh good! I do so like to dress properly for these occasions."

Tim looked at the Mullins. They both stood there with their mouths open and their eyes very big. Tim said, "What is the problem Pastor?"

Frank shook his head, "And I had the presumption to tell her about being a servant of Yahveh." He stepped over to Laura who had just put on her body armor and was checking her rifle for load and function. He reached up and gently touched her on her arm. She looked at the Pastor and smiled at him. "Are you all right Pastor?"

Frank licked his lips and asked in a small voice. "What is it like?" When she didn't say anything, he said, "When you have that armor of God, what is it like?"

Laura understood his question then. The team was very used to Laura "going gold" but this man and woman didn't even know about it. She realized the double whammy it must have been after the firefight and escape from the building with the explosion and then to see a demon, probably for the first time, and then her armor and sword. This must have been a heck of day to them. She smiled again. "It's like you suddenly are the arm of Yahveh battling the soldiers of the enemy. A Holy anger comes on you and if you agree to do God's work by praying then you are anointed to battle along with the angels. It's pretty tiring and heady at the same time."

Frank blinked a couple of times and said, "Thank you."

At that time the truck swayed and lurched around the corner out of the alley it turned north. Through the open tops of the back doors they could see the front of the hotel where their fourth-floor room had been. There was a crater three rooms wide and two floors high

That part of the front of the building looked like the Murrow building in Oklahoma City had looked after the truck bomb. Frank, Tim, and Andrea prayed for any people that could have been caught in the blast that had been sent for them. Blessedly, it had been early afternoon and, hopefully, there few people were in their rooms at that time.

After they finished putting on their body armor and Kevlar helmets the team ranged themselves around the back of the truck in the event the enemy located them and gave chase.

Laura sighed to herself. It was becoming a familiar routine. The sudden violence and her reaction to it. People dying and trying to kill them. It still went against the image she had always had of herself, but, Yahveh willed it and she wasn't going to walk away from what He wanted. Still she felt that part of her longed for a quieter, more romantic lifestyle for her and Jack. Thinking about a life of quiet, uneventful living she realized what a useless, boring, and selfish life that would be and then she knew it was one she really didn't want at all.

As she watched for more enemy action she knew that Jack was actually enjoying himself being a protector of people who couldn't take care of themselves against the enemies of both this world and the spiritual one. Then it dawned on her that she was truly doing what the creator of the universe wanted her to do and that filled her spirit with love and gave her a real lift. Checking the load in her M8 and flicking the selector to three-round bursts she thought, "I'd like to see any fashion model walk this runway."

In the cab Mark finished talking to the American Embassy on Roxas Boulevard. Sarah had jumped in the front of the truck cab along with Mark to act as shotgun guard. She also made a cellphone call but this one was to Israel.

Laura called everyone's attention to three black sedans that were quickly catching up with the truck. Their intentions became clear as they drew closer and rifle barrels poked out of the windows on one of the cars. Having done this before, Jack watched the other car and saw the 4.5 kg warhead on an RPG sliding out of the back window of the second car. Grabbing a box and pulling it open he yanked out an American-made LAW, or light antitank weapon, and armed it by extending the tube. Everyone else went to the sides of the truck away from the front and the back of the rocket launcher. Not having time to aim, Jack fired it out the back of the truck from the hip and scored a hit on the radiator of the car. The explosion blew parts of the motor back into the car and put an end to the plans for the RPG. It fired but went almost straight upward. When it came down it blew a large chunk out of the guardrail portion of the roadway. One of the pursuing cars veered to the left. Finding an open lane it accelerated quickly past the truck.

Three men in a single car following them opened the sun roof and then started to fire at them with automatic rifles. Bullets slammed into the truck body and some went through it. One round hit Jack and spun him to the floor of the truck. Praying for Jack, Laura carefully aimed and fired three quick tri-bursts from her M8 at the windshield of the car. The nine bullets smashed through the windshield and took out both the driver and the front seat gunman. The car suddenly whipped to the left and ran into a lorry being driven by a fish merchant. Both vehicles flipped and fish and bodies went everywhere.

Jack sat up and rubbed his ribs where the trauma plate had stopped the incoming round. As the flattened round fell to the floor of the truck Jack knew he'd be sore in the morning but at least it didn't penetrate. His sincere prayer of thankfulness was from the heart. Ignoring the soreness, Jack pushed himself back to his feet and checked to see if the others were uninjured.

The third car had worked its way around traffic and had gotten ahead of the truck on its left side. As the truck neared, the car switched lanes to a lane further away and an RPG poked out of the rear window on the right hand side. Mark saw it and realized that there was nothing they could do to avoid it. All of a sudden a big Mercedes convertible with the top down, driven by a blonde-haired woman, started to pass between the car and the truck. As the woman raced by the slowing car with the terrorists she came face to face with the RPG. Seeing the weapon she let out an "Eek!" and slammed on her brakes. As the convertible dug in with its front wheels and slowed down it veered closer to the terrorist's car and the left hand pillar of the windshield impacted on the grenade end of the RPG slamming it back into the terrorist's car. Apparently the impact made the shooter pull the trigger and the RPG fired directly into the ceiling of the car. The car exploded from the inside out and became a rolling ball of fire. The blonde in the big convertible roared around the other side of the burning car waved her hand in the air and Mark clearly heard her yell, "My bad! Sorry!" and she disappeared into the traffic. Mark shook his head. The enemy had them cold and would have killed them if the ditzy blonde hadn't been there. Sarah squinted her eyes. "You know, it looked like she did that on purpose." She looked at Mark and together they said, "Naw!" As Mark continued to drive for the embassy, they both kept a sharp lookout for more trouble.

As they neared the embassy Sarah said, "To the left!" Two more black sedans came out of a side street and started firing at the truck. A pack of traffic separated the two terrorist vehicles from the truck which limited the amount of return fire the team could bring to bear.

Most of the traffic raced away or screeched to a halt to avoid the gunfire. A long, black limousine with two security cars going the same direction as the truck was caught in the middle of the battle. As Mark urged more speed out of the truck and it sped away from the shooters, it suddenly seemed that the attackers had forgotten them completely.

The two black cars switched their aim to the two supporting vehicles with the limousine. Riddled by over a hundred rounds, the two support vehicles became rolling tombs for the inhabitants. One of the cars caught on fire and burned brightly blocking the path of the limousine.

Laura watched as the occupants of the two attacking cars jumped out and shot out the front side windows of the limousine. They then smashed their way into the back of the long car. As they dragged a man and a woman from back seats of the big car they threw a grenade into the limousine. The blast blew out all the windows in the big car and bulged out the roof. The blast killed the wounded driver and whoever else was inside that hadn't been already killed by the gunfire. They forced their hostages back to their cars and fled the scene before the first police car arrived.

Mark looked at Sarah and shook his head. More innocents caught in the battle without a chance.

Mark brought the truck to a halt in front of the embassy and everyone jumped out. Sarah and Jack formed a back guard as the others presented themselves to the U.S. Marines at the front gate. Surrendering their weapons the team placed themselves and the missionaries in the capable hands of the Marines. There was a heavily armed squad of Marines in combat gear present in response to Mark's call.

Inside the embassy they dictated their stories which would be verified by the embassy before being accepted. Laura was concerned that the red tape could endanger the Mullins and asked the embassy personnel to contact the office of the President in Washington for their bona fides.

After that, things went much faster and within the hour the missionaries and Pastor Tim were being transported by a heavily armed convoy to the Ninoy Aquino International Airport.

While they were waiting to hear that their three friends made it successfully out of the country, the team learned that the couple the attackers had kidnapped from the limousine were the Philippine Secretary of Foreign Affairs and his wife, Juan and Anna Badar, who had been headed to the American Embassy in response to the attack on the Americans at the hotel.

Mark and Sarah suddenly felt a heavy burden to pray together. After praying they talked and came to a consensus. Calling Jack and Laura over they offered what they felt they were given.

Mark started, "We feel that Yahshua is directing us to be His weapon against these terrorists in response to their kidnapping of the Secretary and his wife. Why don't you guys pray about this and see if you get a confirmation?"

CHAPTER SIX

Frank Mullins watched the runway come up to meet them as they landed in Hawaii at the Honolulu Airport on the island of Oahu. Having flown in and out of Hawaii many times Frank knew that Oahu is the most populated of the Hawaiian Islands and Honolulu is the state's largest and busiest airport. There was considerable amount of aviation activity going on at the airport and they had to wait over a half an hour before they could be refueled.

Frank was in deep prayer about the events on Mindanao and his concern for the Crossfire Team. His focus was to seek Yahveh's will concerning both his and Andrea's next actions and the team's needs.

Frank felt the gentle heaviness as the Spirit of Yahveh drew nearer. He went into receive mode and waited. It was actually quite pleasant. His body was comforted by the soft seating in the aircraft and the cool air in the cabin. His spirit was comforted by the nearness of the Holy Spirit of Yahveh.

As he waited patiently he heard the words of his Savior telling him that he would stay at his home in Denver until he had instructed the team concerning His Name. During that time, he would spend his energy working to bring his assembly to a new height in service to Yahveh.

As the U.S. government jet lifted off from Hawaii into a bright and cloudless sky and banked for home, Frank joined Andrea in praying for the Crossfire Team and giving thanks to Yahveh for sending the warriors to save Andrea and him.

Back in Manila, Jack and Laura were asking for direction and clarification for the team and Yahveh's will concerning their part in dealing with the terrorists and rescuing Juan and Anna Badar.

Jack suddenly understood a complex set of data. There was no learning, or training, or anything. He just had this clear understanding of what the team had to do. He knew it was from Yahshua and it remained in his mind, crystal-clear and vibrant. He thanked the Savior and sat up in his seat. Looking over he could tell that Laura had received the same message. Pulling out his laptop Jack started to put the information down so that he could convey all of it to the others.

Jack called Su Li at the airport and asked her to come to the Embassy. He was still putting the finishing touches on his presentation when the beautiful young Oriental pilot walked into the room. Calling the rest of the team together he presented a summary what had happened for Su Li and to get them all on the same page.

Jack threw a map up on the projection screen in the conference room. "The war on terrorism is being fought all over the world, in places like the Middle East and Afghanistan. But experts are pointing to Asia as being the new front in the war on terrorism. Numerous groups in Indonesia and the Philippines, some linked to al-Qaeda, have claimed responsibility for scores of bombings, killings and kidnappings like the one of the Secretary and his wife."

Sitting back Jack continued, "In the Philippines, a predominately Catholic country, the island of Mindanao is one of the most violent and unstable regions in Asia. Considered the "Wild West" of the Philippines, Mindanao was once mostly Islamic and then Zultarian. The Philippine government encouraged Christian settlers to move there. First Mindanao's Islamic minority and later the Zultarian minority which is about 10% of the present population, has been fighting for independence, forcing hundreds of thousands of people from their homes and sowing the seeds for new rebel and terrorists groups."

Using a laser pointer Jack highlighted the southern half of the island of Mindanao. "Troops from the U.S. Special Forces are presently training the Philippine army to stop the violence by such terrorist groups and the number of bombings has gone down significantly since the U.S. troops' arrival. The terrorists' goal is the destabilization of the government of the Philippines so that they can reinstate a Zultarian state on the people of the Main Island as well as Mindanao. The recent violence by the Crescent Dagger group has actually been a major setback to Zultarian goals."

"Our incursion to save the Mullins was approved at the highest levels of both the American and Philippine governments. The resultant terrorist attack of the hotel will not go unpunished, but the kidnapping of Juan and Anna Badar cannot and will not be tolerated. I've heard from the Chairman of the Joint Chiefs of Staff, General Miles, apparently the President knows the Badars personally and is really upset by their abduction. He wants it handled top priority. They are sending our special operations group, "Miles Marauders" to the Philippines to help us find and rescue the Badars."

Mark raised his right fist in the air and brought it down sharply. "Yes!" Then he had another thought. "Wait a minute. I was under the impression that we had taken out the Crescent Dagger in the jungle the other night. I figured that another branch of the Zultarian rebels were the ones attacking us in the truck and at the hotel. If we are we being directed to go after a main body of Zultarian rebels it will take a lot more than forty people."

Jack smiled at the question from his friend. "The group we took out in the jungle turns out to be only a part of the Crescent Dagger group. They have used misinformation to hide their numbers. Each cell group pretends to be the whole organization. In actuality there are still over two hundred of them left."

Jack then continued with the briefing. "The Messiah gave me an insight into the numbers and dealings of these terrorists and where we need to strike them." He pointed to a small island in the sea just south of Mindanao. "This is Basilan Island, the present and secret home to the leaders and the remainder of the Crescent Dagger terrorists.

Isabella, in the north, is the largest town on Basilan Island. The Crescent Dagger group has plagued the island so much that the government is applying pressure in the form of additional troops dedicated to their elimination. Through the presence of U.S. and Philippine troops, the island has become more secure. But this is a false peace. The headquarters of the Crescent Dagger is actually located on the west side of the island, about halfway between Maluso and Canas. The base is in caves carved out by the sea several thousand years ago. The base is so well hidden that the terrorists are able to continue full operations even with American and Filipino troops roaming the surface in daytime. They can even evade detection by satellite and aircraft surveillance. Needless to say their above-ground operations are conducted at night. In Tipo-Tipo town on the southeast part of Basilan Island the joint U.S. and Philippine armies train and run operations across the southern half of the island. Yahshua showed me that they are aware that the Crescent Dagger has a base somewhere on the island but haven't pinpointed its location as yet. Still, the heightened pressure has led to a decision by the terrorist group to relocate their base away from Basilan Island this Saturday.

We need to strike it no later than six p.m. local time, three days from now. After that the base will be abandoned. Since there are over 7107 islands in the Philippine Archipelago we want to hit them before they fade away to some other island and take their hostages with them."

Su Li raised a question. "Why not just bomb them off the face of the earth rather than send in our troops and risk casualties?"

Jack smiled, "Good thought, it was the first one I had too. But, the base is not only underground but spread out sufficiently so that even bunker busters probably wouldn't get it all. Plus, the Badars are probably being held in the base. We have to go in there, rescue them and then locate the enemy and wipe them out."

Laura tipped her head to one side. "And the reason for not using a regular army unit from the Philippines or the U.S. groups on the island is?"

Jack looked at her, "Because there is a definite spiritual aspect to the battle that requires the Crossfire Team to deal with the added dimension of the conflict. Yahshua confirmed that there are, not one but two, strong men in charge of the spiritual affairs of the Crescent Dagger. One is named Oberon and the other is named Terror."

Sarah asked, "Did Yahveh give you any specifics on how we are to confront the strong men and the terrorists. You know, like march around the place seven times and shout. Something like that?"

Jack laughed at the reference to Joshua and the walls of Jericho. "Yes he did but it is hard to decipher what he meant by *"As with Bitterness, the enemy is overtaken and destroyed."*

Su Li blinked on that one. "What does that mean?"

Jack shook his head. "Don't know, yet." Jack took on a somber mien. "That is not all." He had definitely gotten their attention with that.

Su Li asked, "How do spiritual strong men stop a normal physical attack group?"

Laura stood up and answered the question. "Traditionally demons work through human beings who sin and make their lives available to demonetization. They lure, tempt, corrupt, and intensify the sin in people's lives and can pretty much get them to do whatever the demon wants them to do. In these last days we have seen them transfer physically into our dimension from the spiritual dimension. Su Li, on your first mission with us you saw a large demon in our world yourself in China. What could you do to it?"

Su Li thought for a second, "I shot it twice and it didn't seem to notice. Yet when we've shot others it kills them. What's that all about?"

Laura shrugged, "I don't really know. We're still new at this and why a strong man demon that has transitioned into our dimension isn't affected by bullets while normal demons are killed has something to do with the legality of their entry."

Laura looked at Jack and continued, "The strong man has strength and power similar to that of an Archangel except it is used for evil. There is little known about their operation in this dimension except that they are able to control unbelievers and those with a false faith in Yahveh. Physically they can do great damage due to their physical makeup. I would say that a single strongman would mentally disorient a normal attack group if it doesn't have prayer coverage and render them ineffectual and vulnerable to the human agents he controls or he could inflict damage on the troops himself. Two of them would increase the problem exponentially.

Jack looked at his wife for a few seconds. "The savior also told me that this is just the tip of the iceberg for this operation. There is something much bigger we will have to tackle in the near future. What that is, I also don't know as yet."

Mark nodded, "We'll work on that. In the meantime, let's get all the research we can on that base and the area around it. Jack, you and I will work with the alphabet agencies and the Philippine government. Su Li, you and Sarah get in touch with the Mossad and the Crossfire fortress in Denver. See if David Zahavy or Charlie Wu can give us anything about the place, the number of troops involved and anything else. Laura, do what you do best, pray for guidance and coordinate with the incoming spec ops people. Let's move it guys, we are on a real short string here and the numbers are falling fast."

CHAPTER SEVEN

As it turned out, almost nothing was known about the secret base. NSA, CIA, the Mossad, and others had no knowledge of the web of caves and their use. Charlie Wu had a brilliant idea and was able to get a very good structural outline of the caves from a new version of LANDSAT-8 geology satellite. He was working on utilizing the thermal imaging capability of the LANDSAT-8 to determine troop numbers and locations within the caves.

The caves began within a few yards of the Sulu Sea and ran up and down the coast for almost a half of a mile. The largest cave was close to six thousand yards wide. A total of seventeen caves, mostly small ones comprised the network the Crescent Dagger was using as a headquarters. All of the caves were from twenty to ninety feet below sea level with a covering of rock above the uppermost caves. The thickness of the rock above the caves was a minimum of twenty feet thick and covered with natural vegetation. This provided the terrorists with a perfect hide-away that normally defied detection. They had improved on the natural drainage of water from the caves so that they were essentially dry.

There were three levels to the cave with the largest being below the smaller ones. There didn't seem to be any vehicular traffic because there were no roads leading to the cave area. There could be an underwater sea entrance but the LANDSAT-8 didn't detect it.

Mark stared at the arrangement of the caves and noted many things about them that could be used by the raiders. He also noted many positions that would be very advantageous for the terrorists if they were aware they were being attacked inside the caves. The entrances were small, maybe big enough for one or two people at a time. Natural ambush points if you know the enemy is coming. The Crossfire Team and the Special Operations Group would have to find a better way to make an entrance or the whole affair could become a siege. Then there were the two strong men. Mark spent two hours on the sat phone from the Embassy talking to Pastor Tim and Gary Eisenthal. He was still no closer to determining what to do about the spiritual conflict part of the battle than he had been to start with. He called Laura over and asked her to concentrate in prayer on how to combat these strongholds.

Mark was not happy with his efforts. Any way you looked at it, it had the potential to become a bloodbath for the raiders.

Laura sat in a comfortable lounge chair and prayed in tongues to her Elohim. She was at ease in her prayer time and felt the heaviness that let her know that the presence of the Holy Spirit was with her. As she continued to praise Yahveh in her prayer language she felt a sudden lightness as if she was floating. Her eyes were closed and she chose not to open them. The peace that settled over her was like the most wonderful mist or shower or rain. Little pieces of quietness with harmony settling all over her. It was something she had never experienced before. As the pieces of peace became more numerous they joined together and spread over her. The feeling was so calming and serene she quit praying and just received. After an unknown amount of time enjoying the calmness that defied explanation, she opened her eyes. At first, what she saw didn't make sense but she was so peaceful there was no worry or panic. She just waited.

Soon she recognized a field of grass and she was standing in the grass. The room at the Embassy was missing and that didn't bother her at all. A delightful breeze flowed over her. It was a perfect temperature and the texture of love. Looking around she saw that the field she was in was perfectly trimmed and looked to be mowed, not a blade of grass was too long or too short. The grass moved gracefully in the gentle breeze. Looking to her left she saw a wide area that was also grass but several feet lower than where she was. The lower area was bounded by glassy walls that looked like pearl. There were people standing in the lower area walking alone or talking to each other in pairs or small groups with their hair or clothes blowing gently in the breeze. There were probably fifty people in all but the expanse was so large the groups were separated considerably.

Behind her was a walk of the same material as the walls. The walk ran at right angles to the lower area and came from her right to her left, passed behind her, went down three steps to the lower area and across to an identical set of stairs in the other low wall about six hundred feet further to her left. The expansive grassy area that made up the lower area came from an immeasurable distance behind her and went away in front of her until it was beyond her visual range. It was like it never ended, it just got smaller and smaller in her vision as the distance increased in both directions.

Across the lower area and above the other wall, the walk continued past three buildings on the right side of the walk. The buildings were probably ten stories tall with no noticeable windows. They were the color of gold. After the walk passed the buildings it continued going away until it went out of sight. On the other side of the walk from the buildings were tall trees, like a perfect forest the limbs moving in the gentle breeze.

Sensing a presence Laura turned around and saw the angel Rose standing on the walk, watching her. Laura walked through the soft grass that felt like cool water over to where the angel was and smiled. "Hello Rose, it's good to see you again."

Rose's gold coloring was predominating and the fierce whiteness was muted this time. Rose smiled back at Laura and said, "Laura, you are looking lovely, how are you?"

Laura thought about that for a few minutes. "I've never felt so much at peace as I do now. What is this place?"

Rose laughed, "That would be extremely hard to explain to you at this point. You don't have the references necessary to understand why this place exists let alone where it is. Don't let it worry you though; it is part of Yahveh's domain. He wants us to talk about your task on Earth."

Laura nodded, "Good that is what I was praying for."

Rose floated slowly around Laura and stopped in front of her again. "You have grown in your spirit and your capabilities since we last met. That is good. There is a new strength backed by a calm conviction of who you are in Yahshua. That is better than good!" The angel smiled slightly. "Your time with the Master was beneficial." This was a statement rather than a question. Laura thought back to the time she had been wounded and had been transported by an archangel to Yahshua for healing. It had become a major rock for the foundation of her faith.

The whiteness surrounding the angel brightened and overshadowed the gold somewhat. "The place you're going to attack is defended by two formidable strong men of the enemy. Their job is twofold, first to get the people in the Crescent Dagger to do Satan's will. The second job is to prevent Yahveh's servants from interfering or defeating the people. For His purposes, Yahveh has allowed them, and their servants, to spread death and destruction in their part of the world for a time. That time has now come to an end."

Irritated by the loss of innocent lives, Laura asked the angel, "Why? Why has it come to an end now and not a year ago, or last month?"

Rose studied her, looking for rebellion against Elohim. Finding only sadness due to compassion, she answered Laura. "Because of the influence of the strong men, the leaders of the Crescent Dagger have changed their goals from fighting for their people's rights to a single-minded policy of pure hatred for anyone not like them. They have now declared war on the saints and Yahveh will not allow that to happen.

Laura knew Yahveh loved all people and He wouldn't allow Satan to sacrifice good people unless it was in His will that their time was done on Earth. Her compassion for life and her love for the underdog made her heart hurt that so many were taken but knew that it was beyond her capacity to help the ones that were gone. That didn't mean that she couldn't be Yahveh's sword to prevent more death by this group. She felt the anger burn against all the terrorists in the Crescent Dagger and especially in their evil overseers.

Sensing a great fear for her life and the lives of the rest of the team Laura asked, "How can the Crossfire Team possibly defeat these strong men?"

The fierce whiteness flared up around Rose, "Yahveh says, *"Laura, do not be terrified; do not be afraid of them. Your Elohim, Yahveh, is going before you and He will fight for you, as He did for His children He brought out of Egypt.*

He will go before you like a devouring fire. He will subdue them before you. And you will annihilate them quickly, as your Elohim has promised you!"

Rose's color softened back toward the gold color as she began to fade out of sight. Laura heard her last comment as a whisper. "And I will be there too."

Laura woke up and noticed that while the fear had disappeared the peace was still there even with the anger. She felt stronger and more confident knowing that she was to be the instrument of the strong men's destruction. She got out of her chair and went to find Mark.

CHAPTER EIGHT

The clock was running as Laura talked to Mark and Jack and told them what Rose had told her about the strong men.

Mark was impressed by Yahveh's anger with the enemy. "We have a weak plan right now and I'm glad to hear that. But it still doesn't give us the victory without a lot of casualties on our side. That subterranean cave site is just too easy to defend against invaders!"

Jack felt something gnawing at the back of his mind and he went back to the room that he and Laura had been given at the Embassy. Sitting down, he prayed for guidance and then sat and waited on the Savior to help him recall that fragment of knowledge that was eluding him. After a few minutes he realized the thing that was bothering him was the statement, *"As with Bitterness, the enemy is overtaken and destroyed."* Jack couldn't make sense of that. He needed more knowledge than he had.

Taking out his cell phone he called Charlie Wu in the Fortress. "Charlie, I need you to run a statement through your computers and see what you can determine as to its meaning."

He gave the statement to the computer whiz and waited as the ultrafast CRAY computer net chewed on it. It took only six seconds before Charlie had the results. "Jack, the key to the statement is, of course, the word "Bitterness". In the context of the scriptures the word corresponds to the name "Wormwood" in Revelation. It's the third trumpet judgment. It goes like this; Revelation 8:10-11. *"The third angel sounded his trumpet, and a great star, blazing like a torch, fell from the sky on a third of the rivers and on the springs of water--- the name of the star is Wormwood. A third of the waters turned bitter, and many people died from the waters that had become bitter."* Charlie added, "Wormwood in Hebrew means "Bitterness".

Jack thanked him and returned to prayer. "Master, how does this apply to the enemy in the caves on Basilan Island?"

As he sat there he watched a series of pictures come into his mind. First he saw the Egyptians dying in the Red Sea as it rushed back to its normal place. Then he saw a great waterfall with the water crashing down into a valley. Lastly he saw a picture of the surface of the sea, calm and unbothered. "Okay, I get it, thank you Yahshua!" Jack shouted as he jumped up and went to find Mark.

CHAPTER NINE

Mark went over all the scenarios for the tenth time. He was beginning to think that they'd have to risk at least a partial bombardment to even the odds.

The SOG had arrived and was encamped in the basement annex of the Embassy for the moment. Captain Wollard had been promoted to the rank of Major. Most of the people making up the SOG had gained in rank during their pursuit of America's enemies.

This special operations group had been formed by the Crossfire Team with the approval of General Miles, the Chairman of the Joint Chiefs of Staff. The SOG had been formed by Yahveh drawing only top soldiers who believed in Yahshua. The SOG was made up of ten women and twenty-five men between the ages of 24 and 31. Experience in SpecOps and elite groups was a major factor in the history of each of the members. There were eight Navy SEALs, none with less than four year's service, two team leaders, and two squad leaders. Twelve top Army Rangers six of which were women from the little known Ranger regiment that secretly recruited and trained women on the same level as their male counterparts. Nine Force Recon Marines all with extensive combat service. Mark had not been surprised to see both Craig and Kevin Steel in that group. The two Marines had fought alongside the Crossfire Team in Israel.

The last five members were U.S. Air Force Special Ops personnel, three of them were women from the PsyOps group. These people were a distinct advantage for the Crossfire Team in dealing with their world-wide enemies.

Mark thought, "Even with all the talent we have, the terrorists still have the high ground advantage in an all-out assault. They could bracket our people and chew them up without us getting clear shots at them!"

Jack walked into the planning room and sat down across from Mark. Jack had a big grin on his face. Mark looked at him in frustration. "Just what do you have to grin about?"

Jack watched his friend's face change when he told him about the dream and the conclusion he'd come to in the last few minutes. Mark lost the irritated frown and got a feral gleam in his eyes. Mark nodded as Jack finished, "Let's check the LANDSAT-8 data again. If the walls of the caves where they meet the sea are thin enough, we could really wash up the whole deal."

Laura walked in on their conversation and listened to the new information from Jack. She thought about it for a few seconds and asked, "That's great, but where does that leave us with the strong men and the Secretary and his wife?"

Jack had considered that. "A select group has to go in and rescue the Secretary and his wife before we move on the destruction of the terrorists. Didn't you say that Yahveh will weaken the strong men? He will subdue them before us. And you will annihilate them quickly?"

Laura nodded, "Yeah, that pretty well covers it doesn't it?"

Mark looked at the two of them. "What?"

Jack said, "Elohim says that he will subdue the strong men but that Laura has to annihilate them. If we flood the place it won't affect spiritual beings even though it could kill their troops. The question is; will flooding the place drive them out as the Master told us to do it?"

Mark threw down his pen. "Kids, we're in the last few minutes of the fourth quarter here. Just make a decision because we only have a few hours to plan the entire assault."

Jack sat there in prayer and thought. Looking up he said, "Why don't we do this. Send in UDT teams if the wall can be breached. Have them set explosives and evacuate the area. At that point we initiate an assault that bottles up the people in the caves. But, we don't attempt to enter and get into those deadly cross fires they have set up. Won't that bring out the strong men to defend their territory? If it does, then we take them out and set off the charges which would eliminate the rest of the rats in the caves."

Mark shook his head. "Good idea and not a bad plan but you're not thinking of the other possibilities." Mark's greater experience in planning assaults and his analytical mind saw the flaws in Jack's simple plan.

Standing up, Mark used a laser pointer to indicate the cave locations on the drawing they had on the wall. "There are over a dozen entrance/exits that we can see in the LANDSAT8 scans. There is a reasonable possibility that there are others they could use to escape through and possibly counter-attack us from the rear. Also, we don't know about reserve troops they could have living in the area that could be brought to bear on us quickly. Next, even though Elohim said that we were to annihilate the strong men, He didn't say how long that might take or even in what dimension. How would you cover those contingencies?"

Jack pondered the question and said, "Okay, how about a more flexible, but faster assault? What if we set off charges at the middle level of the caves and start flooding them from the bottom up? That will drive the terrorists upward as the caves fill up and we can engage them on our terms on the surface. We will deal with the strong men as they come."

Mark considered Jack's plans as he presented them. "We really don't have the fineness of charges to drop just a segment of the cave wall. Most likely the whole thing would go and flash flood the entire cave structure and that won't be good for the Secretary and his wife."

Laura had been praying the whole time they were discussing the options. "I think you've both got the solution in hand. We go in, get the hostages out, set the charges, evac and then blow them. We will deal with the troops that survive and the strong men above ground. Although, I'm pretty sure that we need to create a spiritual distraction to engage the strong men before we try to sneak up and plant the charges."

Mark nodded, "But, we still have a problem of timing. We don't have the underwater charges here and it will take way too long to get them here." Mark suddenly smiled as a concept appeared in his mind. "But, I think I've just been given a way around that."

Mark pulled out his cell phone and started calling in favors as "General Connelly". Fifteen minutes later he put the phone away at his belt and smiled. "Our plan is set and we need to advise the troops to be ready for action tomorrow night at midnight local time."

Laura asked, "What did you arrange?"

Mark smiled, "I made a package deal. At 10 p.m. local time tomorrow, the U.S.S. Stingray will torpedo the wall of the caves which have been defined by GPS locations. That takes care of the munitions and the delivery without us risking personnel or having to wait while they return and change into combat gear. Now let's figure a distraction that will draw out the strong men so we can destroy them."

CHAPTER TEN

The next evening a little after nine o'clock local time, Oberon felt his will simply wilt and he felt defeated. His competitor and sometimes ally, Terror, had inexplicably also lost his desire to inflict death and destruction and he too felt like giving up. These two mighty strong men of Satan had lost their drive and interest in the Crescent Dagger group's terroristic goals.

Oberon didn't even want to tease Terror into a rage like normal. Suddenly the whole thing was a huge waste of time. Leaving the cave area, Oberon journeyed to the surface of the island. He was intent on getting as far away from the idiots and sniveling cowards as he could. He knew his orders were to continue to manipulate the humans into every evil thing possible. Well, he had done that for four of their years and it hadn't amounted to much. Everything had been a waste of time actually. He was joined by Terror a few minutes after leaving.

Terror didn't like Oberon at all. In fact he hated him. But, tonight he just didn't care. They talked in their tongue for a few minutes when Terror caught sight of something out of place. He started to go towards it to investigate it when Oberon knocked him aside and went toward the light himself. Terror would normally have gone berserk and attacked Oberon with the intent of killing him for such an insult. Tonight he ignored the snub and simply trailed Oberon over to the light in the jungle.

Both strong men were in the spiritual domain and could only slightly interact with the human's physical world. So, when they approached the three humans standing by the bright light pointed straight up, all they could do is hang there and wonder what was going on. Each one of them attempted to place fear in the hearts of the humans but were rebuffed by their close relationship with the strong men's hated enemy, Yahshua. His closeness to them and the spirit of Yahveh living in each of them angered them but kept them away from controlling even one of the puny humans.

The two men and one woman were setting up an altar and were starting to pray to Yahveh. These were indeed miserable Christians and needed to be destroyed. Not being of a mind to require the services of the human terrorists for only three puny humans, Oberon violated a bunch of spiritual laws and covenants and stepped into the human world with destruction in his heart. Not to be outdone, Terror joined him one step behind.

As they appeared, Laura's armor appeared at the same time. She raised the Sword of Faith which was streaming with the power of Yahveh in white streams of light. Oberon withdrew his massive black sword and attacked the weak human female. In the physical world he was about nine feet tall and built massively like a black rock. He had easily destroyed dozens of soldiers at one time. This would be easy!

As Oberon stomped up to Laura he swung his black sword in a terrific crosscut. Laura raised her sword to meet the larger blade. The black blade crumbled to pieces when the two struck. Laura swung her blade at Oberon's midriff but he jumped nimbly out of the path of the blade. As she brought her blade back to a frontal guard position Oberon feinted to the left. As she turned to her left and moved the blade to cover that direction the large black demon suddenly reversed his path and came directly at Laura from behind. Laura used both hands to drive her blade over her head to the rear. Oberon's arms were almost around her when he stopped suddenly and Laura's blade plunged into his chest. It was like the demon lit up from the inside with the bright white light. Without a sound he exploded and disappeared. Laura spun around on her right foot and went to high guard position facing Terror.

Terror was filled with mixed feelings. He was glad to see Oberon defeated, but that left him face-to-face with the one that defeated him. Deciding he was overmatched he turned to flee back into the spiritual dimension but came face-to-face with the angel Rose. She was in her fighting mode with the bright white light of her anger exploding from around her. The calmer gold color was no more than a slight hue.

Confronted front and back gave Terror the backbone he normally didn't display. He screamed his defiance and raised his sword to attack Rose. As the demon turned to attack the angel Laura charged at the demon's back. Laura drove her blade directly through his back and out of his chest. He disappeared with a whimper.

Rose's fierce whiteness decreased after Terror was dispatched. She smiled at Laura and faded from view. Laura quit praying her battle prayer and her armor faded from view which left only the light they had used to draw the strong men to them illuminating the area. Mark reached over and turned the switch extinguishing the light and the jungle was plunged into darkness.

Laura and the two men got down on their knees and prayed together. They thanked Yahveh for the battle and the victory since it was His. They prayed for all the people in the SOG and the team when they went to save the Philippine Secretary and his wife.

CHAPTER ELEVEN

The team and the SOG troops moved into positions near the two main entrances to the Crescent Dagger cave system. It was to be strictly a holding action while four members of the team searched for the government official and his wife and a support group mined their end of the cave system.

Suited up for combat Mark walked over to his wife and the Malones to discuss their penetration of the caves. Sarah mentally inspected him and his image as he approached them. Mark was dressed in black rip-stop nylon trousers and blouse covering his body armor and trauma plates. His combat boots were also black as was the combat harness that held a supply of grenades, knives, garrotes, and other tools of mayhem. He had a tactical holster on his right side with a .40 caliber Glock at hand level for a quick draw and four magazines in two pouches to the left side. He was wearing a black combat helmet with his night-vision glasses above his face and his tactical radio with bone-conduction microphone and speaker nestled close to his right neck and cheek. His lead weapon, the M8 was slung over his right shoulder where he could bring it on-line very quickly. Sarah knew that Mark also had a.357 magnum in a pancake holster on his right side under his uniform and a four-barrel derringer in his boot. All in all a very dashing figure even with the combat cosmetics coating his face and hands.

Sarah knew that the rest of them were decked out very similar to Mark. It was a professional image that tended towards the functional more than the chic.

Mark was talking to Charlie Wu halfway around the world in Denver. He finished up the conversation and hit the recall button on his battle comm pack. The rest of the SOG slipped out of their positions and zeroed in on Mark's location. Mark looked up at the others and smiled. "Charlie has been busy. He got the U.S. forces on the south side of the island to lend him a Predator. He has been using the Thermal Imaging on the drone to look for anything in the cave system that would show us where the hostages are being held. He thinks he knows where they are, but better yet, he just told me that all but about six of the terrorists are grouping together in the big cave. It must be a major meeting or something and it gives us an opportunity to infiltrate our search and rescue team. When everyone is here we'll assign teams and go.

Twenty of the warriors were tasked with remaining above ground and interdicting any reserve troops that could be called from other locations or handling any attempted escapees. Twenty people doesn't sound like a major force but in this case it was more than sufficient. They retained all the heavy weapons and had both satellite and Predator coverage to pinpoint targets if necessary.

Mark assigned teams with Sarah, Jack, Laura, and himself as leaders and gave Laura's team the job of locating and rescuing the hostages while Jack's team held at the cave entrance and provided support and combat coverage for team one in the event things got hot. Mark's team would go in a separate entrance and place explosives to assist the torpedo strike in bringing down the cave structure.

Four SOG specialists from Jack's team went in to the closest major cave entrance and took out the guards, put static loop tapes on the cameras, and bypassed the alarms without alerting the rest of the terrorists. The two teams of Crossfire warriors slid quietly into two different entrances to the cavern system on the lookout for cameras, trip wires, Claymores, or more terrorists. They were outgunned ten to one and it would be better to get the hostages and leave without a fight. They only had forty-six minutes until the sea came calling anyway.

Laura made her way carefully but quickly towards the GPS coordinates that Charlie Wu had given her as the location of the hostages. There were twists and cross paths that had to be decided on and quickly. Charlie had also indicated that there were at least two more terrorists very close to the prisoners.

The dark, dank cave system would have been scary except for the night-vision gear the team was using. The AN/PVS-7 Delta Night Vision Goggles were the latest version Gen-4 gear which rendered everything in shades of gray and looked a lot like an extremely clear black and white television picture without the raster pattern created by beam fly back.

Spotting a device at floor level she held up her left hand in a fist. Everyone on the team hunkered down and didn't move. Laura pointed two fingers at her eyes and then pointed at the device. Stacy Deville moved quietly forward past Laura and examined the strange contraption. Stacy was one of the team's electronics and weapons experts. It only took her a few seconds to determine that the small box was a single-point retro reflective infrared detector that would set off a remote indicator when a person passed its location.

Taking a small bottle out of her pack, Stacy sprayed the small box with the liquid nitrogen for a few seconds. Satisfied that the entire device was frozen to a crystalline state she stepped on it and it crumbed into frozen dust on the floor of the cave. Pressing the green button on her battle pack got everyone moving forward again.

Coming to the correct GPS coordinates Laura noticed a diffused glow on her right. This turned out to be a heavy canvas acting as a door covering to another room. Raising her NVD she took a small device out of her kit and slid the fiber-optic lens past the curtain. Surveying the room beyond the curtain she saw the Philippine Secretary and his wife sitting on a couch and two of the terrorists watching them. The guards weren't expecting any trouble and their weapons were leaning against the wall as the two burly thugs played some kind of card game. But, they had handguns and were far too close to the hostages.

Checking the room again for anyone she'd missed, Laura withdrew the small lens and whispered to the two men behind her as to the location and preparedness of the guards.

Silencers in place the team members quietly pushed the canvas curtain aside and entered the room. Both of the terrorists died without alarm before they knew anyone had entered the room.

Laura held a finger over her lips in a universal sign to stay quiet to the Badar's. They did as they were told and got up quickly. Two of the team members quickly dressed them in body armor and the whole team flowed quietly back into the rough-hewn hall with the ex-hostages enclosed in their formation.

While Laura's team was rescuing the hostages, Mark had his team placing explosives at every predetermined place to multiply the damage when the submarine fired its torpedoes. He moved as close to the big cave as possible in an attempt to spy on the gathering. As he slid around a jutting wall segment he suddenly came face-to-face with one of the terrorists bound on some obscure errand.

Not wanting to shoot him and possibly give away their presence, Mark raised his M8 as a threat and pointed it between the man's eyes. With his finger on the trigger it was clearly evident to the Zultarian that any attempt to alert his brothers-in-arms would result in his immediate death. He slowly raised his hands above his head in submission. Mark drew him back away from the entrance to the big cave and two of the team members grabbed him and covered his mouth to prevent any cries for help. One of the warriors had his combat knife out with the razor-sharp edge right at the man's throat. The Specialist looked at Mark for his decision. Normally Mark would have eliminated the man as a possible problem but he felt Yahveh's leading not to do it this time. Mark shook his head and whispered to bind the man and they would take him hostage to see if he would reveal anything to them later. The man was quickly bound with riot cuffs and two of the team lifted him off the ground and headed back to the entrance.

One of the SOG warriors slipped up to Mark and tipped his head for Mark to follow him. They ventured down a side tunnel that wasn't lit. At the end of the tunnel was a door standing partially open. Mark gently pushed it open and looked out on a large section of the cave that was obviously a manufacturing area. There seemed to be no one there at the present but a level down on the main floor were all the machines and work stations required to make, something, Mark wasn't sure what it was for. He spotted about four hundred small crates banded and ready for shipping standing to their left on the cave floor. He pointed at them and went up in the air with his fingers spreading out in opposite directions indicating an explosion. The SOG warrior smiled and nodded. He took off his backpack and primed the remote control for eight pounds of C4. Carefully tossing the backpack into the middle of the crates the two men exited the room and hurried back to the rest of their team. Mark worked his way over to the doorway to the main cave and glanced inside. He pulled his head back at once.

There seemed to be a general stirring in the big cave indicating the end to the meeting and Mark decided that they needed to be elsewhere very soon if they didn't want to take on the two hundred terrorists in a pitched gun battle. Mark hit the Extraction button on his battle pack and his team moved quickly back to the surface without any more contact with the enemy. He noticed several lenses pointing in their direction that they hadn't seen before. Oddly there hadn't been any reaction to their presence. "Too late to worry about them now!" He thought as they hurried as quietly as they could to and out the entrance.

On the surface Mark saw that Laura's team had the hostages safely away as well as the prisoner his team had captured. Checking the time on his watch he saw that the Navy's contribution to the cave system was less than a minute away. Signaling the rest of the teams to move back away from the cave system he ran with the troops for twenty seconds and then went to ground.

On the submarine the Captain ordered the torpedoes to be fired to the predetermined stress points in the cave wall.

The MK 48 Torpedo is the standard U.S. Navy submarine launched torpedo, with advanced capability (ADCAP). A highly capable weapon, the MK 48 can be used against surface ships or submarines, and has been test fired under the Arctic ice pack and in other arduous conditions. The torpedo is propelled by a piston engine with twin, contra-rotating propellers in a pump jet or shrouded configuration. The engine uses a liquid mono propellant fuel, and the torpedo has a conventional, high-explosive warhead. The MK 48 has a sophisticated guidance system permitting a variety of attack options. As the torpedo leaves the submarine's launch tube a thin wire spins out, electronically linking the submarine and torpedo. This enables an operator in the submarine, with access to the submarine's sensitive sonar systems, initially to guide the torpedo toward the target. This helps the torpedo avoid decoys and jamming devices that might be deployed by the target. The wire is severed and the torpedo's high-powered active/passive sonar guides the torpedo during the final attack.

Nineteen feet long and weighing over a ton and a half, each MK 48 has approximately 650 pounds of high explosive in its warhead. The Scorpion fired four MK 48s at the cave wall.

Arriving almost simultaneously at their targets the combined 2600 pounds of explosives destroyed the entire wall of the main cave and most of the walls to the seaward side of the smaller caves. The tremendous blast effect roared through the caves destroying almost everything in their path. The explosives planted by the SOG added to the complete destruction through its blast wave front going the other direction. The eight pounds of C4 obliterated the pile of crates in the manufacturing area even before the force of the sea water released into the cave system smashed anything that the explosions missed.

After a few minutes the sea surged back and forth and then claimed its new territory and a new quietness came to that portion of the island. Even though they waited on-guard for twenty minutes no one came out of the Crescent Dagger headquarters to fight with the team or the SOG.

There was a low growling sound that jellied the insides of the warriors on the surface. With a silence that belied the half-mile surface area involved, the entire roof section to the cave area collapsed into the cave area and was submerged almost at once. The team and the SOG were standing on the shore to a new inlet for the sea. The collapsing roof structure effectively entombed anyone that could have survived in the caves. Laura looked at Jack, "Well, that's the first time we've taken out over two hundred terrorists at one time." She shook her head at the death and destruction the terrorists had brought onto themselves.

Mark arranged for the extraction of their personnel and the Badars to the military base at the southern part of the island.

One of the Sysops warriors had been talking in Farsi to the prisoner and motioned Mark over to her position.

Leaning close so he could hear her Margo told him that they had gotten a real find with this man. The team needed to do a deep debrief on him as soon as they landed.

Mark nodded and motioned for the other team members and the SOG commander to link up with him on the silenced intercom. Once they were all there he told them, "Guys, we need to keep the news about the demise of the Crescent Dagger to ourselves for the time being. Okay?" They agreed and Mark got on the radio to provide a concealed arrival and stay at the Combined Forces base.

After the choppers had landed, Juan Badar came up to Mark and asked if he could speak to him for a minute. Mark nodded and led the man to the side of the off-loading operation. Mark looked at the smaller man with gratitude that the team had been able to accomplish Yahveh's work in freeing both him and his wife.

Shaking Mark's hand the Philippine Secretary smiled at him. "Both I and my wife want to thank you for saving us. They were going to demand a ransom and then kill us publicly whether they got it or not. They were an evil people and I am glad that you destroyed them."

Mark shrugged, "There were a lot of people working to save you two. The President of the United States made your rescue a priority."

Juan nodded his head. "I will thank him personally when next we see him. But, I would like to talk to my government about finding a way to thank you and the men and women that were involved in this operation." He indicated the rest of the warriors with a sweep of his hand.

Mark appreciated the man's integrity and honesty. "Thank you for the offer. It will be payment enough to know that you remember these people in your prayers."

Juan stared at the big man for a second. "Si that will happen." Then he walked back to his wife who was talking to several of the women warriors from the SOG.

CHAPTER TWELVE

Ysmael Santos sat in his cell and considered his future. These people shouldn't be treating him like a prisoner. He was a Moro, a Zultarian of Mindanao. He was also an honored member of the Crescent Dagger organization. He wasn't sure but he also thought he might be the only surviving member of that organization. No one told him what had happened at the headquarters after his capture but he felt that he understood the violent shaking of the ground, the collapse of the land over the caves, and the fact that none of his brothers came out after the attack. His horror and sorrow at the loss of all of his friends was muted. He hated their loss but he was a practicing realist. He knew that Zultar was fickle and that these things happened. He would make the best of what came his way. He practiced his non-emotional face and waited for the questions sure to come.

Mark, Jack, and Margo watched the transformations on the terrorist's face in the monitor. Ysmael didn't know that there was a camera on him 24/7. The PsyOps specialist checked the time. "We've given him enough time to build some tension within his mind as to what is coming. He should be fairly pliable now."

Jack studied the terrorist again and asked Margo what it was that she thought he had that was so special.

The trim brunette thought for a moment. "While I was talking to him after his capture he tried to imply that he was an important person. An emissary of great accord. Normally I dismiss talk like this as pride or an attempt to make his position better. This guy said two things that caught my attention. First, he named two names, Abdullah El Sawayah, and Carlos Midrando. Each of these men is just about as high as you can get in the Middle East terrorism organizations and the Cali Cartel in South America." She looked at her two superior officers and smiled. "It's possible that he just heard those names and was parroting them for importance. But, I don't think so. Second, he said "Special meeting" in Farsi. There have been a host of rumors and enticing tidbits in the PsyOps world in the last few months about a unique meeting of terrorist groups about to happen. I think this guy is in on that."

Mark thought back to the statement by Jack that Yahveh had told him that they were going to tackle something major real soon and the leading he had to keep this guy alive. Too many coincidences. "How do you want to get him to talk? He is a terrorist and possibly a leader and would know how to extemporize and mislead."

Margo nodded as she stared at the man's image on the screen. "I have a little something that should give us what we want without the BS." She took her backpack and opened it. Taking out a small kit she pulled out a vial and a hypodermic. Properly loading it and purging the air she put the vial back in the bag and brought out a spray can. Hiding the hypodermic she motioned for Mark to open the door.

Walking into the cell she smiled at Ysmael and walked over to him. She then sprayed him in the face with the aerosol. She backed up quickly and waited a few seconds. Ysmael didn't change expressions or move. Margo bent down and put the spray can on the floor and walked back over to the terrorist and with her left hand on his chest pushed him back into a prone position. Putting the hypo down she pulled out a rubber tube and tied off his left arm. Plumping up a vein she picked up the hypo and injected the contents into the vein. Then she pulled the tube off and let the injection spread into his blood stream. Picking up the can as she walked out she returned with a tape recorder a minute later. Smiling at the two men she pulled a chair out and sat down and stared at Ysmael.

About three minutes later he twitched, gasped, and suddenly sat up. Shaking his head he looked at the others and asked in Arabic, "What is going on? Where am I?"

Margo smiled at him and patted him on the leg. In flawless Arabic she answered his question. "You're in our safe house and you're secure now."

Ysmael visibly relaxed and blew out a big breath. He apparently didn't see either Jack or Mark. Margo asked him, "Are you all right?"

He looked somewhat confused but nodded his head.

Margo clicked on the recorder. "Let's go on about the meeting we were discussing and your part in it. If you're going to be there we don't want any mistakes, right?" She was quietly authoritative and friendly at the same time.

Ysmael thought for a few seconds and frowned. "Where did we leave off?"

Margo pulled a small notebook out of her back pocket. Leafing through the pages she stopped and read. "I am to represent the Crescent Dagger at the meeting." She looked up at him and said, "That's where we were interrupted."

Ysmael nodded. "Yes, I am the representative for the Crescent Dagger. We are only a small organization among the attendees but we have a critical part in supplying the materials for the devices." "We will receive the sums that the cartel has promised or we will not cooperate."

Margo looked a little uncertain. "But we thought the cartels were in charge."

Ysmael laughed, "Yes, in a way they are but they report to the executor. He is the power and he told us that we will succeed with our demands."

Margo nodded, "Very wise. Will the executor be there or will he arrive after you?"

Ysmael thought for a few seconds. "I believe he will be there first. I don't arrive until the second Tuesday of next month. The countdown will be started on Friday. Seventy-two glorious hours and then we will own the entire world!"

Margo stood up and raised a fist. "Yes, we will destroy them all!"

Ysmael smiled at her enthusiasm. "Yes, America and Britain will exist no more as world powers and Europe will cave in within a month. Zultar will be happy with a truly Zultarian world."

Margo nodded. "Do you have your bona fides to attend and do you know where do you have to be?"

Ysmael looked confused for a second and then he grinned. "I know my way around Saudi Arabia and Riyadh. Right under the noses of the Americans. Hah! Of course, my DNA goes with me wherever I go."

He looked a little lost and then said. "I'm very tired and need to sleep. Leave me now."

As the three warriors walked out of the cell, Ysmael lay down and closed his eyes. Margo dimmed the lights in the cell and locked the door.

Turning to Mark she had a very worried look on her face. "What you heard is the truth. He thought he was among friends and had no reason to be careful. I would say that this meeting scares me more than what happened on 9/11.

Jack agreed with her and asked. "I don't understand why he would open up like that. Isn't that a truth serum of some kind?"

Margo smiled ruefully. "Not really. It is a psychedelic hallucinogen that removes any fear or hesitation on the part of the drugged person. Ysmael didn't have any reason to worry about what he said. His world was completely rosy and upbeat. The drug makes the person feel that they are completely in charge of the situation and therefore they can be open and honest which is what they always want anyway."

Mark had been quiet during the exchange. "That was "Cherry1" wasn't it?"

Margo looked at her boss and her estimation of his knowledge went up a notch. "Actually it is "Cherry3", they were able to remove the worst of the side effects."

Mark nodded slowly. "You mean like lifetime dementia or being brain dead?"

Margo shrugged, "You have to break eggs to make an omelet. The worse thing Ysmael will have is a two-day headache and a real bout of depression. Plus, he is strong and young so he can go on being a murderous terrorist for a long time."

Jack saw the problem from both Mark and Margo's sides. "Mark, can I talk to you for a minute alone?"

Mark nodded. "Okay Margo, we can talk later about this. I really don't want Psyops drugs being used unless we have no other option. Are we in agreement?"

Margo nodded and left the room to go back to the SOG camp area.

Jack sat down with Mark. "I understand your being upset by her unilateral action with Ysmael and we need to let them know that they have to approve these things through us. But, I would suggest that we approach it as an overall operation directive so we don't destroy the incentive or creativeness of the SOG personnel. She should have asked but we did need that information more than we need to protect terrorists."

Mark had already cooled down and knew he'd over-reacted. He needed to mend a fence with Margo before his reaction could cause a division in the SOG. "Yeah, you're right. It just worried me because of the fatal reputation of the Cherry drugs. I jumped the gun on that one. I'll straighten it out and we'll hold a meeting to see if we can't get us back to full teamwork status."

Jack knew Mark would take care of the problem.

CHAPTER THIRTEEN

Jack called the team together for a quick brainstorm session.

Su Li listened carefully to the tape Margo had made and nodded her head. "It sounds real. What devices are they talking about?"

Mark shook his head. "We aren't sure yet. It is obviously part of a delivery system for some form of destruction in the U. S. and Great Britain."

Laura had been praying but hadn't gotten anything that would help the discussion. "What do we do now?"

Jack said, "It is my opinion that this jumbo meeting of terrorists and drug cartel people is being orchestrated by this "Executor". This person must have some real pull in the dark world if they can get all the warring factions in those two worlds to pull together in a plan to destroy the free world. Most of those groups hate each other as much as they do us. Also, if there were two strongmen assigned to the Crescent Dagger there will probably be even more demonic power involved in this meeting."

Mark had been thinking about a proper response to the meeting and decided to share his thoughts with the others. He stood up and got their attention. "Guys, besides the leading that Jack got about our having to handle something big soon I think this will have to be handled by us."

The number of concerned looks caused Mark to elaborate. "This meeting has had to have been scheduled for a long time to involve this many organizations and the security has had to be really tight for there only to be clues or hints out in the world. That would suggest demonic help to keep it under wraps. The Father himself was the one that kept Ysmael alive by telling me to make him a hostage rather than just to eliminate him so this may be the first real leak. If we tell the government or even the other agencies the chances are very good that someone will leak the knowledge back to the bad guys and the meeting will be moved or cancelled. We need to take advantage of this heaven-sent opportunity."

Laura shook her head. "Mark! Do you realize what you are suggesting? If we take this on and don't tell anyone else about it, then if we mess up, the destruction of the free world will be completely on our heads. Probably millions of people will die and societies destroyed because of our unilateral action. If we bring in the other forces and attempt to stop them then we will have done all we could to prevent the chaos. If we go it alone then . . ."She left the thought up to the others to flesh out the implications.

Sarah was considering those implications when the newest Christian in the group, Su Li suggested, "Why don't we ask Yahveh what he wants us to do?"

Laura smiled and pointed her finger at Su Li. "Bingo."

The team started to pray when there was a knock on the door. Mark opened it slightly and saw many of the soldiers from the SOG standing in the hall. "Yes?"

The Spec5 at the door spoke for the rest of them. "Excuse us General Connelly, in the last ten minutes we have all received a real burden to pray with your team."

Mark smiled at him and opened the door all the way. "Come on in."

But since the entire SOG was present they retired to the SOG quarters to find enough room for everyone.

Mark summed up the situation and the dangers for the entire team and SOG if they weren't one-hundred percent in Yahveh's will. They all began to pray sincerely. The heaviness that was present when the Holy Spirit or the heavenly host was near fell on everyone. The praying took on a new intensity as each person sensed the presence of Elohim. As a group they were petitioning the Father for his leading as to what to do with the middle-East meeting.

Mark had never felt the closeness of Yahveh when praying in a group and was awed by the absolute correctness of the world at that time. The praying became praise and worship that merged together and took everyone to a new height in their faith and belief.

When the heaviness lifted, Sarah sat down in a chair and watched the others come back and arrange themselves. Laura raised her eyes to her husband and asked him, "Did you get an answer as to what we are to do?"

Jack nodded and looked around. Finding a spiral notebook he tore off one page at a time and handed it to each person. Finished, he said, "I want each person to write down what you received concerning this super meeting and what you believe Yahveh is telling us to do." He sat down and started writing on his sheet.

Ten minutes later he collected the sheets and sat down. Reading each one quickly he put it in a pile. When he had read the last one and put it down he wasn't surprised to find only one pile. Standing up he nodded and spoke. "People, all forty of us got the same message. Oh, your words are different, but your message is the same. The first thing we have to do is be responsible which means we need to tell the President and the CJCS what we know and what Yahveh has instructed us to do. That way we have backup if we fail and we are working as a sanctioned operation rather than as a rouge unit. If the President and Joint Chiefs of Staff veto our operation then they are not hearing from Elohim which will not make sense. I know they pray and obey just like we do. Therefore, if they are in the loop then we have legitimacy and their backing. Our job is to spy out this combined group and determine what they are up to. Then the President can call in the rest of the free world for an organized response on how to stop them."

Mark pulled out his cell phone and called the Joint Force Commander at the base they were at. "General Bartlett, this is General Connelly. I need to see you immediately." He nodded and hung up the phone. Tasking Su Li to start making arrangements to get the combined team and SOG to Saudi Arabia in the next forty-eight hours, Mark told the other four team members to prep for a trip to the U.S. He then told the Colonel in charge of the SOG to make their preparations for the trip to the Middle East.

Explaining the situation without providing any details about the upcoming meeting or the interrogation of the prisoner Mark was able to convince the base commander to keep the lid on the disappearance of the Crescent Dagger terrorists and their complete organization. Jack showed the commander the videos they had taken of the raids and the execution of the group. The commander was visibly impressed when the land above the caves collapsed and sunk. He assured the team the information would be held back until his commander instructed him to talk about it.

Back in their room Mark looked at the five member team. "How are we going to find out what goes on at that meeting?"

Sarah smiled, "Easy, I saw it right away. With the right haircut and a little cosmetics Judah Maritz could be a twin brother to Ysmael. I'm sure that David Zahavy would be glad to join us in this venture and that Judah would be up for impersonating Ysmael.

Mark nodded, "Yeah, but what about the DNA identification?"

Sarah smiled at her husband. "We will cross that bridge before they test Judah. But, we need to know more about the location of the meeting, the timing, and what it was the Crescent Dagger is to provide."

Laura wasn't fazed by the needs list brought up by Sarah. She knew that Yahveh would see that they got what they needed before they needed it. One of the calls made by Su Li was to get their flight path to the U.S. approved. She received a clearance for the flight.

At a villa in Mexico a message was received giving the same information concerning the flight of the Citation X and the times involved. The woman who received the message picked up a phone and gave the man on the other end the green light for his operation based on the information received.

The team boarded the Citation X in Manila at 4 a.m. for the seven hour flight to Los Angeles. They would arrive at LAX slightly after noon West Coast time. The SOG would leave that afternoon for a direct MATS flight to Riyadh, Saudi Arabia.

Six hours later, at eleven o'clock Pacific time, a three-plane flight of U.S. Air Force fighters left Edwards AFB on a secret mission. The flight had interdiction orders to bring down a single aircraft carrying a deadly cargo.

CHAPTER FOURTEEN

Piloting the Citation X as it winged its way across the Pacific Ocean towards the United States, Su Li thought about her involvement with the Crossfire Team and her understanding of Yahveh's will.

She knew the truth now. It had been a long and difficult path for her for the last few years but she was finally on the right path and had become a child of Yahveh and his Son Yahshua. She was capable of discerning the truth and relaxing into Yahveh's arms. It had brought a peace to her that she had never known before. It had also brought a new amount of suffering and reorganization of her priorities.

She made two adjustments to their course and checked in with their FAA controller for the civilian flight they were at this time. The Citation X was a sweet transport plane for a pilot with every leading-edge Techno-gadget at her fingertips. This one had military modifications too. But, it wasn't an F-22 Raptor with even more stuff and a ride that set your hair on fire.

As the flight settled back into a boring routine, Su Li realized that she had come to the understanding that she was where Yahveh wanted her and that was the absolutely the best place she could be even if it didn't line up with what the world thought was best. Deep inside she was content and even happy.

Her introspection was interrupted by a communication from Charlie Wu in the Fortress in Denver. He kept a sharp watch over the team through every means available. His ability to use both U.S. and foreign satellites was based on his time as a leading spy for the Chinese government. He was using a Russian spy satellite that gave him a wide view of several hundred miles around the Citation X and it's path back to America.

He had spotted a cloaked three plane flight of modern fighters on an interception course and had been trying to determine their nationality and their orders. He had been unable to get any information on the flight. So the next step was to warn Su Li of the possible problem. It could just be a training mission by the Air Force. But then again it could be something more sinister.

Su Li checked the advanced military radar that had been installed in their business jet. Nothing showed as yet which was puzzling since Charlie's information should put them within range.

Charlie put a call into NORAD and checked with their contact there. NORAD was tracking the unknown radar-elusive flight also. Since the flight was outside U.S. territory in the Pacific Ocean there had been no interdiction efforts as yet.

Su Li called Mark up to the cockpit and explained the situation. Mark slid into the empty co-pilot seat and buckled in as he studied the radar. Calling NORAD as General Connelly he got priority service. Since the premier defense system in the U.S. couldn't identify these planes Mark mentally labeled them as hostile and thought about their options.

First, the rapidly approaching aircraft were probably fighters which meant the Citation X couldn't out-run them, out-maneuver them, or out-fight them. He immediately called for fighters to be scrambled from the western seaboard of the U.S. but, they wouldn't get there in time to help. Whatever was going to happen would happen in the next ten minutes.

Mark also knew that until their intentions were made clear, the oncoming flight really could not be labeled as hostile. Looking at Su Li he smiled. "Let's get ready for them in case they are aggressors."

Su Li nodded. In her mind the on-coming aircraft were definitely hostile just by their interception course. She flipped two switches on her left switch panel. This activated the flare and chaff dispensers and brought on-line the radar jamming circuitry. Mark used the intercom to warn the rest of the team of the problem and to suggest they tighten their seat belts in case sudden maneuvering was necessary.

Three warning alarms went off suddenly and Su Li dropped the right wing straight down toward the ocean and snapped the bizjet into a right turn directly into the oncoming fighters. This presented the smallest radar image to the approaching fighters and missiles. Chaff and flares were released automatically by the computer when the missiles were detected.

The sudden turn and the decoys worked for the first pass of the fighters and no missile came within three hundred feet of the aircraft. The second pass wouldn't be as easy now that the attackers knew the civilian jet had some military capabilities.

Mark was using the classified frequency to talk to the Air Force about the attack and the attackers. "We were just attacked by air-to-air missiles from three MiG-MAPO 1.42s. Looks a lot like a Tomcat with canard wings. Very fast and stealthy. I doubt that we will get a second break. Our mods allowed us to dodge their first shots but I'm pretty sure they're going to finish the job on the next pass. See if you can track these birds back to their origin. I've been sending an open SOS but the scopes are clear. I'm guessing we have less than two minutes before they are back here."

Su Li drove the Citation X past its limits in an attempt to evade the next pass of the fighters. The threat board was clear but that didn't mean anything because the radar couldn't detect the aircraft until they fired their missiles and that would be too late.

The bizjet was vibrating from the maximum power application and Su Li waited for the next move by the attackers. What happened next baffled her.

Three brilliant explosions off to their left lit up the cockpit. Mark got up and leaned over behind Su Li and tried to make sense of the smoke trails falling to the sea behind them. Mark commented over the radio. "I don't know what just happened but I think the enemy is now missing three of their aircraft."

Su Li snapped her fingers and pointed out the right hand window. Mark sat down and looked at one of the most beautiful sights he'd seen for a long time. Flying formation off the right side of the business jet were three F-117 fighters. Mark got a low energy radio message that wouldn't be heard by anyone else.

"Crossfire Team. Thought you could use some help. We were on a classified CIA air interdiction operation and heard your SOS. So much for the "superior" Russian stealth fighters. We had them painted from the time they attacked you but they never saw us coming. We flew right down their tailpipes and blew them out of the sky. The question I have is why the Russians are trying to down your aircraft so close to our country."

A stronger signal broke in, "Crossfire Flight, Predator Flight Two is closing on your position. Do you have a fix on the bogies?"

The low power signal came back, "Crossfire, here comes your sky cap. When they ask who trashed the Ruskies, tell them it was Robin Hood. They'll understand." With that the three F-117s rolled to the right and went into afterburners. They quickly disappeared into a gathering cloud front.

Several minutes later a six plane flight of F-22 Raptors formed up around the business jet. Mark talked to the flight commander and explained their recent salvation by "Robin Hood". He got back a cautious "Ahh, Roger that sir."

The remainder of the flight was uneventful and the team landed at Edwards AFB in Southern California. Mark made a point of thanking the Raptor commander and his pilots. He also silently thanked the F-117s.

After refueling, Su Li took off immediately for Andrews AFB in Camp Springs, Maryland just outside of Washington, D.C. The Citation X landed at 2:57 p.m.

CHAPTER FIFTEEN

At precisely four p.m. Mark walked into the Pentagon in an icy cold state. It was a tightly controlled balance between peaceful calm and screaming mad. He had been praying all the way in from Andrews AFB for calmness. The fact that three of the newest Russian jet stealth fighters had just tried to kill him and his friends wasn't giving him happy thoughts.

Reaching the office of the Chairman of the Joint Chiefs of Staff of the military services he barely glanced at Angela, General Miles secretary. She saw he was coming with a full head of steam. She pointed at the General's office door and pressed the access button. Mark walked in and saluted the five-star General.

General Miles shared Mark's feelings about the attempted shoot-down and waved him to a seat in front of his desk after returning the salute. He had the phone to his ear. "Yes, General, I understand, please get back to me as soon as you can." He hung up the phone and stared at Mark.

The Chairman frowned and shook his head. "Mark, I extend my apologies that we weren't on top of this and they got a shot at you. I understand your pilot managed to make them miss on their first pass. Is that true?"

Mark nodded, "Yes Sir, that is true. Su Li is an excellent pilot who has surprised many with her skill. I just don't understand what was behind those three MiG-144s targeting our jet. Have the Russians declared war on us or are they just plain nuts?"

General Miles held up his hand to silence the young man in front of him. Assuming a fatherly look he told Mark, "I personally believe a lot of the senior ranking officers in Russia are significantly unbalanced, but then that's just my personal opinion." He shook his head. "It looks like the Russians weren't behind this. They are going bananas trying to figure out how they lost three of their most prized warplanes. They are so upset that they have even resorted to speaking the truth to us about it. The General in charge of the airbase where these three aircraft were stationed has no knowledge of how his signature and voiceprint approval were generated that released the three planes to a special Spetsnaz group." This happened two days ago. The system they use is similar to ours. Aircraft and weapons are assigned a flight, armed, and fueled only by direct orders from the base commander. This flight had that authorization and when three Spetsnaz pilots showed up with the correct credentials, they were allowed to fly off with the planes."

The General shook his head. "Everyone thought it was a routine operation. That it was a phony didn't come to light until seven hours later when the planes didn't return as scheduled from their mission. The Russians checked and found that there was no special Spetsnaz group or pilots."

Mark was at a loss. "You mean to tell me that Russia fell for a ruse and lost three of their new super-stealthy leading-edge fighters?"

General Miles nodded his head. "Yeah, and to confirm their report they released the tail numbers and armament on each of the craft."

Mark sighed, "Great! Well tell them that those three tail numbers are resting at the bottom of the Pacific Ocean about eighty miles off the western U.S. seaboard. I'll get them the GPS coordinates and the little bit of gun camera film available to verify their destruction."

The General's eyebrows went up a notch. "They were destroyed? What, did you shoot them down with a handgun?"

Mark shook his head, "No, a secret CIA flight of F-117s caught them off guard and wasted them before they could turn our airplane into flying scrap metal."

The General called up the information on the Russian fighter that went under various code names such as the MIG-1-44, ATF-Ski or MIG MAPO-1.42. It had a speed of 2450 km/h and was supposed to be very good and agile at air combat. Looking up at Mark he commented, "This aircraft is supposed to be the equivalent of our F-22 Raptor, possibly even better. The program was delayed a dozen times by financial problems but finally got to production four years ago when the Chinese and two other countries bankrolled the Russians to compete with our jets.

These things are costing the Russians over two billion rubles' each. I'm amazed that the Wobblin' Goblins would be able to take them. Also, it would take an extremely well-informed and capable team effort to swipe one of the Russian planes, let alone three at once."

Mark smiled, "I doubt that the pilots of the stolen MIGs had anywhere near the capabilities of top Russian pilots. Also, I'll wager that those guys were so focused on splashing us that they didn't check their sixes for other radar-stealthy aircraft. Now, do we have any idea where the MIGs came from? They have a range of 2500 miles. Cut that in a third for combat time and a return trip, they had to be fairly close, no more than 800 miles at launch."

General Miles called in his aide. "Any information from NSA as to the origination of those fighters?"

The Captain nodded and handed a sheet to the General and left the room.

General Miles scanned the sheet and gave it to Mark. Mark studied it for a few seconds. "A carrier! They flew those things off of a carrier. They would know the Air Force would be after them after they shot us down and they probably didn't plan to land them. Probably ditch them somewhere and get picked up by a ship. Okay, now the question is, whose carrier?"

The General shook his head, "The NSA didn't get a registration for the carrier because it wasn't a problem at the time of launch and the historical photos that show where the aircraft came from doesn't show anything other than a water-based launch. My guess is that it would have to be a Russian fleet carrier or the Chinese Kuznetzov-class carrier Varyag. Maybe your man in Denver can give you more information."

Mark agreed that Charlie Wu might be able to get more information on the carrier. Then he brought the General up to date on the information they had on the terrorist/cartel meeting in Saudi Arabia. Mark showed General Miles the video tapes he had of the destruction of the Crescent Dagger headquarters and the interrogation of Ysmael. He then asked if they could take point on penetrating the meeting to determine how they planned to strike the U.S. and Britain.

General Miles thought for a few minutes and then leveled with Mark. "I'll take this to the President and we'll see what he wants to do. I take it you have prayed about this?

Mark nodded and told General Miles that the leading everyone in the SOG and the team had received was that they would be the point of the spear.

The General picked up the phone and called the White House. When he was finished he had a meeting that afternoon with the President alone. He looked at Mark, "I won't kid you. With this much of a threat it is probable that the Security Council will be consulted and your team's role may be down played considerably. Some on the council are still not thrilled with the Crossfire Team after the false accusations the Senator made against you."

Mark stood up and saluted the General, "Thank you Sir, sorry to take so much of your time."

General Miles returned the salute and turned to other matters as Mark left.

Mark was wrapped up in his thoughts about the attack and who could have engineered such a con on the Russians. The day was pleasant as he walked to his car in the Pentagon parking lot. He heard a distinct "Uhuh" and a thud.

He eased his pistol out and ducked behind a car to his left. Creeping two rows over he glanced around the next car and saw a man laying on the ground with his neck at a really bad angle and a silenced gun in his left hand. Standing over the man was a vaguely familiar woman with dark brown hair with reddish highlights wringing her hands together. She was well built and stylishly dressed in a light gray dress and white high heels. She had a darker gray sweater over the dress and a necklace of pearls.

Mark holstered his pistol, stood up, and walked over and looked at the man on the ground. Looking up at the woman he asked, "Who are you and who was he?"

The woman looked at Mark and he was taken by the bright blueness of her eyes. She smiled at Mark and said, "I'm Alexis." Looking down at the dead man on the ground and shrugged as she said, "Him I don't know."

Mark bent down and took the gun out of the dead man's hand. He looked at the young woman and asked, "Do you know how he came to be so dead?"

She looked anxious and somewhat puzzled and said, "No, I don't know. I think he tripped over my foot and fell and his head hit the tire on that car." She pointed at the car the man was laying against and smiled at Mark in the hopes he would be pleased now that she had summed it up.

Mark squatted down and quickly frisked the dead man. There was nothing in any of his pockets except a pair of car keys on a remote fob. The guy had definitely been a professional hit man.

Mark stood up and turned around. The woman was gone. She had left silently and was nowhere to be seen. It was almost like she vanished. He continued to look around but she was long gone and he knew two things. The woman was an enigma and she'd probably saved his life. The guy on the ground had the look of a stone cold killer and the gun Mark held in his hand was definitely an assassination weapon that Mark felt had been meant for him. She seemed too naive to have taken out this killer and then it hit him. "She was the blonde in the car in Manila." He was sure it was the same one. He called the Pentagon Police and waited until they arrived.

While he waited he pushed the door button on the key fob. He was rewarded with a dual note from several cars over. He walked over to the area and pushed the button again. A rental car responded and Mark walked over to it and opened it up. Again, the car was clean, nothing to reveal the identity of the man. He locked it up and went back to the body. The police showed up and he gave them what he could, including the unfired gun and a description of "Alexis". They had no record of either the man entering the lot or of the woman. Puzzled, Mark left to join the others of the team.

CHAPTER SIXTEEN

While Mark was in General Miles office an ultra-secure, encrypted communication was taking place between a ship at sea and a nondescript house in London, England.

The quiet but authoritative voice of Mr. Beta was obviously strained as he responded to the report from Mr. Tau. "You're telling me that none of the aircraft returned to report and that the jet they were to attack landed intact?"

The deep bass of Mr. Tau's voice boomed out of the earpiece. "Yes Sir. I'm at a loss as to what happened. The one message I received was that our investment was making the attack on the business jet with an overwhelming number of missiles. After that, nothing and they have not returned to the pick-up point. According to my sources there was an explosion in the air at the point of attack."

Mr. Beta confirmed the information and broke the connection. Thinking for a few minutes he then dialed another overseas number and waited until the line was encrypted and secure before talking. "Mr. Beta here, I have to report a failure of the Crossfire attack. I believe it was a total failure. Mr. Tau has not seen any of the MIGs return to the pick-up point."

The soft voice of Mr. Alpha on the other end of the line was a precise English with little hint of his origin. "Is Mr. Tau confident that the pilots didn't abort the mission and take the aircraft elsewhere? Two hundred million in assets is a big inducement."

Mr. Beta had already thought of that possibility. "Doubtful Mr. Alpha. Those men know some of our capabilities and understand that they wouldn't live to spend any money they could get, even if they could find a buyer that we weren't connected to. I don't think that they survived the encounter with the Crossfire Team."

Mr. Alpha's tone deepened. "This team is even more of a pest and obviously more dangerous than they were in the past. No doubt they will attempt to find whoever was responsible for the attack. Did you take care of the loose ends?"

Mr. Beta nodded and then realized that wouldn't be sufficient. "Yes Sir. I will initiate retrieval of the funds paid to the pilots accounts. The Russian aircraft carrier is completely in the dark assuming that the flight was an authorized Spetsnaz secret operation. None of our people have been associated with the acquisition of neither the aircraft nor the carrier operation. Any information concerning us died with the pilots."

Looking at his laptop computer screen, the leader of level three of the Omicron Cartel asked a further question. "I see that one of the pilots used three hundred thousand dollars of his payment already. Do you know what he did with it?"

Mr. Beta had gotten a report on this two days ago. "Yes Sir, He paid for a manor in Barcelona, Spain. It seems he did have a wife and two children he neglected to tell us about."

Mr. Alpha didn't like that. "I assume you will resolve that possible leak?"

Mr. Beta answered quickly, "Oh yes, it's being taken care of as we speak. I put Mrs. Delta on it. Plus we have arranged through a lawyer to gain control of the house thanks to the paperwork he signed. We will be able to sell it for a profit and recoup our money."

Mr. Alpha thought for a few seconds. "No, don't sell it. We can use it as a meeting place in the near future for Operation Frugal."

Mr. Beta agreed and asked what their next step should be concerning the Crossfire Team.

Mr. Alpha's analytical mind had considered that while they had been talking. "We will do nothing for the time being. Now that they are on the alert for some form of aggression against them we will let them beat their heads against the Russian bear until they run out of leads."

He thought for a few seconds. "Their involvement in our efforts in the Philippines unfortunately resulted in the destruction of the triggers along with the Crescent Dagger organization. This could be a major delay if we can't replace them. They have to be shipped no less than twenty-four hours from now. I have discovered another source of same type of triggers that we might be able to get in time. You will contact the African terrorist group Tigre to supply us with some of the trigger assemblies they have stolen from their military. Too bad, that will cost us considerably more. Mr. Zeta indicated that he had negotiated with Ysmael to supply us the triggers for less than two thousand dollars U.S. each. See to it that the African group can supply the triggers in time regardless of the cost. Also, if anyone shows up from the Philippine group we need to eliminate them immediately. That would be an imposter sent by the Crossfire Team."

Mr. Beta frowned. "I am concerned about this last minute substitution. The trigger assemblies from the Tigre haven't had been tested like the ones the Dagger built. How do we know that they will work as well?

Mr. Alpha thought to himself. "The impudence of this man!" He told Mr. Beta, "I'm sure that they will work and that is all there is to it. See that they are shipped on time."

Mr. Beta knew he had stepped over the line. So, in an attempt to placate Alpha he added, "Well, I say It was a good thing you thought to have those extra cameras installed so we could monitor the goings on in the Basilan cave. Even though the Crossfire Team eliminated several of our cameras we had enough left not only to identify them but to witness the destruction of the caves without losing any personnel. It would have been interesting if we could have warned the Dagger about the incursion before they were eliminated".

Mr. Alpha hung up at that point knowing that Mr. Beta would accomplish everything he wanted done. Anyway, he had roses that needed tending.

In Barcelona, Spain, a beautiful young woman with red hair opened the door to the bright red Porsche Cayman and stepped out. Her long legs and expensive high heeled shoes garnered the desired attention of the attendants who hurried to hold the door for her. Standing up, her full figure and pretty face finished the picture for the on-lookers. Class, pure class. The outfit she was wearing cost hundreds of Euros. She walked with a model's poise to the front door of the up-scale restaurante and entered. The Maitre'd quietly accepted the E 200 bank note and took the lady to the best open table in the house, the one with a view of the Plaza.

Waiting for her order Ms. Delta casually checked the time on the diamond-encrusted watch on her delicate wrist. "Very soon" she thought. There was a crash as a waiter fell over a tray full of dishes on a stand. He had been staring at the beautiful red head and not been watching where he was going. Ms. Delta dismissed the waiter and his problem. She knew she had that effect on men, especially European men.

Her order arrived and she tasted the delicate pasta dish with relish. It was excellent and her taste buds were thrilled.

Twenty two miles away, her earlier handiwork made itself known.

Ava Depaldi was driving down the mountain road from her new house on the way to Barcelona when her Audi made an uncharacteristic sound. It was a muffled "pop". The hill she was on was steep and had a sharp corner to the left coming up. The guard rail separated the road from a three hundred foot fall to rocky riverbed below. Ava stepped on her brakes and the petal went to the floor. She felt a cold fear wash over her and she pulled on the emergency brake as the car picked up speed. The brake handle came up far too easily with no effect. Ava tried to downshift but the synchros couldn't handle the speed and it jammed in neutral. Ava looked up with a horrifying cramp in her stomach as the three thousand pound car slammed into, and through the guard rail. Her last thoughts were of her husband and her two little children back home with the nanny. She screamed as the car smashed into the rocks with such force it broke into several pieces before sinking in the river.

As Ms. Delta savored the fruity white wine in her glass she smiled.

The two men in the Volvo behind the Audi saw the accident and called it into the police. The police that responded had a hard time getting to the wreck down in the river gorge but eventually were able to retrieve the body of the driver and most of the car. Because it was a new car suspicions were raised as to why the car had gone through the guardrail without leaving any skid marks whatsoever. The witnesses swore that she continued to accelerate towards the rail, not brake.

Twelve hours later the investigation into the crash determined that an extremely sophisticated device had been used to kill Ava Depaldi by eliminating her ability to brake. The report was routinely sent to the American FBI for any information they could offer. It was also routinely scanned by the CRAY computer complex in the Crossfire fortress in Colorado. The fact that Ava's husband was a top-rated fighter pilot from Spain who was missing also matched a software inquiry that Charlie Wu had set up to locate any pilot that could have flown the MIGs that had attacked the Citation X.

The report came up on Charlie's main screen. He reviewed the report and printed it out for Mark's evaluation. He also sent a message to the FBI concerning their interest in this case.

Charlie had been intrigued by the device used on Ava's Audi. It apparently had a small charge fastened to the brake master cylinder lines for both circuits and one on the emergency brake cable. That was fairly routine but the activating circuitry was unique. It used a simple microprocessor called a process controller. The Spanish investigation team had determined the sequence of events from the programming still intact in the processor's memory. It seems that the car had to be travelling down a 16 degree slope for at least two hundred meters at a speed of at least seventy kilometers per hour before the device triggered the charges.

Charlie nodded his head. "Yeah, I've seen this arrangement before." The victim had to be at the right place before the charges go off and disable the brakes so that the accident is assured. A high Chinese government official had been killed with an identical device three years before. Charlie and his wife Linda had investigated that and determined that a shadowy international organization had been behind the assassination. A young red-haired girl had been suspected of planting the device but had eluded the authorities. This could be a major lead in the attack against the Crossfire Team if this Spanish woman's husband turned out to be one of the MIG pilots.

Charlie sat back in his ergonomically designed chair and relaxed for a few minutes. He had been at work for the last twelve hours without a break and it felt good to relax in the air conditioned office he had designed.

He thought about how he and his wife came to be major players in what he knew to be one of the top anti-terrorist organizations in the world. It was all because Yahveh led them there. There was no other explanation that would answer all of the questions to their convoluted path from Chinese agents to American agents.

Charlie and Linda Wu had abandoned their native land when they had found Jesus in the most unlikely of places, a Manchurian prison. Charlie's mind suddenly flew back to that time as he sat in the cool quiet of his office.

-----------------------------******-----------------------------

He had been one of the Chinese government's agents and he had improperly fallen in love with another agent. This was frowned upon by the people in charge. But he had always been a wild card, toeing the line only to get to where he wanted to in the Communist Party and in the spy business. He knew when to act correctly and when to break wind at an official function. He had pulled strings and gotten himself assigned to an investigation strictly so that he could be near the woman with whom he had fallen in love.

Linda had not known the brash young agent she was working with very well because they had only met twice before in the normal progress of their careers. The man was a great agent and very talented. Why he would want to work with a relatively new agent like her had mystified her.

As they pursued the enemies of the state across the vast land that is China she became drawn to his good looks and professional mannerisms. It became clear to her that he was interested in her in ways that weren't official when she had caught him staring at her like a moonstruck calf one day. Even though he denied it, she knew. After that it became obvious to them both that they were attracted to each other in many ways. Over the months of the investigation and intrigue they had become deeply

79

committed to each other. He was careful to not damage her reputation and left the sexual part out of their relationship until after they got married. After all, she had been the daughter of a prince and one maintained honor above all things!

As their knowledge of each other's techniques and capabilities grew they begin to function as a team with almost instantaneous reactions to the other person's lead. Both were good agents with excellent fieldcraft and had been trained to take on more than one opponent at a time. Together they were awesome in action.

Both Charlie and Linda were modern Chinese without need for religion or worship per the party line. They held their morals high because it was the right thing to do. That all changed on the day they went to the prison in Manchuria to question a suspect involved in the investigation.

They identified themselves at the prison entrance and were admitted. They had the prisoner brought to a small room to question him about a variety of leads they were following. As they were talking to him a loud disturbance outside the door suddenly burst into their room in the form of three men with homemade knives.

The agents jumped up from their seats and flowed into action like a well-oiled machine that had already rehearsed this exact event. Disarming and disabling the three men was relatively easy. The problem came from the prisoner they had been interviewing. He yelled at the two agents to stop hurting the attackers.

Charlie and Linda drew back but watched the defeated trio carefully. It had been very obvious that the three had meant to kill the man they were talking to and eliminate them as well. The men they were investigating were powerful and had a long reach. Someone didn't want their prisoner to talk.

As they watched the man at the table staggered to his feet and blood fell on the table. One of the attackers had managed to throw a knife and the handle of it was sticking out of the prisoner's chest. But, despite his injuries he drew himself up to his full height and faced the three men. His words startled everyone in the room.

He ignored the knife and the bleeding and in High Mandarin stated "Do not injure them on my behalf. They don't know what they are doing." He looked upward and said, "I am the beloved of Jesus Christ and I know that I am on the upward path." The serenity of his expression made the deadly injury completely unimportant. He smiled and walked past all five of the stunned people in the room and out the door. They watched as he reached the sunlight flooding through the high window in the hall. He just opened his arms and raised his hands in silent acceptance of his Lord's magnificence.

It looked to Charlie like the life flowed out of him in a rainbow ribbon and up into the sunlight. His body collapsed like it was boneless. Nobody said anything for several seconds. Then a half of dozen guards came rushing down the hall and into the room.

Awed and shaken by what they had seen, the two agents left the prison and began the journey back to Beijing. On the train that afternoon, they went over the events in their minds and discussed what it would be like to have the security and peace that the man had shown. But how? Like most couples the woman seems to be the investigator when it comes to the heart and Linda was no exception. She suggested that they contact one of the underground Christian groups they knew of and see what they could tell them about this.

One week later Charlie held his first Bible in his hands and began to read the sections outlined to him. The Holy Spirit led his heart and his mind followed quickly. Three days later both Charlie and Linda gave their lives to the Lord and were baptized into Christ's body in one of the underground groups they were chartered to destroy. This total change of mind and heart would be impossible to hide and it hadn't been much later when they had heard from a friend in the service that they were to be arrested. They hurriedly decided to leave China and seek their path as directed by the Lord. That path had led them to the United States,

The FBI worked with them and they provided a great deal of new information about the internal affairs in their old country. After their information was verified they were allowed to become American citizens. Neither of them had been allowed to hold positions in companies doing sensitive or secret work or to enter the security services of the U.S. They had been recommended by a mutual friend to a martial arts instructor in Denver, Colorado. Sensei Grady had recognized their potential and brought them into the first action involving what became the Crossfire Team. Their unfailing loyalty and willingness to sacrifice their lives for Yahshua, who they knew then as Jesus had endeared them to the other team members and they had grown with the group as they literally fought the agents of evil around the world.

Charlie's Chinese name was Zhijian Chochun and Linda's had been Lin Chochun nee Chang. They adopted their English names for both ease of use in America and to help break the trail to China. Charlie realized that he had been trained in China so that he could do Yahveh's work in the West. He had prayed for direction and he had been given one that had led to where he was now.

-------------------------*****-------------------------

Charlie was so glad that he had been on God's mind and that he had not been forgotten.

An urgent message came in and he went back to work.

CHAPTER SEVENTEEN

General Miles met with President Bollen for over an hour. Part of the hour was prayer. When they were finished praying they discussed what should be done to counter this coordinated attack against their country and that of England.

The President shook his head, "Miles, I don't know what to do on this one. It seems that Mark Connelly is right that Yahveh wants them to lead this effort but will that give us enough time to counter whatever it is?"

The General had learned over the last eighteen months to listen to the leadings he got from what he still called God. "Mr. President, I suggest we give the Crossfire Team thirty-six hours to determine what the terrorists plan to do. During that time I believe that we need to get Homeland Security to raise the threat level and start hardening the sites that they can. We still don't know what these combined terror organizations are planning or how they plan to deliver their weapon or weapons. Until then, we're like sitting ducks."

The President thought for several minutes. "The word our security teams, especially the CIA, have gotten is that there will be hundreds of strikes against America. We have to assume that there will be multiple strikes against England too. Okay, give the Crossfire Team their three days. In the mean time have every group work any angle they can think of that would allow these people to strike hundreds of targets at the same time all over our country and that of Britain."

Mark got the word seventeen minutes later. He was already back at Andrews AFB and Su Li was preparing to take off. The Citation X ran down the runway and lifted off. It quickly curved into a westerly heading and disappeared into the cloud cover.

Five minutes later a four plane flight of F-15E Strike Eagles raced down the runway and sprang into the air. Forming up, the flight curved to the right and headed out over the Atlantic Ocean on an easterly heading. The Air

Force had been very supportive after the CJCS called and made his request. Three of the best F-15 pilots were assigned to three of the aircraft while Su Li flew the fourth one. Each of the E models carried two people and it was the quickest and safest way to get the Crossfire Team to Saudi Arabia. Laura flew with Su Li while Jack, Mark, and Sarah each rode in the back of one of the other birds. The 2.5 Mach capabilities of the aircraft is full combat speed with afterburners and would have been prohibitively costly. But the routine cruise speed of Mach 1.4 would get them there. Since this was primarily a ferry mission the range of the aircraft with conformal fuel tanks and three external fuel tanks was 3,000 nautical miles. The trip to Riyadh Air Base in Saudi Arabia would take two refuelings and about seven hours.

By the time they arrived they needed several hours down time to recuperate from the hard trip. Anyone that says flying in a modern jet fighter is easy has never sat in one let alone flown in one. The SOG had been there for six hours when the team arrived.

Jack stretched his six-foot, four-inch frame to relieve any remaining kinks and stood up in front of the group in the room they had been assigned. Looking out over a sea of very intelligent and dedicated faces he smiled. "Okay, here's what we know and what we don't know. First, we know that there is to be a meeting here in Riyadh at which the majority of the world's terrorist organizations will be represented. Second, we know that several of the South American drug cartels will also be here. Third, we think we know what this is about. According to our single source, a Crescent Dagger terrorist named Ysmael; this is the final meeting before a combined group attack against both the United States and Britain. Fourth, the overseeing force for this arrangement is a person named "Executor". Fifth, we know that we don't know enough. The attack is scheduled to take place six days from now. We have twenty-eight hours to determine what is going to happen, who is going to do it, where they are going to do it and how they're going to do it."

Mark frowned, "Access to the meeting is by DNA scan which makes sneaking in an operative unlikely at best. Okay, I want good possibilities."

Maria Olson, a second lieutenant stood up. "General Connelly, if we can determine the location of this meeting is there any way we could bug it electronically or eavesdrop at a distance?" She sat down.

Mark turned to his wife. "Sarah, what are our chances of doing something like that?"

Sarah stood up and addressed the lieutenant. "Maria, I'm fielding this question because of my background. As a Mossad Agent I've probably bugged more places than everyone else here combined. So, to answer your question, I'll cover some basics. To get audio or visual Intel from a closed area, like a hall or a house, you need to get access to the audio waves or vision sources within the structure. Most modern counter-surveillance techniques strive to reduce the availability of such access. We would need a window that is facing the area we are interested in to use a laser, an active phone line to get audio off of, a portal where we could insert a camera. All of these accesses are known by the people we are up against. They will do everything they can to limit our access. If we can determine the actual site soon, we will attempt to "create" an access that they won't know about. This will be difficult because I'm sure they will be using live guards, CCTV, IR, and thermal scans to watch for anyone approaching the site prior to or during the meeting." Sarah sat down.

One of the ex-SEALs asked, "What if we just waste the whole group?"

Mark shook his head. "They will have thought of that and will have a backup plan in place if that happens. The problem here is that we are not dealing just with radical terrorists and myopic drug lords, we're dealing with a sophisticated planner that probably won't make rookie mistakes."

One of the ex-Navy planners suggested, "If we can determine the site, why don't we wait until they disperse and grab a couple of them and sweat the intel out of them. They will have been there and will have the information we need."

Jack took that one. "Again, we don't have time to risk everything on grabbing one or two people. They may not know what we need. By then, the plan is in full swing and we're still in the dark."

Other suggestions were made, underground approach, phased MASER beams for an invisible microphone, UTD type microphones on the outside of the building. None of these were feasible considering the security that would be employed.

As usual, Laura was praying and asking Yahveh for guidance in this matter. A water bottle came to mind. A water bottle? She thought for a few seconds and when everyone was quiet she stood up. "Would it be possible to get a microphone and a video camera into the meeting in a water bottle?"

Everyone chewed on that for a few minutes. Then Sarah stood up and said, "If we know where the meeting will be, and if we can get a shot at their vendors, yes, we could do it!"

Jack looked somewhat confused, "How?"

Sarah looked at him. "Some of the latest Mossad efforts have been in reverse OLEDs. Printable LED screens but reversed so that they operate as a microphone or a video camera of sorts. Let me call Tel Aviv." She took off for the phones.

Mark knew his wife knew her stuff. "Okay people, half of you have been in this city before, another third of you are seconded from Psyops. Go find out what we need to know. The rest of you start taking incoming information and coordinating it. You know what to do, do it."

CHAPTER EIGHTEEN

Larry Hampton had been stationed in Riyadh for eight months a year ago. He knew his way around the town, although it wasn't for sightseeing or souvenir hunting this time. A city of over four million inhabitants covering over six hundred square miles it is a mixture of Arab culture and modern western design. The city itself has received a great deal of exposure in the western press as one of the places many American service men and women worked and left from in the various conflicts in the area. The war in Iraq for example. There was a large American presence in Riyadh and the Zultarian authorities were not in favor of any terrorist activities because the negative world reaction.

Therefore, the majority of the city was not practical for a meeting of well-known men of the terrorist world or for the cartels. Larry grudgingly gave credit to the organizer of the meeting for holding it in the midst of so much western military presence. Also he had been warned to be on the lookout for any demonic presence.

But the African-American had an idea on how to locate the meeting site. He stopped in a local shop and purchased a Thobe. The Thobe is the traditional clothing for men. The Thobe is a loose, long-sleeved, ankle-length garment. He also purchased a Tagiyah, a Ghutra, and a Agal. The Tagiyah is a white knitted skull cap The Ghutra is a square scarf, made of cotton or silk, which is worn folded across the head over the Tagiyah. The end of the scarf can be draped across the face as protection in the event of sandstorms. Lastly the Agal is a thick, doubled, black cord which is worn on top of the Ghutra to hold it in place."

Properly outfitted Larry started searching for a particular street vendor. Locating one on King Abdul Aziz Road, Larry made the traditional Arab greeting in Farsi. He then asked if the man was privy to the lesser known activities going on in the city. Assured that he was in on the events in and around Riyadh, Larry inquired as to a meeting that would include foreigners from South America.

The man suddenly became very suspicious and asked why Larry needed this information. Larry knew that this guy would sell his interest to the terrorists if he wasn't convincing. So Larry expressed his outrage that these men come from another land and took advantage of his daughter. That they snubbed his demands for reprisal or remuneration and went away from the land laughing at him. He heard that they were coming back and he wanted to extract revenge for his daughter's shame.

The man truly sympathized with Larry's loss and shame. He told him that the foreigners were going to an estate fifteen miles outside of the city center. The man gave the location to Larry but he gave him a warning too. Looking closely at Larry he said, "There are going to be many, powerful bad people there and the security is very tight. If you are seeking revenge you would do well to find another time and place."

Larry paused like he was considering the advice. "You may be right, but I don't know if I will have another chance."

The man laughed, "I assure you that you will. They are buying their own place here and perhaps living here. That is when I would take my revenge."

Larry acted encouraged. "Thank you my friend. Allah will be honored at the right time." Bowing low, Larry walked away from the man. Going around a corner he waited two beats and then looked back around the corner. The man was still patiently waiting for his next customer.

Larry went into an alley and used his miniature transmitter to send the information to the SOG base.

Larry was about to head back to base when he sensed a spiritual and physical presence behind him. Turning around quickly he saw an unsavory looking type in a burnoose and a dingy robe. None of that mattered because the man held a long sword with a wicked looking blade and was smiling an ugly smile as he prepared to run the American through. Larry could sense the presence of a demon egging the man on in his quest for blood. Larry started praising Yahveh under his breath and felt relieved when the spiritual assault faded away. He didn't know if the demon had left or had just moved to the background so the human he rode could take care of the warrior on the physical plane.

Just then a woman all covered in black came into the alley and saw the confrontation. She spoke in Arabic and told the man to stop bothering people. She walked past Larry and scolded the man as a public nuisance. The man was enraged and raised the sword to attack the insolent woman.

Larry started to move forward to intervene when the woman caught the heavy blade with her bare hands which blocked the man's attack. The woman snap kicked the man in the stomach and took the sword away from him in two moves that were only blurs from Larry's viewpoint. As the damaged man staggered forward she tripped him with her right foot and smacked him a solid blow on the back of the head with the flat side of the sword. The attacker fell to the slimy alley bricks unconscious. The woman stepped over to a trash bin and dropped the sword in there. Dusting her hands off she stepped back to confront Larry. "Arab Scum Patrol." The words were conveyed in excellent English and in a sultry voice.

Larry asked her what her name was and she shook her head. All he could see was her blue eyes above the veil. Larry said, "How can I thank you?"

The woman stepped into Larry and hugged him. He could feel the curves and warmth of her body. She kissed his cheek through the veil and said, "You can watch your back in this town". Then she stepped back, turned and left.

Larry Hampton's information was received and correlated to other reports and sent to Mark's attention. Four different accounts of a meeting between foreigners and known heroes (read terrorists), at the same location. Mark nodded and told the SOG staff to recall the other members. No use alerting the bad guys by too many references on the same day.

Determining the exact location on two maps and an aerial photo of the area, Mark sent the GPS coordinates to Charlie Wu in the fortress. Midge Frampton had been able to determine who the suppliers to the large home were and when they supplied the various items. Water went out every other day.

Mark asked Sarah if she had gotten in touch with David Zahavy and if they could get them technological help in time. Sarah smiled, "It's on its way as we speak. It should be here this time tomorrow in time for us to rework some water bottles and get them to the supplier the night before the delivery.

Jack and Laura came over and sat down. Jack asked Sarah to tell them how the reworking of the labels on water bottles would get them what they needed.

Sarah grabbed some paper and drew some sketches. She started to explain the functions. "An organic light-emitting diode or OLED is a thin-film light-emitting diode or LED in which the emissive layer is an organic compound. OLED technology is intended primarily as picture elements in practical display devices. Our scientists discovered that you could reverse the process by the addition of special atoms to the mix of the OLED. This actually allows an OLED to record a visual record of whatever is in front of the OLED. Multiply a different set of atoms and the OLED will record audio waves and store them for transmit. The amount is limited but then a special burst transmitter will cause them to transmit and a special receiver can pick the signals up and rebroadcast them so that we can receive them."

Laura asked, "How can we get the special receiver and transmitter into the meeting area?"

Sarah smiled, "They are going in as the lining in the boxes the water is delivered in with a financial reward for returning the empty bottles in the boxes. That should have the people keep the boxes."

Mark nodded, "If this place is like the hotels here there will be at least ten bottles of water on each table. We'll just sort through the various OLED broadcasts until we get the one we want and concentrate on it or others if it is used. Charlie is working up a sensitive receiver that is going to become a part of the roof over the meeting hall. It will attach itself the night before the meeting."

Jack stood up. "All right guys. Good work. Let's relax until the stuff gets here tomorrow."

Larry Hampton came up to the front and asked to talk to Mark. He told Mark about the scuffle in the alley. Mark listened and said, "I think we've got a guardian angel. This is the third time she has kept the enemy from hurting us. Keep your eyes open and see if you see her again. Don't look for hair color though, that seems to keep changing."

Larry smiled, "She's definitely human, I can vouch for that!" He nodded and left. Sarah had been listening and looked at Mark. "Is there any chance this chick has bright red hair?"

Mark thought that one over and prayed about it. "No, I don't think so. This one is definitely on our side. But, I don't have a clue who she is or what group she could be working for. She seems to speak several languages and is very capable."

Sarah grinned, "And she seems to have a corny sense of humor, Arab Scum Patrol!"

CHAPTER NINETEEN

Over the next twelve hours the SOG and team members identified over thirty known terrorists or cartel members arriving at the airports or by car and being delivered to the large home outside Riyadh City.

At three o'clock in the morning, local time a small UAV or unguided aviation vehicle approached the home. It detected the two guards stationed on the top of the house and avoided them and remained undetected. When both guards were looking away from its target space the UAV moved quietly to its desired place and settled lightly to the roof. Gently releasing its package the UAV silently ascended back into the night. On the roof, the package moved slowly until it was under one of the clay shingles that made up the roof. It continued to move until it was completely covered and invisible unless you looked directly into the space. Even then, it was black and looked like a shadow. The lithium-ion batteries came on line and energized the transceiver. There was no signal so the device went into idle mode to conserve battery power.

The OLED devices came in from Israel and a select crew carefully fixed them around the bottles of water below the normal label. The OLED advertised the rebate return reward in Arabic. As each bottle was finished it was tested for function and approved.

Eight of the SOG members took the altered bottles to the supplier's warehouse to switch the cartons of water with the ones marked for the target house's address.

As the eight warriors waited in the shadows for the night guard to finish his rounds, Kevin Steele felt the touch of the Father's spirit and a warning sprang into his mind. He hissed at the others of the team to stop them as they started to move. The leader of the raid, a SEAL team leader named Nance Barlow, moved back to Kevin's position and looked the question "What?" at him. Kevin made the hand sign for sentry on duty and tipped his head to the side. The two men moved away from the warehouse so they could talk softly.

Kevin looked into the other man's eyes. "There are several demonic watchers located inside the warehouse. The Holy spirit showed them to me. They won't bother us but they will alert the guards of our presence when we enter the building."

Nance sighed, "How do we handle them?"

Kevin frowned, "We need to pray and ask for the Father's help to blind them to our presence." Nance nodded and they went back to the other six members of the team. Nance made a quick explanation and then as one stayed alert and on guard the other seven asked Yahveh what was the right course. As they were led they began to pray for a spiritual blindness for the demons watching the warehouse so that they could achieve Yahveh's will. They all felt the breakthrough and the leading to proceed.

They quickly infiltrated the warehouse and replaced the water order for the target residence with the altered bottles. Taking the original water with them they left the warehouse without a trace of their incursion. The demons on watch continued to wait without noticing the SOG warriors.

When the meeting began, the team had nine hours left before their thirty-six hours were up.

Charlie Wu orchestrated the OLED camera/microphones through the receiver, cleaned up the images, and sent the four clearest ones to the team in Saudi Arabia. While not motion picture quality the reception from some of the OLEDs was sufficient to see who was talking and listen to their conversations. Charlie worked to clear up the other pictures with limited success. He finally called Mark and told him. "I think the problem is that some of the bottles were refrigerated or ice cooled before being brought into the meeting. It seems to have affected the transmission capabilities of the OLEDs."

Twelve of the SOG members spoke Arabic, Farsi, and or Spanish; as did Sarah. Each one translated the conversations that they were monitoring. After a great deal of chest beating and "Yeah we be the power" speeches the group got down to business. An unknown Caucasian man took the central podium in the room with the tables placed around him like an open square. He was a big man, probably six foot tall with a weight-lifter's physique. He had close cropped brown hair and a jutting jaw. His pale blue eyes seemed to thirst for power.

His translated comments were; "Hello, I am the Executor. As you may know, my job has been to arrange all phases of this operation and to bring all of you together to complete the mission. As of now I have accomplished everything I was supposed to do. You may be asking, why risk a meeting at this point. For two reasons, first to synchronize the timing of your people for the after strike cleanup. Second, we wanted to bring you all together so that we can network your groups and provide you with suggestions for the breakdown of territories and control after the attack. I urge you to continue to work together after the west has been defeated. My group has determined who gets what spoils and new territories in the United States, Britain, and eventually, Europe. The entire world will be under Shari 'a law in less than two days." A tremendous ovation occurred with this statement.

After the crowd settled down the Executor set the strike time for five a.m. on the east coast of the United States. "This will allow all your operatives to reach their targets across America in the quiet of the morning hours with minimal delays due to traffic, construction, or interference." Another fit of clapping ensued.

The Executor looked at the tables full of expectant faces. "Two years ago I approached the Colombian Cartels represented here and proposed a plan to get the Americans and the British off of their backs. The Zultarian groups were able to provide the dedicated personnel to deliver the strike in the two countries. Today they are a common and expected sight everywhere they go. In two days, each of these teams will do more damage than that accomplished by the heroes of 9/11 at the New York World Trade Centers."

Another cheer and exaltation.

"As we speak, those teams are being armed with the explosive power and detonation devices. It will be a glorious day for Zultar and the cartels."

A great cheer went up that took five minutes to settle down.

The Executor held up his hand for silence and then continued. "The targets selected, in many cases, have been barricaded to prevent attacks. These barricades will be taken out as the time approaches, allowing the team to reach its target. To prevent one person from giving away the entire plan. Each of the teams is autonomous and thinks they are the only ones involved. There is no command and control for the western agencies to find and attack. They will all attack at the same time in both countries. So, we will succeed and by the dawn two days after tomorrow it will all be done.

Each of you will return to your organizations to prepare for the cleanup. There is a package for each one of your organizations being passed out now. Detailed operations will be accomplished on schedule and without complaint. Does everyone understand?"

There was a shouted agreement and the meeting broke up into small groups and individual conversations. Charlie shut down all of the links and melted the transceiver in the event it was discovered.

Margo came over to the team's location and added the information she had gleaned from a side conversation between two of the attendees. "This is interesting." she said. "One of the cartel guys was speaking Spanish to another cartel leader. He said, "What about the prohibition against drugs in the Zultarian law? We'll be out of business once they take over." The other guy laughed and said, "No, you don't understand. Their law is flexible if they get some of the profits. They will allow us to supply them, make a decent profit, and they'll distribute the drugs as they see fit. That makes our operations legal and with an assured, captive, user base. It's a win-win situation with no DEA, CIA, or local cops busting our chops. Neat, huh?"

Jack thanked Margo and looked at the rest of the team. "We have the timetable but no information on how they plan to strike and our time to get the rest of the good guys involved is almost up. What do you propose we do to get the information we need?."

Su Li asked, "What about the slime out at the house, can we go after them and grill them?"

Mark nodded, "Select three of the attendees and take four man teams to snatch them. Remember that we do not have a sanction in this country and if caught it will mean Arab jail time or death. Make it clean, quiet, and quick.

Take one of the PsyOps people with each team and use whatever means you need to get the information. Understood?" Mark looked directly at Margo and said, "Margo you are with my team". She nodded back.

Major Wolford started setting up three teams from the SOG. Everyone knew they'd have to wait until dark to snatch their targets so they begin coordinating with the Fortress for targeting Intel on select attendees. Many were heading back to the airport but some wanted to see the nightlife in Riyadh. Since the type of nightlife they wanted to see was strictly banned in the Zultarian controlled country they would be going to private homes to have their fun. Three of these people were targeted by the SOG for interrogation.

Jack talked to Charlie and asked him to concentrate on the tracking of the Executor and feed them the Intel as he had it.

Larry Hampton took measurements of Mark's team and hurried out into the city to get appropriate clothing for Mark and Jack. The women would be noticed if they acted improperly on the streets and Larry didn't want to risk trying to get clothing for them because it would cause suspicions.

The two Americans donned a Thobe, a Tagiyah, a Ghutra, and Agal. Although they were tall compared to the majority of the Arabs in the area, there were similarly tall people seen in the city so they would not be totally out of place.

Keeping their bone conduction microphones and earpieces under their head coverings allowed them to stay in touch with each other and Charlie. As they left their building they were met by a smaller Saudi woman who bowed and asked to accompany them. Mark had to look very carefully to see that it was Margo. "You know if you get caught wearing men's clothing it means the death penalty in this area?"

Margo shot back, "Sure, but I think kidnapping, torture, and military operations without permission have the same penalties. So, let's not get caught." Mark silently agreed with the PsyOps soldier.

Charlie assured them that the Executor had not left the meeting area as yet. He knew this because the armored limo that the man had come in was still sitting in the parking lot of the estate with the driver. Mark checked out the setup and nodded. Going to the base personnel office he got a name and called the Captain he'd located.

Carefully racing to the terrorist meeting location Mark counted on a relaxed security stance since the meeting was over and successful. There were only five cars left outside the security wall to the manor house.

Pulling into the parking area in an American H2 Hummer they had borrowed from the Captain on the base they pulled up to the right side of the limo which blocked the view of the limo from the cameras at the front of the building. Margo got out and walked around the front of the long vehicle she came up to the driver's window and tapped on it. The driver powered down the window to see what this person wanted and was rewarded by an aerosol spray that froze him in position.

Mark and Jack exited the Hummer on the driver's side and slid into the back of the limo as Margo unlocked the door electronically. Margo had pushed the driver over to the right side of the front seat and she now gave him a long term sedative that would keep him asleep until the next morning. She then pulled the limo out from behind the shielding Hummer and moved closer to the gate and waited.

A call in Farsi came twenty minutes later and she pulled the limo up to the drive in front of the building and waited. After the vehicle stopped, the man they knew as the Executor came out with two bodyguards. The bodyguards checked the area and opened the back door for the Executor. The man slid into the back seat and saw the silenced gun in Mark's hand pointed at his face. Mark had his finger over his lips to tell the Executor to stay silent. The man did as he was told and the guard, not noticing anything because of the tinted windows, shut the door. Margo pulled smoothly away from the building and headed out for the street.

Jack told the Executor to put his hands on his head and interlace his fingers. Looking very disdainful the man did as he was asked.

As they left the parking lot, a car carrying Larry Hampton and the Captain drove in to reacquire the Hummer.

In the back of the limo Jack changed seats and moved next to the Executor. Reaching up he fastened one end of a set of handcuffs to the man's right wrist. That was when the man made his move.

Lunging toward Jack, the man attempted to head butt Jack while at the same time lashed out with his right foot to knock the gun out of Mark's hand. In the movies that might work, in reality it didn't fare as well. Mark calmly avoided the kick as Jack leaned back so that the man fell into his lap. Using his left elbow Jack struck downward on the right side of the Executor's neck with enough force to stun him.

Using the handcuff he had already attached, Jack wrenched their captive's right arm around behind him. Shoving the stunned man roughly to the floor Jack grabbed his left arm at the wrist. Yanking it back he finished tightly handcuffing the man.

Margo pulled the limo off the road at a water stop and the Hummer pulled alongside. Unobserved, the three warriors changed vehicles with their prisoner and left the limo sitting alone at the highway stop.

Pulling back onto the base went well as the Captain was well known by the base guards and they didn't check the floorboards where the, now gagged, Executor was being held down by three pairs of feet.

CHAPTER TWENTY

Mark called the Commander of the Riyadh Air Base on his cell phone and apprised him of the impending interrogation and that it needed to stay as a strictly need-to-know basis. The Commander had been given strict order by the office of the President of the United States to provide any and all efforts requested by this group and he agreed immediately.

Hanging up Mark told the Captain to take them to the old base BOQ that had been marked for demolition since a new one had taken its place. The area was deserted and as the team stepped out onto the tarmac into the blistering heat they saw an awesome sunset in progress. The desert sky was awash in purples, pinks, blues, and light shadings of gray. The air was dry but hot. Mark and Jack hauled their prisoner out of the back of the Hummer and into the dilapidated building. Larry and the Captain stayed outside to prevent any curiosity seekers from barging into the festivities.

Jack held the Executor as Mark searched him for tracers, weapons, or anything else for that matter. When Mark was done all the man's pockets were turned inside out and hanging outside. Jack sat the man down in the darkening room and used two more sets of handcuffs to lock him into a swivel chair that was bolted to the floor. Jack then removed his gag.

The man looked at his captors with a venom that would have soured an apple orchard. He spoke in a low voice. "You have no idea who you are messing around with. I won't give you any information and my people will be coming for me and for you very soon."

Margo smiled at him and said, "That's nice." and sprayed him with the aerosol. He froze in mid comeback and she pulled his sleeve up past his elbow. The injection routine went the same as before. She brought her tape recorder back and waited until he came to. This time she took a different tact with the prisoner. "You have angered the council! It is time for your debriefing and if you miss a beat, you will be tortured until you get it right. Do you understand?!"

The confusion was apparent in his eyes. "What are you talking about? I did everything I was supposed to do."

Margo slapped him across the mouth. "Do you understand?!"

Licking his hurt lip he simply nodded. Margo said, "Your failure was in underestimating the reaction time of the western security services. They were able to intercept almost all of your Zultarian lackeys before they could strike their targets! Why!"

The man flinched fearing another blow to the face. "That is impossible. Our plan was perfect. Each team would arrive at their target at the appointed hour because they were each aware of the time."

Margo laughed at him. "Nice words, but most of them were stopped. How do you explain this?"

The Executor shook his head. "I can't explain it."

Margo appeared to soften her voice somewhat. "Then it may not be your fault. Go over the plan in detail, leaving out nothing. We may be able to figure out who the real culprit is in this mess."

Believing he had found a reprieve he was glad to comply. "Certainly. Two years ago we manipulated the South American drug cartels into fronting eight hundred million U.S. dollars into our trucking company. We were able to purchase the four hundred tanker trucks in the U.S. and Britain and get the teams familiarized with their areas as well as letting them become commonplace and well known. The fuel for the fuel-air bombs was purchased and shipped to the proper locations on time. The African trigger assemblies were a substitution required due to the destruction of the ones from the Crescent Dagger group. They were rush shipped in at the last moment and installed in all of the trucks. At twenty hours before the strike the trucks were fueled and armed. At eight to ten hours before the strike the trucks were moving towards their targets. At the appointed time all of the three hundred trucks in America and the hundred in Britain were to be at their target locations and waiting for support teams to clear the way or to set off their bombs on the hour. I can't see what could have gone wrong."

Margo concurred with him. "You seem to have been organizing the movement of the truck bombs efficiently but what about the targets? Did the selection of targets give the western security services the clues they needed to stop the trucks?"

He seemed to think for a minute. "That was a list approved by the council. Perhaps there is a leak on that level."

She rattled some papers behind him. "I don't have a copy of the approved target list here. Where is it?"

He flinched at the anger in her voice. Quickly he said, "It is on the L2 website!"

Margo looked at Mark and rolled her eyes and shrugged her shoulders. "I don't have authority to get into the L2 website. How can I find the target list? Without that list I will have to carry out the council's orders and terminate you for incompetence!"

He was starting to get tired and confused but realized his life was on the line. "I have a backup copy on my passport in the right eye of the picture. You can see that it is all there. I just wan t..." He fell asleep and his head nodded down to his chest.

Jack rummaged through the man's belongings and found his passport. "Got it!" Mark uncuffed the man and they carried his heavy body out to the Hummer. It had gotten completely dark while they were having their chat with him. Mark told the Captain and Larry to take the man to the brig and have them hold him under a terroristic warrant until notified. He told them to give him the name John Weath. Jack, Mark, and Margo rode as far as the base operations office and asked for the Criminal Investigation Division.

Rousting a CID agent they were given access to their lab and a microscope. Two minutes later they had the microdot off of the passport and were printing out copies of the target list. It took almost twenty minutes to print it out and get it scanned into a secure computer. Mark ran encryption software and sent the encrypted list to the Chairman of the JCS.

While Mark was working with the computer, Jack called back to the SOG and got the results of the other teams.

The answers were the same. The only difference was that they had the target list.

Jack and Mark put in the call to the President and the CJCS with two hours to go on their allotted time.

CHAPTER TWENTY-ONE

The President and General Miles were alone in the Oval Office when they took the conference call from Saudi Arabia. After Jack and Mark had shown them the pictures, the target list, and detailed the information about the operation they sat there numb from the sheer immensity of the undertaking ahead of them. The President thanked them for acquiring the information and told them, "You'd better get back here. We're going to need all the help we can get. After disconnecting the call they started discussing how they could get an adequate response to such a horrific and huge attack and do it in time.

Two hours later President Bollen looked at the people he and General Miles had assembled to meet this latest crisis. Every agency in the U.S. was represented from Homeland Security to the FBI, CIA, NSA, Interpol, State Police, local Police, and the head of a specialized organization involved to counter terrorism called Highway Watch that worked out of the Homeland Security umbrella. The Prime Minister of England and his Defence Minister were attending by video conferencing.

The President opened the meeting with these fateful words, "Ladies and Gentlemen, I cannot stress the life and death importance of this meeting. Your way of life, if not your life itself, depends on what we do in the next twenty-four hours."

He went ahead and presented the information to them without editorializing. When he had finished with the actual footage of the meeting in Saudi Arabia and the tape of the Executor's confession he added one more statement. "In the next twenty-four hours we need to identify, locate, and prevent four hundred tanker trucks from fulfilling their mission. How do we do it?"

The consensus was that neither the United States nor Britain could afford to let the terrorists get to their targets but, stopping them could result in horrific collateral damage and deaths caused by frustrated bombers.

In the end of the meeting it was decided that all tanker trucks would have to be frozen in place until they could be searched and cleared. Not only would this be a monumental effort, but the upheaval in the daily life of everyone would be costly. Tanker trucks deliver everything we buy that is in liquid form.

The cost would be borne because the alternative was unthinkable. Now, how could they enforce such a plan? The President would authorize all states to call up the National Guard and the Air National Guard. Martial Law would go into effect at the time of the announcement. Any tanker truck attempting to move from its location would be fired on and destroyed where it was found. Obviously, the collateral damage would be taken into consideration, if possible. The President himself would go on the air at eight o'clock EST that night and explain the problem and the solution to the people of the country. There was no other option than to have the nation itself help stop the terrorists before they could reach their targets. The Prime Minister of England agreed to take the equivalent steps in the British Isles.

Right after the meeting the calls went out to the National Guard, the Air National Guard, and as many active military units that were available from the Marines, Navy, Army, Air Force, and the Coast Guard. Standing orders were: No tanker truck shall move until it is inspected, cleared on a national database, and marked with a special GPS marker. These markers were already stockpiled at military bases all over the nation for war games. Now they would serve a far different purpose. Truckers on the road would be required to pull over immediately and wait for clearance or face being killed when their truck was destroyed.

The President stood next to his wife at the window overlooking the rose garden at the White House. She recognized the anger, frustration, and sadness that this massive attack against the country was causing her husband. She watched him stare out the window, his mind a million miles away from that peaceful view. She put her arm around him and held him to her. He looked at her and shook his head. "I don't know how we're going to prevent massive death and destruction this time. We've got a heads-up with the information on what, where, when, and how and we still may not be able to prevent it."

She could feel the heart wrenching passion he had for the people of the country. He didn't care about politics as much as the souls he was charged to protect. Now he was faced with another peril without a solution. She knew that even if the military stopped the vehicles from reaching their targets that they could blow up wherever they were and cause widespread death and destruction. These truck bombs were professionally designed and built. They were probably ten times as powerful as the one Timothy McVeigh set off in Oklahoma City in 1995. That one not only killed 168 people, the bomb injured over 800 people and destroyed or damaged more than 300 buildings in the surrounding area, leaving several hundred people homeless and shutting down offices in downtown Oklahoma City. The concept of what three hundred bombs ten times as powerful could do was mind-numbing. She started to cry with her husband as they stood there.

The team and the SOG were on a C-5 Galaxy aircraft on the way back to the U.S. when Mark was called to the cockpit level for an incoming telephone call. Mark picked up the headset and said, "General Connelly."

Mark was surprised when the voice on the other end of the line was General Miles. "Mark, good work in the Middle East. Listen we have been scrambling to get troops assigned in every major strike area. We have a gap in our defenses in Boise, Idaho I'd like your team to fill for me. I know it's not your home town but two of the targets are critical and we really need some experienced command and combat experience there. I'm going to need to scatter the SOG to run things between Atlanta, Georgia and the North Carolina area. You'll find good men to assist you at the Boise ANG base."

Mark smiled, figuring the times for a diversion of the C-5A to Atlanta, getting another flight and reaching Boise which was almost on the West coast. "Yes Sir, we'll be there in eight hours."

CHAPTER TWENTY-TWO

Boise, Idaho is an island of trees and water in the middle of the Northwestern high desert. The sixty-four square mile area of the city runs along the foothills of the Rocky Mountains from northwest to southeast. It is a beautiful sight and has many natural attractions to attract visitors and sightseers. In size it is on a par with the other cities of the Northwest with a metropolitan area population over a half-a-million people. That includes the cities of Boise, Meridian, Nampa, and Caldwell.

What Jack and Laura noticed from the air as their Air Force Jet Commander circled to land at the Boise Airport was a relaxed look to the city of Boise. This was reinforced as they traveled the area later.

Their aircraft taxied away from the commercial airport complex and stopped at the 124th Wing, Idaho Air National Guard which includes two flying squadrons and 12 support units based at Howard Air National Guard Base.

Boise Airport also serves as the primary commercial service airport in southwestern Idaho, but its service area (with a population in excess of 500,000) extends well into eastern Oregon.

The 124th Wing, a reserve component of the US Air Force, is one of the few Air Guard units in the nation with three separate federal missions. Mark was glad to see F-16 fighters and A10 anti-tank aircraft lined up in flight status. They could come in very handy if they had to stop trucks on the run.

Disembarking from the aircraft Mark was met by a collection of military, state, federal, and local agents. Word had passed that Mark was in charge of the defense of the Boise Metropolitan area and everyone wanted his attention or wanted to know what to do.

Mark assigned one of the team to each group of officers present and tasked them with determining what assets each agency had available. He would then determine their overall strategy.

Commandeering a large conference room with video and map capabilities he brought out a copy of the target list. He was surprised to see that there were only five truck bombs planned for Boise City. He gave the local list to an airman technician and asked him to superimpose the locations of the targets on the large illuminated map of the area.

It took twenty minutes until the eight targets showed up as bright red dots on the map but it was worth the wait. Mark called in the group that met him at the aircraft and showed them the map. It was a much more subdued crowd after that. One of the ANG air force officers pointed out that there was a bomb set to go off in the middle of the area they stood in at the moment.

Mark looked at the dispersion of targets and then studied the assets he had on hand to interdict the bombers if they refused to obey the pending Presidential order to stay put. Something kept nagging at his mind and he needed to resolve it before assigning tasks. He told everyone to study the targets and possible routes by tanker trucks to those targets. Then he pointed at Sarah and they went into a small office away from the conference room and sat down. Mark looked at his wife. "I've got something pestering me like I've forgotten something important. You got any idea what it might be?"

Sarah thought for a few seconds. "No, but we know who does know."

They sat there and prayed for guidance and revelation of the missing pieces of the puzzle.

Mark sat up suddenly and said, "That's it! I just wasn't thinking properly."

Sarah smiled and waited. Mark got up and paced as he thought out the concept he discovered during his prayer. "I've been thinking of the Omicron Cartel as a typical low-life terrorist enemy. They're not that, they're really very smart, in an evil sort of way of course, but very intelligent. I realized that if I put myself in their place at this time I would change things. Why? Because their main man and several others involved in this attack have disappeared. I would assume that meant that the other side, that's us, had gotten hold of these people and rung them dry of information concerning the strike."

Mark stopped pacing and smashed one fist into his other hand for emphasis. "I would go to plan B or even plan C. We have to assume that the target list is a phony, planted on the Executor as a ruse in the event he was captured. I'm sure of this now. No way would this elite criminal group leave themselves so vulnerable. And I fell for it and convinced the CJCS and the President that it was genuine. Forgive me Father for being so gullible!"

Mark took out his cell phone and called the CJCS. In several minutes he got in touch with General Miles. "General, I've got a sneaking suspicion that we have been snookered. I realized it when I looked at the targets in the Boise area. They didn't make any real sense. Schools, parks, even a water park for Pete's sake! The target list is a phony to misdirect us. I think the Omicron Cartel upper council planted it on the Executor just in the event we did get our hands on him. Think about it. They are going to go after the infrastructure that makes the country run. Power plants, water sources, governmental entities. That makes more sense out of the comment the Executor made at the meeting that targets that were already barricaded would be cleared just as the strike occurs. Not too many water parks are barricaded."

The General was quiet for a few seconds. Mark was about to ask if General Miles had heard him when the man spoke. "You're right, several of my people have been questioning the targeting as inappropriate and now I see it. All right, scratch the list as far as targets go but I think the numbers of trucks per target area may be correct. The balance seems right for the number of targets in the given area. It will be the effort to keep them from moving that will make them stick out. Because the mind set here from all the experts is that the terrorists will not stay put as ordered but make a run for their real targets. I suggest an area defense based on known, pre-established high risk targets."

Mark offered another suggestion. "General, I'm also afraid that some of the truck bombs may already be at their destinations, simply waiting until the time to strike. They won't be moving but if we check the high-danger target list then we can investigate any tanker trucks nearby."

General Miles agreed. "Good hunting Mark, I'll get the word out to the troops."

Mark hung up and looked at Sarah. "Two hours until the President speaks and eight until the strike deadline. Let's set up our troops to check the local area around any existing high-danger targets such as military, civilian governmental, utility, or specific targets that we are aware of in and around the city. This could still be devastating to the country even if they set them off where they're sitting right now."

CHAPTER TWENTY-THREE

Mark called Charlie Wu and asked if he could use any satellite imaging to isolate tanker trucks in the Boise City and surrounding city areas. Charlie said he'd get on it right away.

Going back to the conference room Mark and Sarah got the attention of everyone there. Sarah started it off with, "People! We need to lean on your expertise. Those red lights have turned out to be a red herring. Please remove them from the map."

The red lights disappeared one by one until they were all gone.

Mark picked up the discussion."You all live and work here. We believe that the bombers will go after infrastructure targets that will cause the biggest destruction to the way of life and continuity of business. What targets can you suggest? Make a list and prioritize it in the next ten minutes."

The team discussed how they would divide the control of the responses over the three cities of Boise, Nampa, and Caldwell. When the ten minutes was up they collected the lists and had an airman use a computer screen to show the various targets in descending order of importance. One that seemed to be on most of the lists was an earthen dam called "Lucky Peak". Mark looked to the local disaster manager and asked why."

"Lucky Peak is an earth-filled dam 2,340 feet in length and 340 feet high. Luck Peak's reservoir is 12-miles in length and its storage capacity is 300,000 acres-feet of water. It is fed by three other dams. If Lucky Peak were breached, the water released would rush down the old riverbed through Boise, Eagle, Nampa, and Caldwell at a volume twenty times the capacity of the rivers to contain it. It would result in flooding in Boise City at an average of five feet minimum and pretty well destroy everything. All the population and business development below what they call the "bench" here would be erased totally. In short, it would be the end of Boise."

Mark pointed at the ANG commander. "We need eyes in the sky at Lucky Peak Dam and it probably wouldn't hurt to check the other three dams for trucks also."

The Commander made a note and assigned two of his pilots to the tasks immediately.

Sarah had been working with the airman specialist to light up the targets that had been selected by the group. There were over a hundred possible targets. Mark's phone rang and he answered it. Charlie was on the other end, "Mark, Crayton has identified thirty three tanker trucks in the area of discussion."

Mark asked, "Who is Crayton?"

Charlie chuckled, "Sorry, computer humor, that's what we call the assembly of Cray computers here. They seem to be developing a personality similar to the TV star Raymond. Anyway, back to business. The majority of those tanker trucks are clustered at fuel stops along the I-84 Interstate that runs through all three cities. Let me talk to whoever you have displaying your map information and I'll download the present picture. If they have the equipment I'll update it every three minutes automatically."

Mark gave his phone to the airman specialist and listened to him talk to Charlie in what seemed to be a foreign language. Ports, IP Addresses, baud rates, handshakes, and a myriad of other details. The airman smiled and gave Mark's phone back. Green blips started appearing on the wall-sized glass map. Several of the green blips appeared right next to the red target indications.

Mark watched the green blips appear and told Charlie thanks. Charlie added a comment. "Mark, some bad news. My investigation of the information provided by the other three attendees we "interviewed" indicates that the truck bombs are going to be fueled by Astrolite A-1-5. I'm sending you an info packet on it now. Stay hard and don't let these bozos get away with this." Charlie hung up and Mark went to his laptop and opened the file Charlie had just sent him. He studied it for several minutes. It bothered him that Charlie's safety and that of everyone at the fortress was in the hands of others. But, Mark knew who was in charge and it certainly wasn't him.

Mark then asked the State Police, and an Army backup to check out the trucks near the targets to see if they were truck bombs. Everyone stopped what they were doing and looked at Mark. The head of the State Police asked, "How do we know it's one of the truck bombs and what do we do if it is?"

Mark looked at the assembled crowd. "The U.S. military and law enforcement agencies often call a truck bomb a VBIED, an acronym standing for Vehicle Borne Improvised Explosive Device. Mark shook his head. "We believe that this VBIED scenario is fueled by a completely new family of explosives that has been developed with entirely new properties.

Our interrogation of one of the meeting attendees revealed that the VBIEDs in this case are going to be fueled by Astrolite A-1-5, said to be the world's most powerful non-nuclear explosive." Mark read from the file Charlie had sent him. "Astrolite explosives are a product of advanced rocket propellant technology. They were discovered quite by accident in the 1960's by research personnel investigating a so-called rocket propellant that proved so powerful that it consistently destroyed rockets on the test stand. This explosive is remarkably safe to handle and can be mixed from nondetonable components.

Astrolite explosives are formed when good old. cheap, readily available, and easy to get ammonium nitrate is mixed with anhydrous hydrazine. Extensive solvolysis occurs with the liberation of large amounts of ammonia gas and a new compound called hydroxonium nitrate is formed and remains in solution. This produces a clear liquid explosive called Astrolite G. When 100 mesh or finer aluminum powder is added, it forms Astrolite A-1-5.

The aluminum powder in the A-1-5 does not react with the two main components but remains in solution to give added power to the explosive when it is detonated by an explosive detonator capable of generating a 2000 degree heat source. The tremendous explosive power stems from Astrolite's amine-based chemistry which releases nitrogen and hydrogen gases. These expand more forcefully than the gases produced by the usual hydrocarbon explosives.

The Astrolite A family of explosives of which A-1-5 has proven to be the most powerful is totally unrelated to any existing explosive compounds. Side-by-side field tests have revealed that Astrolite A is twice as powerful as TNT. Yet the Astrolite A family of explosives is 40 times safer than nitroglycerin explosives under adiabatic compression and impact shock. In demolition, Astrolite A produces crater volumes 3 times greater than C-4 plastic explosive."

Mark looked up from his computer. "Another note, there are several nuclear power sites in our target area. These must be defended at all costs. The NRC has done a lousy job of defending the reactors because it would cost too much of their profits. The damage would be horrific. For example, an NRC environmental impact statement for the San Onofre nuclear power plant near Los Angeles estimated up to 130,000 acute fatalities, plus 300,000 latent cancers and 600,000 genetic effects. The cost of off-site mitigating actions was estimated at $35 billion. This was nine years ago.

Sarah picked up the talk. "Attacks on reactors may have an escalatory effect as well. As Bennett Ramberg, perhaps the leading scholar on the subject, has argued, attacks on nuclear reactors with conventional weapons may provide nonnuclear nations or sub national groups a near-nuclear capability. A power reactor contains about 1,000 times the long-lived radioactivity of a Hiroshima bomb. Use of conventional attacks on nuclear energy facilities as a form of radiological warfare may provide the escalatory link between conventional attack and nuclear response. You have to know they will go for any nuclear source with one of these powerful VBIEDs."

Mark drew a large drawing of a tanker truck on the white board. Pointing at the tank portion he said, "The think tank in Washington believes that the detonators will be dropped into the mixture so that it is completely hidden, and then detonated remotely by a trigger device. So, you won't find any blinking lights or count-down timers like in the movies."

There was a roar of laughter. "But, you can easily detect these VBIEDs through the use of a unique, aerosol-based field test kit for the detection and identification of compounds containing inorganic nitrates for example our enemy's weapon of choice. Expray™ is used as a pre-blast, analytical tool, with a level of sensitivity of 20 nanograms or less. The testing process is fast and efficient. Results appear in seconds. The identification/detection process requires no special training and testing can be performed "on the spot" You will be using Expray 3 to search our VBIEDs. It will detect many nitrate-based explosives which includes ammonium nitrate. "

"The manufacturer was contacted and is rushing to provide kits to all the units in the field. Fortunately there was a supply of the testing kits here in Boise and surprisingly they're stored right here at the Guard base. Someone has already been contacted to get the kits and bring them here. You will only need Expray 3 aerosol can. Spray it near the fill ports of the tanker truck and you will see a vivid pink stain on the fill ports if ammonium nitrate is present. If it is, it is probably a VBIED. Remember there are perfectly legal uses for ammonium nitrate and for the tanker trucks that carry it. Astrolite A-1-5 will show pink, ammonium nitrate will show red."

Sarah explained the "what to do". "If you detect what you think is a truck bomb. Attempt to find the driver or drivers of the vehicle. If possible, arrest them and make sure they have no access to any type of detonators. If you have an RF generator, jam the airwaves near the truck to prevent a signal reaching the detonator. If you detect a VBIED, lock down the area, see if you can get the drivers, and call us. We are arranging for heavy lift choppers to pick the whole tank portion up and move it to a safe area for detonation." Just then two of the reservists came in with several dozen Expray 3 aerosols. They passed some out to the groups going to investigate the trucks close to predicted targets.

CHAPTER TWENTY-FOUR

As the team finished assigning areas for the different groups to locate the VBIED trucks, Jack came over to Mark and asked him, "Are the other sites, especially the nuclear ones, in Idaho covered or do we need to do it?"

Mark looked at his friend, "They are being covered by a federal nuclear task force that has been training for something like this for six years. No, we need to concentrate on this area." He pointed at an area map showing the cities of Boise, Meridian, Nampa, and Caldwell. "There are probably five truck bombs dedicated to these cities and we need to find them before they can hit their targets."

Jack looked at the map. "I see we've got people going out to all the various sites that have tanker trucks marked by Charlie's computers. What about ones that are under cover, that Charlie's satellites can't see?"

Mark felt the fingers of defeat brush against his soul. "We'll find them, we just have to!"

Two thousand, three hundred, and seventy miles ESE of Boise, the President of the most powerful nation in the world was deeply repenting in prayer to Yahveh. His sorrow was not for himself but for failing to guard Yahveh's people from this disaster. He prayed from the heart. "Father, forgive me for the terrible price your children have to pay." The man's heart was grieved sorely by the news his Homeland Security Director had brought to him an hour before he was scheduled to speak to the nation.

Director Hennsen had shown him the predictions that with the best possible detection rate and all factors working for them there would still be thirty to forty bombs that would probably get through out of the original three hundred.

The agony the President felt was for the thousands of people that were about to die in fireballs and explosions so immense that huge sections of cities would be leveled and twenty times more would be fatally damaged. He felt the Father's heart for the people. President Bollen knew that the Creator of the universe loved each and every person on the Earth and it had been his responsibility as Commander in Chief to protect those threatened. He prayed for divine intervention to prevent the evil plans from coming to a successful end.

Running out of words he knelt there and waited to see if Yahveh would give him hope. He felt his concern and grief fade away and a wonderful sense of peace filled him. He actually heard, *"Do not fear. I have heard your prayers and those of many others. I will act and I will overcome and all will know that I am Yahveh their Elohim."*

The President sighed a large sigh of relief and relaxed in the peace until a knocking came at his bedroom door. Climbing to his feet was a chore that was getting harder to do all the time. He levered himself up with his arms and stood beside his bed. He said, "Come in."

His wife opened the door and she knew immediately that something wonderful had happened. Her husband had gone in to pray and looked older and far more worn than he did now. She tipped her head to one side and stared at his face. "Honey, what happened?"

He smiled. "The guy upstairs said that He would take care of it. But, we still have to do everything we can to find these people that would hurt the country." He walked around the end of the bed and took his wife in his arms. She snuggled up to him and felt the positive energy he was putting out. She thought that she'd never felt so safe and protected as she did at that moment. She clung to him for a few more minutes and then pushed back and told him, "They want you downstairs now."

Fifteen minutes later Andrew Bollen faced the cameras as he addressed the nation. "My fellow Americans, as I address you today our nation is under attack by Zultarian terrorists in an unprecedented campaign of horror and destruction. This isn't just another pronouncement of impending threats to our great nation. The attacks will occur at midnight tonight Central Standard Time. It is not a limited attack on one city or building. This attack will shatter the entire country and our way of life if we don't stop it."

He looked at his notes for a second. "The South American drug cartels have financed a massive thrust against us by a combined group of the Middle Eastern terrorist organizations. Over the last two years they have purchased three hundred tanker trucks like the one shown on the screen behind me. For two years these trucks have traveled their routes and done everyday business. In the last two days these familiar vehicles have been loaded with an explosive ten times as powerful as the one that destroyed the Murrow Building in Oklahoma City. Their plan is to drive these truck bombs to their targets by the strike time and detonate them all at once. You can imagine the death and destruction such a strike would cause to our country. There are one hundred trucks already in the United Kingdom to do the same thing to Britain."

The President sighed a large sigh. "To stop this attack I am ordering an immediate, one-day Martial Law throughout the United States. The Congress and the Judiciary have endorsed this action. I am ordering all tanker trucks to remain where they are at this time. If they are moving they need to pull over and stop immediately. I have authorized the National Guard in every state and the full force of the Military to enforce this shutdown and inspection of every tanker truck until all the bombs are found. Any trucker that defies this order has only themselve to blame when their truck is destroyed for failing to stop until inspected. The armed forces have shoot-to-kill orders for any violations of this order. We will stop this attack against us. I'm asking the truckers of this country to make sure every tank truck driver is aware of this order. If they are asleep, wake them up, if they are drunk, lock them up. Make sure your friends and fellow drivers don't die because of ignorance."

He looked directly into the camera with sincerity on his face that was undeniable. "I know that there will be some fanatics that will attempt to complete their mission of horror. When their vehicles are destroyed there will probably be collateral death and destruction. I have prayed for the innocent and the military soldiers and guardsmen that could lose their lives in the defense of our great country. I am hereby calling on the entire population of our country to assist our military, police, and other law-enforcement officers in finding and reporting any tanker truck. We will flash numbers on the screen in just a minute for every state. Call these numbers to report the location or movement of any tanker truck. Remember, there are at least 1500 tanker trucks traveling the roads of our country today. The terrorists are counting on your passivity and lack of interest to accomplish their mission. Show them that they are wrong!"

The President stood up and left the office.

CHAPTER TWENTY-FIVE

The Air National Guard Commander, Colonel Wayne Corless walked up to the team as they were watching the end of the President's speech on TV. He stood behind Mark as the President left the screen and Mark turned around. "Yes, Colonel?"

"General Connelly, my men have discovered a tanker truck parked in a remote parking lot near Lucky Peak Dam. Who do you want to investigate it?"

Mark thought for a few seconds, "Sarah and I will investigate this one since I've assigned almost everyone else to other targets. The odds are pretty high that this one is a VBIED. Jack, you, Laura, and Su Li run the op while we're gone. Sarah get a detection aerosol and meet me at the Tahoe."

Mark got two M-8s and put them in a normal civilian vehicle as Sarah jumped in. He fired up the engine and pulled out onto Gowen Road and headed southeast. He turned on the red flashing lights and accelerated to eighty miles an hour. Passing other vehicles going the speed limit he attracted the attention of an Idaho State Trooper who noted the flashing lights and did not pursue the racing SUV.

Slowing for Federal Way, a major intersection near the Semiconductor Manufacturer plant in Southeast Boise Mark brought the Tahoe back up to speed as they flew into the foothills. Passing large subdivisions on their left they dropped down into the area of the old river right-away. As they started to climb towards the dam they saw a large park area in the river area below the dam. Sarah looked at the map, "That's the Lucky Peak Recreation Area." Since it was almost eight o'clock in the evening there were no visitors still in the park. Mark switched off the flashing lights and drove up the highway that ran past the dam.

Mark reached the turnoff that led across the top of the dam to parking areas on the other side. The buff colored hills rose above them into the darkening evening sky as they drove across the dam towards their target. As they continued down the road on the south side of the dam

Sarah spotted the tanker truck parked all alone at the back of a right hand parking lot. Mark pulled the Humvee into a parking lot to their left and out of sight of the tanker truck.

The light was fading rapidly as Mark examined the truck through binoculars. He turned to Sarah, "There doesn't seem to be anyone in the truck but they have to be nearby both to watch the truck and to be ready to drive it out on the dam at eleven o'clock."

Sarah had her own binoculars and was examining the area near the truck. She couldn't find anyone anywhere. Mark started looking farther afield and struckpay dirt four hundred yards away and slightly uphill from the back of the truck. He saw a small red glow as he was panning over the scrub brush behind the truck. Zeroing in on the glow he was able to see a person under a dirt-covered tarp held up by sticks. There was only a small opening but the person he could see was also panning the area with a set of binoculars.

Sliding down in his seat in the SUV he reduced his profile and Sarah followed suit immediately. Mark said, "four hundred yards behind the truck, uphill to the left by ten degrees. They've got glasses too and are watching the truck. I don't think they've seen us yet. Probably think we're necking or something."

Sarah felt the urgency and danger of the moment and knew Mark felt it too. She reached over and touched his face. "So, you think we should make out to throw them off the scent?"

Mark grinned. "My dear wife, we're a respected married couple. We don't "make out", we are "affectionate."

Sarah grinned back. "Okay, affectionate one, how do you want to take these bozos?"

Mark smiled, "I'm going to circle around behind them while you distract them."

Sarah nodded, got out of the truck and took off her camo jacket. She knew she had an attractive figure and if the guys on the hill saw her they'd focus on her activities and be fairly lost to anything else. As Mark exited the SUV he grinned again and slid down the hill behind the scrub until he was out of the line of sight of the little dugout up the hill. He then began to run hunched over until he was out of sight of the dugout and then he ran up the hill. He could feel the thin air above Boise. The city itself was a half-mile higher than sea level. It was noticeable but didn't slow him down as he was acclimated to the mile-high air around Denver.

He was able to ease in above the watcher's position. He carefully checked the area again to see if there were any backups but didn't see any. It was almost dark at this point. Mark carefully walked down the hill until he was above the little hideaway. He couldn't see into the small lookout position because of the tarp which was artistically covered with sand and a small bush for camouflage. Looking around he found a large rock several yards up the hill. Carefully stepping up to the rock he tested it for movability. It took a lot of his strength but he was able to get it moving and rolled it downhill at the tarp-covered dugout.

As the large rock rolled downhill Mark could see Sarah down at the other parking place taking her blouse off. The boulder bounced just before it got to the position and then fell squarely onto the tarp crushing it down into the dugout. There was suddenly a bunch of screaming and cursing. One man squeezed out of the front of the tarp and turned to help a second person out from under the boulder.

Mark had run back to the dugout area with his handgun out and pointed at the two men. The second man had suffered some serious damage from the falling rock and couldn't use his left leg or arm. He was in a great deal of pain and moaned as the other man moved him. The first man looked up and suddenly saw Mark standing there with his pistol. The man released the arm of the wounded man and was deciding whether to attempt to draw the pistol he had in his belt or to surrender. After all the months of striving and preparing to strike a blow for Zultar he couldn't just give up now.

Then Sarah appeared from behind him with her M-8 locked onto the back of the standing man. In Arabic she said, "You will not be honored by this death. Raise your hands, NOW!" The fact that this came from a beautiful woman who was still partially undressed pushed the terrorist past his ability to reason. He grabbed for his gun and both Mark and Sarah fired at the same time. The man was thrown off his feet by the combination of shots. Dropping his weapon from his numb fingers he died on the way to the dirt.

Mark stepped up and disarmed the other man who had passed out from his rock-inflicted injuries. Sarah had buttoned up her blouse and looked at her husband with a raised eyebrow. "What kept you? I was running out of distractions."

Mark smiled at her. "Honey, I'm married to you; I know you've still got lots of distractions left for any man." Throwing the two terrorist's guns down the hill in case the still living terrorist made a miraculous recovery Mark took the aerosol out of his pocket and headed for the truck. Sarah walked with him and said, "It would be a real bummer if it doesn't turn out to be a bomb, right?" Mark didn't even want to think about that possibility.

Carefully checking the truck for trip wires or booby traps Mark climbed up on the side and sprayed the aerosol at the loading port on the top. In the light of his flashlight everywhere the spray hit the metal it turned bright pink. "Bingo, we've got a hot one. Call it in and get the Sheriff's people up here to arrest the live one." Sarah used her cell phone to make the arrangements. Then there was a ten minute lull while they waited for the various groups to respond.

As they looked at the glow from the lights of the town behind the hills between Luck Peak Dam and Boise Mark realized just how precious life was in all the cities and towns of not only America but the whole world and how innocent the majority of people in those town were. He felt a burden to protect every one of them from the evil represented by the terrorists. Tears ran from his eyes as he realized it was the burden of love that Yahveh had in His heart for all people that he was feeling. The heartache went completely off the scale. He felt a lessening of the burden and a peace that was definitely love flood over him. Wiping his eyes on his sleeve he looked over at Sarah and saw she was feeling the same things. He took her into his arms and held her. She mumbled "Thank you for loving us."

They stood there like that for several minutes until the Sheriff's car pulled over the dam and came towards them. Mark used his flashlight to bring them to the truck. He pointed out the location of the dugout as a Paramedic SUV with big lettering stating ADA COUNTY PARAMEDICS pulled in behind it. Sarah also pointed at the dugout and told the paramedics to take a body bag with them as well unless the coroner wanted to retrieve the body himself.

As the deputy and one of the paramedics were helping the wounded man down from the dugout a heavy rotor beat announced the arrival of the heavy lift helicopter. The chopper landed and two crewmen hurried to the truck with lift straps and cables. They quickly dropped the trailer skids and cranked them into position holding up the trailer. Disconnecting the trailer from the driving unit they then moved the tractor section away from the trailer. They secured the lift straps correctly to the trailer, hooked the cables together, and hooked a large ring at the top of the two cables. The chopper lifted off and hovered over the trailer. The cables dangling down from the chopper were affixed to the rings and the helicopter rose until it took the strain and lifted the trailer off the ground. Once the ground crew was satisfied the chopper lifted straight up and moved off toward the disposal area. The crew left the tractor part of the truck locked up and then walked over to Mark and asked for a ride back to the base.

Heading back Mark realized a darker side to their riding back with him. In the case the bomb went off while being transported then only two men would die, not four. He shook his head and concentrated on his driving.

CHAPTER TWENTY-SIX

The reports were coming in from all three cities when Mark and Sarah returned from Lucky Peak. Six more truck bombs had been detected and secured to the empty plain south of Boise.

One of the curious pieces of information was that twice the terrorists had activated their detonators before they could be stopped. In the first case the military unit had an RF damping field going and the signal never got to the bomb. But in the other case, local and state police had detected a bomb in a truck stop and they didn't have a unit to interfere with the RF signal. The bomber ran out of the diner shouting death to all infidels and pushed the button on his detonator. Nothing had happened and the man was captured before the truck was airlifted away.

Mark studied the report and Sarah read it over his shoulder. She sat down across from him. "Think it was a defective detonator or triggering device?'

Mark shook his head, "I really don't know but we need to determine why that one didn't work. You don't suppose the bombs aren't real and they're just a diversion from the real attack?"

Sarah shook her head. She got up and turned on the large screen TV near the table they were at. Hitting the remote TIVO she brought up the newscast she'd just seen. The news anchor was prepping the tape. "Highway Watch members number over two hundred thousand drivers plying the roads daily. Their calls to their emergency number actually located the first truck bombs in the country. After the President's order to stand down some of the bombers have still tried to reach their targets Watch this piece of tape." The screen showed the logo for the ten o'clock news in California. It showed a spectacular view of a tanker truck fleeing a roadblock at over eighty miles an hour on the I-405 headed into Los Angeles. An Air National Guard F-16 targeted the truck and hit it with an air-to-ground missile. The resultant explosion cratered the highway but spent most of it's blast on empty roadside.

The fireball was so immense the F-16 had to pull up and accelerate to avoid it. The narration began again. "Everything within a mile of the blast was incinerated and several buildings were extensively damaged by the explosion. Eight people nowhere near the actual strike were killed by the blast effects. Six were drivers going in the opposite direction to the truck and had no warning. The film has been widely seen and since then some bomb trucks were found abandoned.

Sarah shut off the TV. "I think that shows that the bombs are real. I don't know why that one didn't detonate but it could have been something else interfered with the signal or the terrorist didn't check the batteries in the remote control device."

Mark sat there in contemplation. A memory of a similar incident came to mind.

-------------------------******-------------------------

As a team leader in the Navy SEALs several years earlier Mark had been tasked to take his team on an unannounced inspection of a tramp steamer that was headed for the oil fields near Houston, Texas. This particular steamer had been listed as a possible terrorist vessel and the rumor had it that intelligence put Akbar Mohammad Tawfig on board. Tawfig was one of the Palestinian terrorist leaders in the killing of sixty-six Americans on a tour of the Holy Lands. He not only killed them but he also displayed them for the world to see on TV as a warning against trifling with Palestinian politics in favor of the Israelis. The sight of old men, women, and young children shot or beheaded was a cruel and blood-thirsty act to shock the world. It did shock the world and Tawfig had been high on the list of wanted terrorists ever since.

One of the elderly couples that had been slaughtered that day were the grandparents of Admiral Keets, then Commandant of the Navy SEALs. He recognized the opportunity this raid encompassed and had given personal attention to the team selected. He knew Mark's reputation and contacted Mark personally by phone before the raid. "Mark, Admiral Keets here. I'm glad you were chosen to effect this inspection. As always I expect you and your team to be careful but I am emphasizing the need for care in this case. You know about my grandparents and Tawfig and I'm not emotionally uninvolved here. But, I want you to get him if he's there. I'm asking you personally to see to it. I've read the reports on your previous raids and I expect no less from you this time. The man is evil so be extra careful for me, all right?"

Mark had understood the pain and anguish the Admiral was hiding. "Yes Sir! If Tawfig is on that ship I will capture or kill him."

The Admiral didn't pause because he had thought this out. "Unless he surrenders, don't try to capture him. He's too dangerous. Understand?"

"Yes Sir, I do." That was the end of the conversation. Mark ran those comments back through his mind as their high-speed attack craft neared the stern of the steamer in the early hours of the morning. It would be light here in two hours but they should be done and gone by then. The water was cold and the night dark. The visibility was even further limited by a slight fog that had settled over this stretch of the ocean. The attack boat bounced and shuttered through the wake of the bigger vessel as they neared the port side.

Two miles away in a blacked-out helicopter, two other SEALs watched the ship through SIB 16x40 gyro-stabilized binoculars. Mark heard the "all clear" through the bone-conduction earpiece on his battlefield comm gear. He raised his hand and pointed up. Five separate grappling hooks were fired over the rear, port side rail of the old steamer. The twelve men went up the ropes quickly and were on the deck in minutes.

Mark used silent signals to deploy his men. He took three with him and made for the wheel house and the communications shack. Each man had seen pictures of Tawfig and had memorized his facial features and height. It was easy to simulate a heavier person but hard to change the height without easily spotted props like elevator shoes.

They ran into no one on the way to the wheelhouse and were outside on both sides when Mark said, "Go". They entered both sides of the wheel house silently and totally surprised the man at the wheel. He was the only one on the bridge at four a.m. Two of the SEALs bound and gagged him while Mark and the other SEAL slipped into the communications shed. The man at the radio was fast asleep and they had him half tied up and gagged by the time he woke up completely. Leaving two of the SEALs to hold the wheel house and keep the ship on course, Mark and his remaining man went to join the other eight SEALs.

They found and bound the crew and then began to search for Tawfig. They had just about finished with the ship and no sign of the terrorists when Mark saw a light in one of the cargo holds. Sliding carefully across the deck he peered into the hold. What he saw was frightening. Tawfig was arming explosives that filled the entire hold. Mark knew if it was set off the steamer would cease to exist along with everyone on board.

Not able to get a shot at the terrorist through the crack Mark signaled two of the SEALs to operate the winch that was already connected to the hatch over the hold. The winch must have been very old because it screeched loudly as it lifted the hatch and Tawfig spun around with a remote detonator in his hand as Mark slid down the ladder into the hold. Tawfig held the detonator up and yelled in broken English, "I will kill us all if you don't leave the ship immediately!"

Mark had his CAR-15 up and aimed at the terrorist's head. "No way, Tawfig, Give it up now!"

The Palestinian's face grew angry and he mashed down on the firing key as Mark triggered a three round burst that removed the scowl, his forehead, and his mind all at the same time.

The terrorist fell backwards and landed on the deck of the hold with a soggy thud. Mark waited to die but nothing happened. He ran forward and pulled the detonator out of the dead man's hand.

Three more of the SEALs had descended into the hold by then. One of them walked over to Mark. "How come we're not all dead?"

Mark shook his head. Looking at the detonator he took a multitool out of his pocket and unscrewed the cover over the batteries. He looked inside and then all the tension came out in a huge laugh. "He put the batteries in backwards." That led to a lot of cheers.

Mark disabled the triggering charge and threw the remote overboard when he got back to the deck.

-----------------------*****-----------------------

That memory made him wonder if the local malfunction could be something similar.

CHAPTER TWENTY-SEVEN

By eleven o'clock on the Eastern seaboard, two hundred and fifty six of the three hundred truck bombs had been located, removed to a safe location, disabled, or had been detonated. An hour before the deadline six of the targeted buildings or structures had been destroyed, roughly one hundred and ninety people had died, a number which included the terrorists, and the frantic hunt for the remaining forty-four VBIEDs was in high gear all over the country. This included Alaska and Hawaii.

The Crossfire Team and the associated military and law-enforcement units in the Boise area had located and disposed of seven of the five suspected VBIEDs in the area. Four of the terrorists involved were dead, two of them were being held on terroristic warrants.

Laura sighed and looked over at Mark as the eleven-thirty mark on the East Coast passed. "What were the two special targets here in Boise that General Miles wanted us to cover?"

"There is a special nuclear development group located in Boise in the downtown area. It's supposed to be super-secret but the location could have been compromised by a mole in the NRC. I've got two Army teams watching the area but they will be strictly reactive and we would have to lose part of the downtown area just to stop them."

Mark looked at his paperwork. "The other target is a curiosity. There's a modern building off of Eagle Road in Eagle which is Northwest of Boise. The request is to defend the building and realize it is a critical target. But, there is no explanation of what the target is other than a building. I've got another two military units and an ANG sky cap on that one."

Laura sighed again. "Ahh well, we should know what's happening in the next fifteen minutes." Mark nodded his agreement.

Mark thought about the truck that didn't explode when the detonator was used. He prayed, "Father Yahveh, I ask for wisdom concerning these weapons of destruction. Let me know what I should do."

Radio chatter increased suddenly. Multiple reports of a tanker truck moving towards the Eagle target area coming in from the Star area on State Street. Mark looked at the map. "There's farmland in the next two miles." He suddenly had a thought. "Stop them there. Shoot only for the tires and the drivers. Do not shoot the fuel tank area. Precision shooting only!"

Jack looked at Mark, "Why do that? The terrorists will likely just detonate their bomb when they are stopped."

Mark nodded, "Maybe, but if we missile it or shoot it directly it will go off anyway. There is a chance it may not be detonated which is better than our doing it for sure."

The two men in the tanker truck pushed it for all it was worth but it just didn't get up to speed fast enough. A helicopter flew alongside and a loud speaker told them to stop immediately or face destruction. They ignored the orders and bore on towards town. As they entered the sparsely populated area the driver saw something in the road ahead. It was all the way over the road and he couldn't avoid it. As the truck hit the nail strips all ten tires on the truck were punctured and deflated. The speed fell off quickly to a crawl and then the truck came to a complete stop. Realizing that they had failed to reach their target the passenger picked up the remote detonator and looked at his driver. The driver said a quick prayer to Zultar.

Bullets smashed into the cab from both sides. The passenger died instantly from a sniper shot to the head. The driver was critically wounded but fumbled for the detonator that the other man had dropped as he was hit. The driver had blood all over his hands and couldn't get his failing strength to pick up the remote unit. He had almost grabbed it when he sensed a presence at the shattered window on the passenger side. Looking up he saw a flash and then only darkness.

The Idaho State Swat Team member that shot the driver opened the passenger door and dumped the body of the passenger out of the cab. Reaching in carefully he picked up the remote detonating unit and put it in an evidence bag. Keying his tactical radio he called the base at

Howard Field. "We have an all-clear on the State Street VBIED. Send a chopper to get this thing out of here as quickly as possible."

Mark and Jack did a high-five and smiled at the rest. Sarah grinned, "There were some incredibly brave people out there tonight. Everyone from the SWAT team including their snipers and even the helicopter crew were in the blast zone if that thing had gone off."

Mark sobered and nodded, "That same scenario is being reenacted all over the country and in Britain right now."

CHAPTER TWENTY-EIGHT

The digital clock in the war room at Howard Field registered ten o'clock which meant midnight on the East coast. Everyone held their breath waiting for the reports of explosions. Locally the night remained quiet, a soft breeze blowing from the West and the stars staying in their places. Mark called into the national command center and listened to the on-going updates.

He looked up and told the assembled crew that there had been nine detonations by terrorists in the U.S. and only one in Britain. There had been four trucks detonated by American forces in defensive attacks in California, New York, near Miami, and one in Phoenix. The loss of life was close to four hundred people. At ten minutes after the strike deadline all but six of the truck bombs had been found and handled.

Mark shook his head. He looked at the assembled leaders for all the civilian law enforcement groups and the active and reserve military units for the Boise area. "I want to congratulate you and your people for a service above and beyond the call of duty. I expect that there will be citations and probably a national service medal for everyone involved in the action today. The loss of life and destruction is lamentable but is so limited compared to what it might have been if each one of you and your teams hadn't put it all on the line." He stood up and saluted the assembly. His salute was returned and everyone began talking all at the same time.

Sarah sat down and pulled Mark back into his seat. "Don't forget, there could still be one truck somewhere out here. You estimated five and we've dealt with eight. Let's not quit yet."

Mark nodded in agreement with his wife. "I know, but it is a job we need to handle ourselves. These people need to go home to their families and reassure them that life goes on." He looked up at Jack, Laura, and Su Li. "We have a mission from Yahveh that is 24/7 and He will give us the strength to accomplish it." He grinned, "Anyway, this is home for us, right?"

As the others agreed Mark flipped open his cell phone and called Charlie Wu in Denver. Even though it was after midnight Charlie answered on the first ring. "Charlie, good work. Listen, we think there might still be one VBIED out here in Boise that hasn't been found. What can you tell me?"

A celebration could be heard behind Charlie as the computer troops realized that the worst was over and they could unwind. Charlie though was all business. "Mark, I see that the majority of the tankers discovered by satellite have been tagged as clear or moved on out of the area. I have three indications that haven't been cleared as yet. Do you think that one of the bombs is still parked out there somewhere?"

"It's possible. Show me the location of the three remaining trucks and we'll check them out."

Charlie highlighted them on the big illuminated map on the wall. Mark thanked the computer whiz and hung up. Studying the map he realized that one of the SWAT team leaders was standing next to him. Mark looked at the man and recognized Captain William Stoegy who had been his go-between for SWAT team activities. Bill Stoegy looked at the three remaining green lights on the map. "One of those you can forget." He pointed at the one to the South of Boise. That one is in a junk yard and I checked it myself this afternoon. Nothing there but a shell, no engine or wheels."

Mark checked the other two locations. "One is at a gas station in Caldwell and the other one is moving south on the I-84 Interstate against the President's orders to remain stationary until they are inspected and tagged!"

As they watched the moving blip slowed and turned Northeast onto Howard Road. Mark looked at the SWAT officer. "The semiconductor chip plant!" He looked around and found the Commander of the Air National Guard standing a few feet behind him. "Do you still have any assets in the air?" The Commander nodded and picked up a radio. He vectored his two remaining aircraft to the truck location. The call came back quickly. "Sir, I have been watching him for the last ten minutes. I think we need to stop him fast."

Mark asked for the radio and spoke to the pilot. "Can you take out the cab and not the load?" The answer came back, "I'll try."

The pilot checked his Integrated Flight and Fire Control Computer (IFFCC) automated continuously computed weapons delivery; He keyed his Sniper XR targeting pod for precision-guided weapons and used his helmet-mounted sighting system. His A-10 "Warthog" tank buster raced out of the sky as the tanker truck prepared to turn South on Federal Way towards the nearby plant.

Coming from the mountains at right angles to the travel of the truck the pilot triggered off a four-round burst from the 30mm cannon jutting from the nose of his aircraft. The four rounds struck the cab and engine compartment of the truck and turned everything there into rubble. The force of the 30mm rounds that destroyed the cab caused the tanker part of the truck to tip over onto its right side and slide into the ditch between the road and the Interstate highway. The pilot flew back over the debris and radioed that it hadn't blown up yet but it was inoperative and they needed to get people out there to remove the tank sections.

Jack alerted the chopper crew and gave them the GPS coordinates and then called the 9-1-1 number and got officers out there to control the situation.

Mark told the Commander to thank the pilot for his delicate slicing and dicing.

Sarah called in the last truck to the national crisis headquarters and learned that theirs was the last of the three hundred trucks to be eliminated.

As the tank part of the truck lay on it's right side in the ditch at the corner of Federal Way and Howard Road one piece of debris from the destroyed cab moved. A cotter pin, weakened by the destruction broke and the spoon flew off of an M-67 hand grenade. Because the tank was laying on it's side some of the liquid was leaking out of the damaged loading port. Four seconds later the grenade detonated. The violent heat of the exploding grenade was sufficient to ignite the Astrolite A-1-5.

The explosion was similar to a tactical field nuclear explosion without the radiation. The shock wave moved out from the epicenter and smashed everything in its path. The four-story main administration building of the semiconductor manufacturer was pulverized into fragments. The outer walls, the cubicles, the furniture, the computers, everything disintegrated and flew away to smash the other buildings near it. The three closest buildings suffered the same fate.

The concussive blast disintegrated the two ramps, four lanes of the interstate and the interstate bridge over Howard Road and then moved on to flatten the Outlet Center across the Interstate from the chip plant. The other buildings within a half mile of the epicenter were also destroyed with structural damage and heat and flame scarring for anything within the next quarter mile. All of this happened in less than three seconds.

As Sarah turned to Mark there was a heavy rumbling sound and the building shook violently.

Mark picked up the radio and called the A-10 pilot, "What happened?"

The pilot was rattled. "The tank section blew up! The concussion almost knocked me out of the air. There's a huge fireball going up back there."

Mark asked him to do a quick damage survey.

Jack was trying in vain to raise the helicopter crew. He quit trying and looked at Laura and shook his head.

The pilot came back on the radio and Mark patched it into the P.A. system in the conference room they were calling the war room. "It looks like a nuclear strike out here. There is extensive damage to the chip plant and there are at least a dozen major fires in the buildings that weren't destroyed. There are some serious chemicals at that plant too. Bettered get HazMat out there immediately." As his plane circled to the north of the huge crater he continued to report. "Most of the shopping center north of the plant is gone. The only sign that there was a fast food restaurant is a bent and burning sign. There are at least twenty-five homes over here damaged and or burning." Crossing the Interstate he looked down at the missing Howard Road Bridge effectively amputating the Interstate south of Boise. "Most of the Shopping Center across the

Interstate is gone and the rest is on fire. The water tower was blown over a half mile away to the Southwest. The Howard Road Bridge was vaporized and both lanes south of the bridge are completely gone for a half-mile."

Mark frowned as a phone rang in the background, "Thank you Captain, come on home.".

One of the ANG airmen ran up to the front of the room with a remote phone which he handed to Mark. Mark grabbed it, "General Connelly."

The voice on the other end was shaky. "General, this is Captain Morse, I am, or was, the pilot of the heavy lift helicopter we were using to move the VBIEDs."

Mark let out a whoop! "Captain are you and your men all right?"

Captain Morse paused for a second. "Yes sir. We've all got bumps and bruises and I think Mac broke his arm but all in all we're still with you. I can't say as much for the chopper. We were about half way to the site when the bomb went off. It slapped us so hard it knocked out all the electronics and dumped us into a field so hard we smashed the landing gear and the rotor blades snapped off. The chopper fell over and it took us forever to find a land line to call in our report. We could use a ride back to the base and maybe to a hospital for Mac."

Mark laughed, "I'll get right on it."

CHAPTER TWENTY-NINE

The damage reports kept rolling in from Southeast Boise throughout the night. The blessing was that the death toll never went above twelve people. Due to the warnings about the chip plant being a high-risk target and the late hour the only people killed were those serving as security for the various businesses, the terrorists themselves, and three members of an early morning work crew who were driving through the area during the time of the explosion.

At least the Manufacturer's management had protected its workforce by closing the plant for the twenty-four hours during the emergency. If they hadn't there would have been hundreds killed and wounded instead of twelve.

The same was true of the other employers in the area. No night shift personnel were on duty and most of the houses in the area were empty as people heeded the warnings and went somewhere else for the night. Businesses had insurance and buildings could be replaced much easier than their work forces. Alternative plans would be put into effect to utilize the work forces in other locations until the physical plants were rebuilt.

Mark turned the mop-up operations over to the Army Reserve Commander and the very tired Crossfire Team were driven to the Boise Airport for a chartered flight to Denver.

During the short flight Mark got a call from the adjutant for General Miles. He listened for a few minutes and then hung up. He called the other four members of the team together. "Investigation into the trucks that were seized and removed to desolate places has revealed that the trigger devices inside the explosive fuel in the trucks would not work. It seems that the liquid in the trucks short-circuited the electrical circuits and drained the batteries. The conclusion is that the last minute substitution of the trigger devices from an African source rather than the original triggers from the Philippines was the reason for the defect. The think tank people feel that

137

the terrorists groups probably trained with and tested the original triggers but didn't have time to do the same with the new unit. This is why the drivers couldn't trigger their bombs."

Laura smiled, "Think about it. Who made sure they'd have to use the African units? Who put a burden on our team to go after the Crescent Dagger terrorists who just happened to have all the tested trigger assemblies neatly stacked where we could throw a bomb at them and destroy them? It could all be a coincidence but I see the hand of Yahveh in it protecting our country and that of Britain."

Sarah laughed, "You're right! Praise Yahveh and Yahshua! They are mighty to protect God's children."

There were high-fives and cheers. Mark then held up his hand and silenced the group. Mark organized his thoughts and then looked up. "This was a great victory for the free world against the forces of darkness. Yes. But, I have several questions we need to answer for the future. The main one and the hardest to speculate about is this. Why would this international group of super smart bad guys really want to bring about the ideal Zultarian world?"

There were frowns and thoughtful looks but no one offered an explanation. Mark waited and then tried to answer his own question. "Because they either had a way of controlling the powers that would be in charge or they never meant for the attack to succeed."

Sarah was puzzled by that line of reasoning. "Why would any group spend two years bringing together a host of radical terroristic groups and drug cartels and orchestrate this whole thing planning for it to fail?"

Mark shook his head. "I don't know for sure but I do know that these world-class bad guy organizations are only after three things. One, money, they probably siphoned off millions from this operation and needed it to fail so they could spend it in a non-Zultarian controlled world. Two, power, they wanted to focus all these groups on this goal so that the organization could acquire new power somehow. Or, three, this is all part of a bigger plan and we don't know what that is. If it is number three, then I'll bet dollars to doughnuts that Satan is calling the shots and it is probably against Israel."

The pilot of the U.S. Air Force Jet Commander called Mark to the cockpit where he took a call from General Miles. "Mark, the only way we could stop the majority of the truck bombs was to involve the populace in both countries. That meant letting them know who was behind the attacks. Now that the attacks are over the hue and cry is swelling for retribution and retaliation against the groups involved in the truck bomb plot. It has become such a rallying cry against the Zultarian religion even though the majority of Zultarians only want peace. This is forcing the President to take some definitive action to satisfy the public. I need to have a high-profile dragnet working to bring the culprits to justice before we have sectarian warfare. Will your team take point on this action?"

Mark was deep in thought about the way things were progressing. "Uh, Hmmm, Yes Sir. That will be all right. We have some team research we need to accomplish first. Thank you for letting us have this opportunity Sir."

The General thanked Mark and reminded him that they needed results quickly. He then hung up.

The plane landed at DIA in Denver and the team was met by Charlie at the security doors. Charlie drove them to the Fortress in one of the armored vans available to the team.

Mark sat in his bedroom in deep prayer. Several possibilities were becoming clearer in his mind and he wanted to bounce them off of the other team members. He went to the big conference room next to the living room. Drawing everyone into the room with their snacks, drinks, and cell phones he finally got their undivided and uninterrupted attention.

He looked at the other people of the team. His wife, his best friends, people he would trust his life to in any situation. "Guys, the way things are going has caused me to question the overall situation. I need your input on what I got while in prayer concerning my thoughts on this. Okay?"

Everyone agreed and sat quietly. Mark reprised his question on the flight to Denver. "What was this attack really about? I'm sure for the radicals involved it was a chance to strike their enemies. For the cartels it was a sure way to give them a free shot at a world market for their drugs. But, what was the motive for the Executor and his group? I think I've got an idea what it might be."

That made everyone sit up and listen harder. Mark got up and paced back and forth near the head of the table. "I was wondering why they would spend so much money and time in what became a losing effort. I believe that this mysterious group is smart enough to foreseen the possibility that the strikes would be compromised or defeated. Even if they didn't tell the radicals or the cartels. So what is their agenda?"

Looking at the others he didn't see any knowledge coming forth as yet. "Okay, my thought is that they didn't plan on winning, or losing. They planned on either event. I believe they wanted the plan to succeed not to destroy the free world as much as destroy Christianity and Judaism. Think about it. The U.S. and Britain are the world seats of Christianity other than the Vatican. Once the U.S. is knocked out, the Zultarians would eat up Israel piece by piece. But, the plan didn't work, or did it?"

Mark picked up a bottle of water and took a drink. "What did they plan if the attacks didn't result in an all-Zultarian world? How about this. The backlash of the "well publicized" massive attacks by Zultarian radicals on the free world would be, and is, huge. The populations of both countries are calling for blood and they aren't too picky as to whose Zultarian blood it is. How does this serve our mysterious group's leaders? By promoting sectarian warfare between Zultarism on one hand, 1.5 billion people, and the free-world's Christians and Jews 2.3 billion people. Surrounded as they are by Zultarian countries, Israel would not last long in a war like that."

Laura said, "Sounds like Satan is at work again to destroy anyone, everyone, and especially Yahveh's people."

Mark nodded. "My thought exactly. So, the enemy wants to destroy Israel and Christians, nothing new, but the mechanism, this mysterious group is new and I believe my leading from Yahshua is for us to track them down and put them out of business. This is also what the President and the CJCS wants us to do." Mark sat down and asked for opinions.

Jack answered for all of the team. "Okay, we need to pray about it, but assuming that is Yahveh's will, how do we get started finding out who the enemy is in this case?"

Mark smiled, "Let's see what Charlie Wu and his computer network can get us."

CHAPTER THIRTY

The team rode the elevator to the computer level and tramped in to see Charlie Wu.

Charlie knew they were coming by the fact that he watched them all the way there on various cameras. He reclined in his ergonomically designed chair and inspected his friends. They all looked tired and a bit haggard. But the fire in their eyes had gotten brighter.

Mark recounted what they had gone through in the island jungles, caves, and Boise. Jack filled in the efforts in Saudi Arabia and Sarah explained the reverse OLEDs they'd used to gather the Intel at the meeting. Mark then explained their brain-storming and conclusions since returning to Denver.

Charlie nodded at that. "Okay. I've got some Intel for you guys. First I think I know who we're after. The street name for the group you have run into is Omicron. It is the name of the fifteenth character of the Greek alphabet but it has a more sinister meaning with these people. Little is known as yet about the cast of characters that make up this diabolical business except that they all use the name of a Greek letter as their business nom-de-plume. For example, Mr.Beta and Ms. Delta are two that have been heard."

Charlie brought up some more information on his computer screen. "When Linda and I were agents in China we investigated the murder of one of the most prolific criminal trackers in the country. He was coming through the mountains on his way back to Beijing when his car failed to make a turn on a particularly steep canyon road. We found that a simple computer device called a process controller had been placed on his car. The process controller has a very limited instruction set. It knew that the car had to be in a certain place before it severed his brakes so that he could not stop his descent and the car went off the road at the worst possible place. A six hundred foot fall ensured his death."

Charlie called up another file and showed them the similarity between two cases. "This woman was just killed a week ago in Spain in exactly the same way. Reports on both cases revel that a woman was seen near the vehicle just before the accident. A red-headed woman. She's somewhat older now than when the Chinese accident was arranged, but I think it's the same woman. I believe she is our mysterious Ms. Delta from the Omicron group. The woman that was killed was the wife to a top Spanish jet fighter pilot who is missing."

Charlie called up a picture of the pilot. "I think this is one of the guys flying the MIGs. He paid off his house in cash two days before he disappeared. I checked into the ownership of the house in the event of his death and discovered that the house has been claimed by the Milsap Realty Company. That is a front company for a lot of mob activity. But, I did some digging in the CIA files and found out that this house is actually owned by the Omicron Cartel through a series of dummy companies. Apparently the pilot signed a waiver that gives them the rights to the house and that sends the dead woman's kids into a state orphanage."

Su Li had been following the trail. "So, you think that the Omicron Cartel paid the pilot to steal one of the MIGs and to attack us. When he was killed, his wife had to be killed to keep his deal a secret?"

Charlie shook his head. "No, I think that they paid him and he didn't deliver and didn't come back. So, to cover their backsides, in the event the pilot had told his wife anything, they killed her to eliminate any possible problem."

Sarah added, "And then they take the only possession the woman had, the house, away from the children?"

Charlie nodded, "That's what it looks like. And these people are smart, I started to follow leads and most of them lead to dead ends or traps."

Mark knew Charlie and his skills as an agent and knew he would never let a little thing like smart bad people slow him down.

Jack looked at Laura, "I want to contact an agency in Spain that will take the kids, love them, and let them grow up educated and in security. Charlie, will you find the right group for me to get in touch with fairly soon?"

Su Li tipped her head to one side. "You'd spend your time and money to take care of the children of the man who was hired to kill all of us including you and Laura?"

Jack smiled, "Yes. First off, they are innocent of any wrongdoing. Second, they were robbed of their chance at a decent life by this Omicron Cartel twice and are being robbed by them again. Lastly, Yahveh teaches Agape love which judges the heart not the ancestry. These are little children who have just lost their parents and now are being stripped of all chances by the same organization we've vowed to hunt down and destroy. I would think you would understand their pain and confusion better than most." Jack was referring to Su Li's loss of her parents when she was young.

The pretty Oriental woman had a tear in her eyes as she nodded. "I do understand all too well. I just wish there had been a Jack Malone there for me."

Laura got up and went over to Su Li. Squatting down she put her arms around the smaller woman. Quietly but with great conviction Laura said, "No man like Jack was there for you but Yahshua was there. He knew where you were heading and what it would take to get you to love Him and become an accomplished warrior for the Kingdom. You have become a bright light in a world of darkness and you had to walk the path you walked to get to this point."

Su Li stared through her tears at Laura and then hugged her fiercely. "Darn right I'm a bright light! Thank you."

Sarah was staring at the screen showing the last image the murdered woman. "Do you have anything else we can work with to locate this Omicron operation?"

Charlie smiled. "Yes I do. Thanks to the cooperation of the NSA I have the exchanges and addresses for the numbers called by the Executor in Saudi Arabia before he became the guest of the U.S. Military. Most of them are to the factions that were there. But, I have three numbers that seem so innocuous that they scream importance. Two are to an address in London, England, and the other is to a flower shop in Barcelona, Spain."

The computer expert manipulated several files and brought up some photos. "This is the house the calls went to in London. Oh! By the way, there were three cut-outs and twelve relays in both of these calls and the conversations were encrypted. This is the type of mystery the NSA thrives on. The house is owned by a retired military man. A Colonel in the British Army. Distinguished record, commendations, etc., etc. Here is a picture of the Colonel."

A white haired, stern looking elderly man stared into the camera.

Charlie clicked to the next file. "Unfortunately, the Colonel must be away because the man living there is this man." Another photo appeared showing a man in his late thirties with a powerful physique, a high forehead, and a cold, cruel look on his face as he exited the side door of the house. He was dressed in gardening clothes and had gloves in his left hand.

Charlie looked at his desk screen. "Photo identification from Interpol shows him to be one Manfred Charles Pendragon. Manny is a British citizen with no known means of support but obviously well-off by the luxury cars, boats, and airplane he owns. Interpol suspects him of being involved in not one, but two of the biggest bank heists every pulled off in Britain. They can't prove anything but his involvement in a dozen different murders and blackmail of public officials is also suspected. They have carefully watched him for the last two years. One mistake he has made is that he answered the phone on a solicitor's call as "Mr. Alpha" then made a joke out of it. I'm pretty confident he is one of the Omicron's leading lights."

Charlie frowned, "That's the good news. The bad news is that Manny has some very high protection in the British government. My guess, some of that blackmail he is suspected of by Interpol and some massive contributions to several political personages of great influence. Attempts to corral him have been squelched by the Prime Minister on advice from several of the Lords of the British Parliament. Other than that slip and his elusive lifestyle, and now the two phone calls from the Executor, we don't have anything on him. But, I think he's as dirty as they come. And, I don't like how he looks either."

More screens replaced the picture of Manfred Pendragon. A tall, extremely beautiful red-haired young woman in expensive clothes, standing next to a red

Porsche was shown next. Charlie smiled, "This I think is Ms. Delta, no real name or identification by any of the world's law enforcement groups. She's managed to avoid all notoriety to date. But, I'll bet you that she's the bomber that killed the pilot's wife in Spain. I tracked her by the flowers ordered by the Executor. The hotel she received them at not only had her passport, which was a phony, but this picture of her taken by a bellhop because he thought she was so pretty. This one reminds me of the female android in the old movie "Terminator 3" starring the then Governor of California. Bad news."

Jack asked, "Any idea where she is at now?"

Charlie shook his head. "No, but I'm looking for both of these characters and anything I get I'll send to you right away."

Mark had thought this through. "Jack, I want you, Laura, and Sarah to go to this house in London and see what you can unearth without having to kill everyone in the area or even just Mr. Pendragon. He may be our only link to Omicron. Jack why don't you see if President Bollen has enough pull with Number ten Downing Street to give you the cooperation, on the sly, of the British government?"

Sarah raised her left eyebrow and asked Mark, "What are you going to do, track down the pretty little thing?"

Mark smiled and spread his arms outward, "Of course, who better to do it?" Which got him a glare from Sarah.

Mark continued, "But, I'm taking Charlie and Linda Wu with me just in case she's more than I can handle."

That was a big concession on Mark's part. Very few people in the world were on the short list of ones he couldn't handle.

CHAPTER THIRTY-ONE

The President's schedule was overfull and he was tired. But when he heard that Jack Malone wanted to talk to him and had a possible lead to the people behind the truck bomb attack; he dropped what he was doing and took the call.

"Jack, how are you and Laura faring?'

"Mr. President, we're fine and, as usual, we need your help."

The President smiled, "Well your batting record is still one-hundred percent with me. What do you need and will this help capture the people behind the bombings?"

"Yes Sir, we think we have a suspect. He got two calls from the "Executor" in Saudi Arabia as tracked by the NSA. He has a probably blackmailed a few of the Lords of the British Parliament who are protecting him from investigation. We would like to ask you if you could persuade the Prime Minister to authorize us to secretly investigate him. His name is Mandrake Charles Pendragon and we believe he is a dirty as a person can get."

President Bollen didn't hesitate. "I'll see to it personally and immediately. I need a break from this meeting anyway. Good hunting Jack." The connection was broken.

Jack nodded and the three of them made their preparations for a trip to the British Isles. Su Li was taking Mark and the Wus to Spain in a modified Air Force Jet Commander that had teeth in the event they met any unwanted visitors on the way. Due to the national security angle the Malones and Sarah were given the services of Major Mike White of the USAF for their trip which was also in a USAF Jet Commander, a twin to the one in which Mark and the Wus were traveling.

The trip to Barcelona was twelve hours while the trip to London was nine hours. During the trip Jack got confirmation from the White House that they had special status to operate in Britain. They would meet with a member of MI-5 at Heathrow when they arrived.

The remainder of the flight was uneventful and all three of the warriors caught up on their sleep on the trip.

Rerouted to a British Military Airfield thirty miles north of London the trio were met by David Thornton, an MI-5 operative who guided them onto a British Army Air Corps Westland Lynx AH Mk.9 for the short flight into London.

Once there, they met with several agents of Scotland Yard and discussed their target and his high-level protection. It was a known fact that Pendragon was blackmailing one of the Parliament's Lords over a well photographed affair with a beautiful, young red haired woman. His wife and three children were unaware of the affair and he was determined to keep it that way.

Recognizing the even higher level of authorization that these people had, the agents cooperated freely with all of their knowledge about Pendragon. It was a surprisingly large amount of data considering the hands-off request from Parliament. One of the agents winked at Sarah and told her that Scotland Yard never liked this particular Lord anyway.

After reviewing the information on the man and his movements. Jack decided they should do a drive by to see the house and the area to determine the course of their investigation. Securing a driver from MI-5 the trio set out for the Park Royal area northwest of London. The driver was grinning from ear to ear and Jack looked at him. The man sobered up and then broke into a grin again.

Jack asked, "Is there something humorous we're not aware of?"

William Codson again sobered up and swallowed noisily. "No sir." Then the grin came back. Glancing at Jack in the front seat next to him he said, "Everyone at the ministry has read about the activities that your team has been involved in over the last couple o' years and I'm looking forward to seeing some action. You know, how quiet and staid most of our investigations are, this should be great."

It was Jack's turn to smile as he heard a giggle from Laura in the back seat. "You may find that this is just as boring as your investigations. On the other hand, you may see things you've never seen before." Jack eyed the man for a few seconds, "How's your faith in God?"

Codson glanced at the tall man next to him. "I'm a good Catholic if that's what you're askin'."

Sarah spoke up from the back seat next to Laura, "No, William, what Jack is asking is how your personal walk with God and Jesus is going."

The agent looked confused, "My personal walk? I didn't know I was allowed to have a personal walk. My priest tells me I need to pray to the church for their help in talking to God. I go to confession and light candles for urgent causes, and I am faithful in tithing and attendance." He seemed actually proud that he didn't know God himself, but as part of the Catholic Church.

Jack nodded, "Good, we should talk later if we get the chance. Okay?"

Codson nodded, "Get set, the house is just around the bend."

As the car rounded the bend and a large English Tutor style house appeared, Laura blanched and sucked in a big breath. Sarah looked at her friend in alarm. "Laura, what is it?"

Laura waved her left hand and said, "Keep going, drive away from here, quickly." She started praying and her golden armor suddenly appeared. Her shield was there but not the sword. The light streaming off of her armor lit up the inside of the car and startled the MI-5 agent. He started to step on the brakes when Jack commanded him. "Don't stop! Drive away quickly!"

Shaking his head as he stared at the impossibly bright image of Laura's armor in the mirror, he accelerated down the straight part of the street. As the house disappeared behind them, Laura's armor faded out of sight and she shuddered. She looked up at Jack with an intensity that jolted him. "Keep driving for a while."

After several miles they were coming up on a park and Laura told the driver to pull in there. He did and parked in a car park on the side of the park. Laura opened her door and got out. Jack did the same and came around to where she was. She tipped her head to one side and started walking. Jack stayed with her. He didn't ask anything because he knew Laura well enough that she would reveal what she wanted to when she wanted to and not before.

Laura stopped several hundred feet from the car and turned to Jack. Taking his hands in hers she looked into his eyes. "Let's pray."

A few seconds into the prayer and Jack knew it was for their protection. He implored Yahveh to protect them as it says in Psalm 91, *"He covers you with his feathers, and under his wings you take refuge; His truth is a shield and armor. My refuge, the Most High- your dwelling place, No evil befalls you, the plague does not come near your tent; for He commands His messengers concerning you, to guard you in all your ways. They bear you up in their hands, lest you dash your foot against a stone. You tread upon lion and cobra, because Yahveh says. He cleaves to me in love, therefore I deliver him. When he calls on me I answer him, I am with him in distress, I deliver him and esteem him."*

Laura stopped praying when Jack did. She took a deep breath and moved against Jack who put his arms around her.

Jack just held her for the minute.

In the car the MI-5 agent looked away from the couple and asked Sarah, "What happened? And what was that golden suit of armor?"

From her years of service with the Mossad, Sarah knew the intensity behind the questions of the other agent. She prayed for the right words and when she thought she had them she said, "William, there are forces involved in the spiritual struggle that the Catholic Church will not tell you about, but they are real and can be very deadly. What happened? Well, I'm not sure, but I would guess that a major demon was in the vicinity of that house. Laura is especially sensitive to spiritual forces and has been given special protection by Yahveh; you would say God, to do battle with demons. The armor appeared because she started to pray but it was for protection this time rather than battle."

William looked at her with keen interest. "How do we know that?"

Sarah smiled at the man, "Because the sword of the word wasn't there." She saw that he had assimilated the information and not freaked out like a simpler person might have. "Don't worry William Codson, remember, our big guy is bigger than their big guy."

150

William Codson sat back and processed what had just happened and the explanation. His world view had just been rewritten and he needed to try to understand the changes.

Laura was telling Jack about the same thing that Sarah had told Codson. "When we came near that house I sensed a demon of immense power! Don't ask me how I know, I just did. I realized that I would give us away to him if I did anything at all. I'm afraid that my armor might have alerted him. I saw a vision of Pendragon bowing down with his head to the floor worshiping the devil. The man is evil but he pales next to the real evil. Oh Jack! I don't know how we can even go near that place."

Jack considered the possibilities. "Let's go back to our flat and pray for guidance."

CHAPTER THIRTY-TWO

Jack closed the door to the suite they had been given by MI-5. He was concerned about Laura. She normally didn't react to the enemy this way.

Laura was in prayer. She prayed for Yahveh to give them guidance as to how they could approach the enemy's house. She was afraid that her closeness to Yahveh would alert the enemy and they could set a trap for her and the others.

As she felt inadequate to the task and pleaded for Yahveh's guidance so that they could accomplish His will, she sensed the approach of something. She was on her guard as she prayed for protection and truth.

Laura felt a force that went off the scale for power and perfection. She heard a voice say, *"My daughter, why do you worry? Haven't I told you that I will protect you? You are my daughter and I love you more than you can understand right now. Stand for me and I will lead you in the fight. I love you."* That was the message.

Laura shook her head and blinked her eyes open to find Sarah watching her and smiling. "What are you grinning about?" she asked.

Sarah smiled, "You. I watched you as you prayed and got an answer. You positively glowed. I love you as a sister but I realize that there is someone more powerful than me that loves you. And, I'm glad."

Laura composed her thoughts, "It's our love of Yahveh and His will that is the key. We need to be operating in love of Yahveh and His Kingdom. He will protect us when we act in His love. Now, how do we act in his love to someone who is worshiping Satan?"

Jack answered, "By knowing His word. We know His word and it tells us what to do. Part of love for Yahveh is righteous anger. Anger against things that rebel against Yahveh and His Name and His Word. This is what Yahshua was doing in John 2: 15-16 when he cleansed the temple of the moneylenders and the merchants that were blaspheming the temple. Our righteous anger against what this man is doing and against what his whole group are doing in Satan's name is love for the Father."

"But how do we do that?"

Jack said, "Let's pray for the answer." They began to pray for Yahveh's will concerning this action because it would be coming against Satan and even the angel Michael did not disrespect Satan when he argued with Satan about Moses' body. *Jude 1:9 But Michael the chief messenger, in contending with the devil, when he disputed about the body of Moses, presumed not to bring against him a blasphemous accusation, but said, Yahveh rebuke you!"*

As they prayed for direction and guidance they felt the peace of Yahveh fall upon them and they rested quietly for some time. Then a voice spoke to them, *"I have allowed these men to do their evil on the world for their allotted time. Their father knows that the time is up. He and his minions will not interfere with you as you deal with their agents. If they do, I will rebuke them for you. Go in my name to my glory."*

Jack opened his eyes to see Laura crying and laughing at the same time. He poked her and said, "What's so tearfully funny?"

She smiled, "I saw a snap vision of the angels Rose and Caleb doing a high five."

Sarah joined in, "I know Yahveh says that the devil and his goons can't involve themselves but let's remember that in the natural these people are highly trained, deadly agents and even without spiritual help are going to be extremely dangerous."

Jack thought about that. "Okay, superspy, what do we do?"

Sarah had given this subject a great deal of thought on the way to Britain. "We break into the house when the resident and the resident evil aren't there and see what we can find. Any leader will have information on his computer, files, notebooks, something that he can use daily to organize and run his business. We just need to think one step ahead of this character. I would suggest we get the best hacker MI-5 has available before we go in there."

Jack nodded, "I'll get with our contact and see what we can get in the way of floor plans, electronic hookups, and the like."

Sarah nodded, "These days the notes are just as likely to be on his personal PDA which he takes with him. But, usually they upload and download to their own computer or a server out in the cloud somewhere."

Jack agreed with her on that. "The chances of our finding any written material are almost non-existent. He's probably using a direct satellite uplink to a server downlink to minimize detection. But, I'll bet you that the NSA can find and track his signals."

Jack called their contact at the NSA and described the GPS location of the house and their suspicions. He gave the contact an override code that would move their request up the priority list.

Sarah also called David Zahavy in Israel and gave him an update on their activities. She also explained their need to get a handle on this group and this was their one address to work with at the present. David agreed to see what he could do to help them.

It seemed that their upgrade in status was considerable. The NSA agent called back in twenty minutes. "General Malone?"

Jack acknowledged his identity. The man continued "Sir, we've actually been monitoring that address for the last two months due to a request from Homeland Security. It seems that the people at that address may have been involved in a rash of attempted break-ins at the secure databases for Homeland Security and the U.S. Army. Are you ready to copy and is your end of the line secure?"

Jack had already checked the line supplied by MI-5 and he told the NSA to go ahead with the information.

"General, the people at that site are very good at trying to hide their information and data storage. Actually, one of the best I've ever seen. It took us almost two days to figure out their schemes. I'm sending you the analysis summary for the last two months." As he spoke he transmitted the data to Jack's laptop. When it was complete he said goodbye and terminated the conversation.

Jack brought up the Intel and was amazed at the detail the NSA had sucked out of the Omicron server. He located information concerning the attack on the Crossfire jet, the summary of the effort to destroy the U.S. with truck bombs, and a great deal more incriminating information. But the best of the Intel was a listing of personnel and their schedules. Everything was still coded and the people were referred to as Mr. Beta and Ms. Delta but it was a heaven sent treasure trove for the Crossfire Team.

Jack thought about it and called the NSA back again. He got the same agent as the first time and asked, "If you had this information about the truck bomb plans, why didn't someone act on it?"

"General, all that information was forwarded to the FBI. They have the mandate to act on it within the U.S. We just collect it."

Jack thought for a few seconds, "Can you get me the name of the person who got that information?"

The agent told him to wait one. "It was an FBI Senior Agent, Lionel Skools. I have an electronic signature and a photo of him as I sent the data."

Jack asked the NSA agent to send a copy of the signature and the photo and then thanked him and broke off the contact. Looking at the Wus he shook his head. "I think we've got a rat named Skools in the FBI."

CHAPTER THIRTY-THREE

In contrast to the official welcome in Britain, Mark and the Wus came into Barcelona, Spain on a commercial flight. They had left their USAF flight at a military airfield in Lisbon and taken an Air France flight to Barcelona. Disembarking with the other passengers the three Crossfire warriors walked separately. Charlie and his wife were ten steps ahead of Mark as they went down the concourse to the terminal. The airport security in European airports is different than that in the U.S. Teams of flinty-eyed Spanish military types with sub-machine guns slung over their shoulders walked the terminal and examined each and every person.

Mark rented a car and picked it up. He then swung around to the terminal again and picked up the Wus. Mark drove to the hotel where Ms. Delta had been staying when the picture had been taken.

Showing their U.S. Homeland Security badges they requested assistance from the hotel staff. The hotel manager worked with them. He showed them the room she had rented but there had been several other lodgers staying there since and the room had been cleaned daily.

Charlie and Linda had been two of China's top intelligence agents before they found Yahshua and went to America to start a more godly life. They went over the room carefully but were unable to find anything that could be identified as belonging to their target. Not a single red hair was left. It could be that the hotel staff was meticulous in their cleaning, but Charlie and Linda thought that the woman was a professional who tried not to leave any traces of her passing.

Mark had been working with the manager to see if there was anything else they could use. He had a make, model, and license number for the Porsche she had been driving but knew it was probably a stolen plate. They could check for sales of that particular model of Porsche but again, it probably was purchased through an agent or by one of Omicron's dummy companies.

As they were preparing to leave with no really good information, the desk clerk came over to Mark and handed him an envelope. It had come for the red-haired beauty just after she had left. Since there was no return address, the hotel decided to hold it for her if she were to return in the near future.

Mark looked the letter over from the outside carefully. The Wus watched him. Charlie said, "It's a backtrack trap isn't it?"

Mark nodded, "Yeah, she probably sent it to the hotel after she left. There has to be something pretty nasty inside."

Charlie said, "Give it to me and I'll see what I can find when we get a room and I can get some tools out."

They had a quick lunch and went to find a suite in a reputable hotel. They found what they wanted in the Majestic Hotel Barcelona, located on Paseo de Gracia in the heart of Barcelona. Truly a five-star hotel that was built in 1918, the suite of rooms accommodated their needs nicely.

Charlie took out his "tools" and began to examine the envelope. He ran several tests on it and then put it under a high-power microscope. Then he did several chemical tests on the seal. When he was done he walked over to the others and sat down. "That's one really professional backtrack trap."

He looked at his notes. "She filled the envelope with blank paper and a botulism strain that causes a very slow lingering death and for which there is no known cure, Clostridium BoNT. This neurotoxin is so deadly that most terrorists shy away from it. She didn't care if the hotel personnel opened it or a mail person did in attempting to see that it was delivered."

Charlie smiled, "There is a redeeming value to this package of death. She accidently left one tiny piece of hair stuck to the flap. I've already run it through Interpol and the FBI, not to mention China's files. Total blank. But, when I ran it through the Russian files I got a match."

He laid a photograph on the table of a very beautiful red head with a winsome smile, she seemed to be happy and almost gleeful. "Her name is Raisa Ivanova; she was born in Kiev, Russia twenty six years ago. She was recruited by the KGB and trained as an assassin. When the

Iron Curtain fell she left the crumbling KGB and disappeared. She reappeared in their records as a member of the Omicron Group. In Russia the Omicron Cartel offers almost everything in the way of services but mainly in the area of wet work."

"According to a file one of her handlers put in her record, she is the smartest and deadliest human on the planet. We know how the Russians like to brag about their own agents." Charlie finished with one more statement. "But after reading her case files, I would recommend immediate termination with prejudice because she will kill you if you don't kill her first."

Mark agreed with Charlie's appraisal of the capabilities of the woman. He had actually run across one of her earlier operations before he became part of the Crossfire Team.

CHAPTER THIRTY-FOUR

Mark thought back to that time almost three years ago.

-----------------------******-----------------------

In the dark night the strobe lights of the muzzle flashes made a crazy quilt pattern out of the side of the motor pool. Bullets reached out seeking Mark's life from three different places. The four-by-eight he was using as shelter was taking a large number of hits. One round punched through the glass on both doors and creased his hair raining glass nuggets all over his head and shoulders. Shaking off the glass fragments and ducking lower he moved next to the front wheel on the left side of the truck for protection. Bullets whined under the body of the truck and slammed into the wheel and tire assembly protecting him. The tire was a military run-flat and didn't deflate even after being hit several times.

Mark had a handgun and two extra magazines. He knew he was up against at least three fully automatic assault rifles, probably M-16s or CAR-15s from the sound of the fire. A lull in the firing gave him time to run to the next vehicle in a crouch. But he didn't stop there, he went three vehicles up and then two more towards the shooters. Slipping around an M1A2 Abrams Tank he spotted two of the men that had been shooting at him. Dropping into a prone position he carefully targeted the more distant man he fired twice quickly. Immediately switching to the other man he fired a second double tap at that target. The nice thing about firing a double tap was that if one shot missed the target, the other one usually didn't. Mark was an excellent marksman and both men went down, one with his finger on the trigger of his assault rifle. The firing stopped when the magazine ran dry.

Mark was about to move toward their positions to find the third shooter when the night became day. Huge lights lit up the entire area and more came on farther away to illuminate everything outside of the motor pool and the building next to it. His backup was finally arriving.

Mark scanned the area and didn't see the third shooter. He stepped out into the light to let the good guys know who and where he was. He started walking towards the first two shooters with his.40 caliber XT at full extension. As he reached the row of vehicles they had been behind he watched an amazing sight. Four of the regular security officers had cornered the third shooter and were attempting to secure the person.

Mark saw a flash of red hair and a blur of motion. She was moving gracefully at high speed destroying the security officers one at a time. Mark was separated from the action by an eight foot fence topped with razor wire and all he could do was watch. The woman used a right hand knuckle punch that crushed the throat of the first man, spun to her left and kicked in the side of the second man's skull. Hardly breaking her motion she then executed a left hand palm heel strike to the chest of the third man. He flew off of his feet as his heart exploded and was dead by the time he hit the ground. The fourth man was shooting at her with a pistol. She dodged and feinted several times causing him to miss each time. She closed with the man and grabbing his gun hand she rotated the gun towards him and made him pull the trigger. The shot was high to the chest and he fell to the ground wounded. The woman turned and looked directly at Mark. She fired a shot from the officer's gun at him which caused him to duck. She then shot the officer in the head killing him. Moving very fast, she dropped the gun and ducked behind a building as Mark fired at her. By the time he could check she had disappeared.

Mark had met the men she had killed so easily. All of them were ex-military and tough guys. The red head had gone through them like they were cardboard cutouts. As the memory ended, Mark was fairly certain that woman and the one that Charlie IDed were one in the same.

-----------------------*****-----------------------

Mark asked the Wus to get all the information they could on her and her activities. They might get a lead as to where she was headed.

Mark used his cell phone to call a friend of his from his Navy days. Al Harris was now an analysis at the National Security Agency. Getting a recording he left his name and number. Hanging up he waited.

His phone rang thirty minutes later and it was Al on the other end. "Mark Connelly, how are you doing?"

Mark laughed, "I'm doing fine Al, how about you?"

It was Al's turn to laugh. "Before I told you, I'd have to run a security check on you or have you terminated. But I'm sure if what I've been hearing about you and that team you're on, this is probably not a social call, right?"

Mark smiled, "Sharp as ever Al. I need some help finding a girl."

Al came back, "I thought you were married"

Mark continued to grin, "Funny. Yes, I am married. The girl I'm looking for is a stone-cold killer and she attempts to stay out of the limelight. I can give you her original Russian name and a description but that's about all."

Al got serious, "Okay, shoot."

Her name is Raisa Ivanova and I think she's about twenty-six by now. She's about five-foot, ten-inches, probably about one hundred thirty pounds, well built and normally has flaming red hair. I personally know of four people she has killed. In fact I watched her disassemble four armed ex-military security officers bare handed."

Al said, "I'll get back to you with anything I can find. I'll tell the man in charge that I'm helping an old friend find a date."

Mark said, "I owe you one." After thanking him Mark broke the connection.

The Wus and Mark went out and had dinner and then turned in for the night.

About five a.m. Mark's phone rang. Mark answered it before the second ring. "Connelly."

"This is Al, I've got some information for you and you need to get ready to move quickly. Raisa is presently a blonde and is going under the name of Estelle for the moment and she is about to enter the Majestic Hotel in Barcelona with four very tough looking men that my equipment say are heavily armed. I believe that is where you called me from earlier so I suggest a hasty exit or a battlefield stand. Call me back if you survive and I'll give you more information." The receiver went dead.

Mark jumped up and yelled at the Wus. "We've got hostiles headed for our suite right now! Move it!"

The Wus were trained and experienced agents. They were dressed, armed, and ready in less than two minutes. Charlie looked at Mark, "Do we stand or run?"

Mark's inclination would have been to stand, but he had been praying while getting dressed and the leading he got was to flee for now. Having learned that Yahveh had a lot better Intel than he had, Mark obeyed. "We run for now. Check the door."

Linda opened the door a crack and then wider. Checking both ways she could see it was still clear. "Clear!" She went out and down the hall to the stairs and into the stair well with her pistol leading the way. Charlie went next and then Mark. After reaching the stairwell Mark closed the door and headed down the stairs quickly and quietly. Reaching the lobby he checked and didn't see any shooters. Opening the door the three of them walked across the lobby and out a side door that led to the parking garage.

Linda had been praying too. "No, not the car, it will be rigged and watched. This way." She headed down an alley and out on the next street. Walking down the street Charlie found a new Mercedes-Benz. While his wife and Mark watched, he broke into the car and hot-wired it. This was something that normally was not possible. Charlie could do it. The car started and the three of them left the area quietly.

Linda sat back in the fine leather seat and asked Mark, "Why did we not fight? We came looking for her didn't we?"

Mark nodded in the dark, "Yeah, we came looking for her. But, the Father said for us to go and not fight this time. So we went."

Leaving the stolen car on a side street after wiping it down to erase their prints, the Wus went to an open car rental agency they had seen and rented a BMW 500 series. They drove out and picked up Mark. Back on the street in a legal way the three of them stopped and had breakfast and planned their next moves.

Mark looked at his companions. "Yahveh knows better than I do when to stand and when to flee. But, I'd be curious as to why we had to run this morning. Knowing the habits of this babe I'd bet she's left us some surprise like watchers or a booby trap. So, we need to operate through someone else."

Charlie sat there thinking. "How do you suppose she knew we were at that hotel?"

Mark shrugged, "She's operating in this area, and maybe she pays the hotel staff to let her know when certain people show up. Or she could have bribed someone at the hotel she stayed at and they followed us to this one. She could have contacts in the NSA and they warned her after my call to Al. Al could be dirty but I doubt that because I shared foxholes with him not too long ago and he called and warned us of the strike. It could be a lot of different things."

Charlie nodded, "I know, I just wondered" Actually, Charlie was relieved that Mark was open to the possibility that his friend was bought and paid for. Charlie knew that they were up against some real competition this time. As the ex-spy looked out at the dawn sky that looked so peaceful he wondered how the group in England was faring.

CHAPTER THIRTY-FIVE

Mark called the Majestic Hotel and asked for the manager. When the man came on the line Mark described the events of the previous night but omitted the cell phone call and their hurried departure.

The manager was rather disturbed and told Mark that there had been a terrible gun fight on their floor last night. The National Police had been summoned and were still investigating the scene. Mark asked to speak to the highest ranking officer at the hotel.

"Captain Enrico Parva at your service. May I enquire as to your identity?"

Mark smiled to himself. "Captain Parva, I am General Mark Connelly, United States Air Force and am presently serving as an investigator for our Homeland Security Administration. I believe that the attack at the hotel may have been targeted for me and my two companions."

Captain Parva came back with, "I see. General, why would these people want to attack you?"

Mark wanted to work with the man but he was stonewalling and that wouldn't do. "Captain, I will call you back in two hours." Mark hung up and dialed an international number. Getting direct access to the Chairman of the Joint Chiefs of Staff of the U.S. armed forces he asked General Miles if he could call his counterpart in Spain and ask him to task Captain Enrico Parva to provide all possible assistance to Mark and the Wus.

The General responded, "I can do better than that. I'll ask the President to call the King directly. I know that President Bollen has a scheduled call to the King today and I'll see if he can bring this up first so that you can get on with your investigation.

Doing research with their wireless laptops until the two hours were up Mark called Captain Parva. When the man apologized for his lack of cooperation Mark said, "Captain, I don't like having to involve our upper management but there is little time and we are dealing with the massive assault on the U.S. and Britain two days ago. Please let me know what your investigation has turned up if anything."

Although embarrassed by having his very superior officer dress him down for not cooperating with the Americans, Captain Parva considered himself a professional soldier. "General, I'm sorry if you felt that I was not cooperating, but understand, I didn't know if you were really who you said you were. My recent phone call from the Director of the National Police cleared up that question so I will summarize what we have determined happened here and what we have deduced so far."

Mark pressed a suction cup microphone to the handset and activated the mini recorder and the speakerphone function. "Captain, I am going to record this. Is that all right with you?"

The Captain's voice came through the phone clearly. "Certainly. At approximately five oh six this morning, a woman and four men entered the lobby from the street. They made no requests of the desk clerk but went directly into the elevators. They went to the fourth floor and exited the elevator. Apparently they went to suite four-sixteen where the four men displayed submachine guns. We know this because one of our two-man teams were in the hotel and had gone to the fourth floor in response to a warning from the desk clerk."

Mark looked at the Wus who were listening to the conversation. Mark frowned and shook his head.

Captain Parva continued, "On seeing the guns, one of our men attempted to call for backup but was gunned down after giving his unit number. The GPS signal in his communications device gave the dispatcher the location and she dispatched a flying squad immediately. We have several seconds of video of the woman and the men before the camera was hit by a bullet. Sadly to say, both of our men were killed. At that point, the roomer across the hall from room four-sixteen heard the shots which awakened him and he looked out the peephole in his door in time to see the woman kick in the door to four-sixteen. The men and the woman went in with all guns blazing. Several seconds later they exited the room and disappeared. In a side note, four more men were seen on the fire escape firing more machine guns into that suite at the same time the group in the hall went in firing. Then there was an explosion consistent with a satchel bomb inside the suite that destroyed the entire suite but curiously did not cause a fire."

"The flying squad arrived in time to confront the men from the fire escape in the alley below. In the ensuing gun battle, all four of the attackers were killed. They had no identifying marks or papers on them. In short, it was a professional job. We are attempting to identify them through dental records and facial features at present. There is no information concerning the woman or the men in the hall at this time although we have issued a full alert for them. The woman was very pretty and had blonde hair. The men were non-descript other than being larger than the average man."

Mark thanked the Captain and hung up. Disconnecting the recorder cord and shutting off the recorder he looked at Charlie. "It seems that they not only had us out-gunned but they knew where to find us and destroyed the suite totally."

Mark called Al Harris back at the NSA only to find that he was off duty. He would be back in six hours. Mark asked if there was a file for him there. The agent on duty located it. It was on a DVD and encrypted. Mark asked him to send whatever was on it to his laptop. The agent loaded the file and did a FTP transfer. Mark received it and thanked the man.

Charlie took a look at the file and the encryption and raised an eyebrow. "They've gotten serious about their encryptions lately. It will take me at least ten minutes to figure this out."

It actually took him more than forty minutes to break the encryption and print out the information for Mark.

Mark read the files Al had gathered for them. A lot of it was old news about their quarry. But there were three things that intrigued Mark. He got the Wus attention. "This gives us a starting place to track this witch. The NSA has noted that several of her phone messages originate at the same GPS coordinates. They've also located the lo-jack signal from her Porsche and we can find that anywhere. The best piece of news is that she has rented an aircraft for tomorrow at Barcelona International Airport. I think we need to be there to greet her, don't you?"

Both Charlie and Linda grinned.

CHAPTER THIRTY-SIX

The crew of Jack, Laura, Sarah, and their MI-5 driver, William, sat in the car and watched the house from a distance. This time they were there to collect Mr. Alpha not his information. They had gotten more information from the NSA than they could have ever pried out of his house and now didn't need to try to out-fox Manfred Pendragon. The stake-out was to identify when the best time to attempt to capture him would be. Laura was their detector of spiritual matters and she was waiting until the presence of evil was no longer at the house.

William watched the operation with a keen sense of adventure that he felt was normally lacking in MI-5 operations.

Knowing that their target was at home, Laura prayed to Yahveh, "Father Yahveh, guide our steps and direct our paths as we attempt to capture this man of the devil."

Jack was about to order the assault when William held up his hand. He picked up a mobile phone and spoke into it for a few seconds. He then raised his eyebrows and handed the phone to Jack. Jack frowned but took the phone, "Malone here."

The voice on the other end of the phone was that of Frank Mullins, the Pastor they had rescued in the Philippines. "Jack, Jack! Listen to me! Yahveh does not want you to attack the house you are at, do you understand me? You are being misled by the enemy. Do not attack that house, it is a death trap!"

Jack was startled by the revelation even as it settled in his own spirit as true. "Pastor Mullins, how did you know what we are doing?"

The Pastor laughed, "The same way I know anything. Yahveh revealed it to me. Call me when you can talk freely." and he hung up.

Jack thought about the situation and realized that there was no other way that a Pastor thousands of miles away and not involved in the operation could have inside knowledge of what they were doing. "William, call in another team to stake out this place and take us back to the hotel." As William drove, the three Crossfire warriors prayed their gratitude and love to the Father for his saving mercy.

After returning to the hotel and the flat provided by MI-5, Jack set up a VoIP video/audio connection between their flat and the Pastor's residence in Denver. Once the connection was completed the team could see Pastor Mullins and his wife Andrea in their living room and the Pastor could see them. Jack started off the festivities with, "Pastor, I really want to thank you for your timely warning saving the three of us and others."

Pastor Mullins smiled and nodded, "You're very welcome Jack, but it isn't me that you should be thanking, it's Him. You know He loves you all very much and has been working with you as you fight for the Kingdom. But, you now need some new understanding of how to operate in Elohim's will."

"Pastor, we try to walk in His will all of the time. Many times he tells us where to go and when to strike or when to run. Isn't that doing His will?"

Pastor Mullins shook his head. "No, I'm afraid not. It's close but only just close. Let me give you an example. If you are a world class fighter and you decide that you want to serve Yahveh, you need to let him become ALL to you. Not just a convenient backup or guarantee of success. If you decide to go for the world title and pray for his protection and help to win. You are just talking to yourself. He will probably protect you because He loves you but you are not doing His will but your own."

"I told you that you need to get closer to Yahveh. That was not just a "good idea", that was the first basic step towards serving Him. If you are close to Him you will hear His voice and then you can do His will. Here's another example. We never go to people we think need salvation or healing. If Yahveh tells us that we are going to go to, say, Russia. We do nothing until He moves a Russian Pastor to call us and ask us to come. Even then we have to hear from Yahveh that it is His will for us to go. Many times we have a vision of where we are going. Sometimes the people that call us know nothing about us but have a vision of who we are, when we'll be there, and even sometimes what we will be wearing."

"You see the difference? There is no "we" deciding anything, there is no "we" making the plans. We wait on Yahveh to tell us to do anything. That way we know what we are going to do will be accomplished. Again, I have hours and hours of teaching on this but you need the crash course in your business. You are all sharp and can pick this up quickly. Take everything I'm telling you to Yahveh in prayer and have Him confirm it or not. Understand?"

Everyone there agreed, even William who was watching this with wide eyes.

Before you take the next step in your battle, go to Yahveh in prayer. Ask Him to tell you or show you what He wants you to do. Then "wait" until He tells you. I know you have to make sudden responses but if there is time, don't do anything unless He directs your path. If you don't get anything, continue to do the last thing He told you to do. Remember, He is also a warrior, as is Yahshua, His Son. Between them they have directed world conflicts for thousands of years. So, I think He will know of your need for timing. Call me if I can be of any more help. Blessings in His name."

Jack thanked the Pastor and broke the connection. He looked at the others, "Okay, the direction of this operation has been handed over to Yahveh. I suggest we pray for guidance and wait for an answer."

William asked, "What if it is something foolish, say, put down your guns in the middle of a battle and let Him handle the enemy. Would you do it?"

Thinking of their recent campaign in China Jack laughed, "We already did that one. Yes, I think I can fill in for Pastor Mullins on this one. If it is Yahveh, nothing He gives you will be bizarre from His perspective or go against His word."

Sarah said, "The Pastor told me that one time they were on a crusade and the Father told him to go to see a popular Christian Minister and tell him that Yahveh was not pleased with his actions and he was in danger of going to Hell. Needless to say, Pastor Mullins was not thrilled with this singular mission but walked it out anyway. The Minister was so idolized that he saw no one. But Frank went to his hotel and told the security guard that he needed to speak to the man. Against strict orders not to admit anyone the guard let Frank and two others in to speak to the man. Frank wanted to tactfully speak of the problem but, like normal, the Holy Spirit spoke for him through his mouth. The Minister heard the word and knew it was true and from the Father. But instead of repenting and asking forgiveness, he stormed away denying everything Frank had told him. Two weeks later the Minister died in a car accident, still unrepentant. Frank had submitted himself to Yahveh even though he didn't want to do it. Instead of being black-balled by that Ministry and congregation, Frank was honored as attempting to help save the Minister's soul. So, if Yahveh says do it, then step out and do it. We really serve Yahveh and the Kingdom not man."

Jack agreed with Sarah. He and Laura knelt down and began to pray. Sarah joined them and William decided to seek Yahveh directly even though he knew the Catholic Church would probably ex-communicate him if they knew.

As they prayed for Yahveh's guidance concerning their operation against Pendragon, the heaviness they associated with the power of the Father settled on all of them. William's breathing became somewhat labored considering he didn't know what the touch of Yahveh was like. After seeking His will they fell quiet and waited. There was a flutter of sound in the room and everyone looked up to see the angel Rose appear in glorious gold and fierce white light. The flat lit up and Rose smiled at them.

She floated several inched off of the floor and regarded each of them. "Yahveh is pleased that you are learning to listen instead of acting. He will never forsake you or leave you and He loves you more than you can understand right now." The radiance pulsated away from the angel and felt like power as it passed through the people in the room.

Rose looked at William. "Welcome to the Crossfire Team William Codson, you can breathe now." At which point the MI-5 agent realized he was still holding his breath at the sight of the beautiful angel. He exhaled with a whoosh and smiled crookedly.

Rose regarded the three members of the Crossfire Team. "Yahveh is proud of what you have done so far, but He expects much more from you and there will be suffering. You know that the Messiah suffered and warned you that to follow Him would cause you suffering. You've had suffering so far but you have accounted it as nothing to do His service. That is what you need to do in the future. The Most High knew that Manfred Pendragon was laying a trap for you but you didn't seek His direction, you asked for His protection. He would have kept you from death because the evil one is behind the trap and the power to harm you. As Yahveh said, that time is past. But, He is pleased that you were willing to seek His direction now. Here is what He wants you to do."

The warrior whiteness heightened and overrode the golden hue. Rose's voice took on a stronger timbre and her eyes flashed like sunlight. *"Yahveh wants you to go to the airport at Heathrow in three hours and set a trap for Pendragon at Utility Hanger number six. Do not be dismayed by his troops or his weapons. Take him!"*

Rose faded out and the room seemed absolutely dark with her going.

CHAPTER THIRTY-SEVEN

In the last rays of sunlight, Mark and the Wus carried a great deal of equipment as they slid quietly along one side of a private hanger at the Spanish airport. The aircraft that was their target was in the hanger. Their plan was simplicity itself.

At a little after six p.m. a luxury car pulled into the hanger and stopped near the plane. Two tough-looking men got out of the car and looked around. One of them went onto the aircraft and came back a few minutes later and nodded. Two more doors opened and two more men got out and these were armed openly with submachine guns. They took a stance between the car and the airplane. At that point Raisa Ivanova exited the car from the open rear door in one smooth movement and headed for the plane.

Linda Wu used the four-power scope on the tranquilizer dart gun to target Raisa's bare upper back. She fired the dart as the woman stood up. The dart impacted on target and Raisa staggered and then grabbed for her back but was quickly overcome by the drug mixture.

As Raisa was hit Charlie Wu pressed a remote trigger. Five powerful flash-bang grenades went off right near the four bodyguards. They had been placed at the bottom of the staircase and under the wing on that side by Mark acting as an aircraft inspector an hour ago. The sixth one went off in the cockpit where he had left it when he talked to the pilot and co-pilot. Most of the windows in the cockpit blew outward from the force of the grenade. The four bodyguards were blind and staggering around holding their ears or their faces.

Mark ran up to the guards and fired pillow shots from a 12-gauge shotgun into the guts of the guards, knocking the air out of their lungs. They all went down without a fight. Mark was headed around the car when another flash-bang grenade smashed through the windshield of the car and exploded inside. A fifth guard who had apparently been the driver was blown out of the front seat through the open door on the driver's side dropping the handgun he had been aiming at Mark. He wasn't in any shape to bother anyone anymore. Mark looked back at Charlie and saluted him.

Scooping up Raisa, Mark ran back to the crates the Wus were behind. Mark laid the unconscious woman on her face on the gurney they had brought with them and put two sets of riot cuffs around her wrists in opposite directions. He then bound her feet the same way. Lastly, he attached a strong rip-stop cord between the hand and leg cuffs to immobilize her completely. Charlie ran a field DNA test and confirmed that it was indeed their target. Linda expertly frisked the woman and came up with an astounding amount of weapons.

When Linda was done, the woman had on underwear, checked for any weapons capabilities, and a one-piece linen outfit. While Mark made sure she wouldn't be able to get off of the gurney by securing her to it, Charlie and Linda changed into medical garb. Mark did a quick switch and added a stethoscope as a convincing prop. Charlie went out and brought an ambulance up to the hanger door. The three of them loaded the unconscious woman into the back and Linda got in with her. The others got into the front and headed for the side entrance to the airport with the emergency lights flashing.

After they were away from the airport Mark turned off the lights and they drove to a large underpass where they had left their car. They switched the "patient" to the car and gave their medical clothes to the officer of the Spanish police and he drove the ambulance out of the underpass. Mark waited until ten or twelve cars entered the underpass and then drove out in the middle of the group and disappeared into the downtown Barcelona traffic.

Captain Parva of the National Police provided them with an interrogation facility and two of their top interrogators. Mark brought them up to date on the deadly capabilities of this woman and her smart mind. The Crossfire Team would watch the interrogation from video monitors and stay out of sight.

By matching DNA evidence from the electronics that murdered Ava Depaldi the police had a lock on Raisa for murder one. In Spain that meant death by hanging. They not only had DNA and physical evidence they also had a witness who had picked her picture out of a set of five as the woman they had seen standing beside Ava's car just before her death.

Mark looked at Charlie. "Ten to one they won't get anything out of her. If she was sufficiently trained in Russia she will be as impervious to their threats as she would have been to our "truth serums. But what I'm worried about is her group and how they'll react to our grabbing her.

As Charlie agreed there was a knock on their door. Charlie checked through the peephole and said, "Looks like the Spanish gang of four incoming."

Charlie's reference to an earlier dictatorial leadership of China wasn't too far off.

Charlie opened the door to admit the Spanish brass and they filed into the room followed by four high-ranking National Police officers. The speaker for the group was not the most important guy there, the one everyone deferred to, but probably the second in command. He looked at Mark and spoke in excellent English. Mr. Connelly, I am Eduardo Pennatas and I am the director of the National Police. You and your two companions are under arrest for multiple murders, violation of Spanish law, kidnapping, and violation of the civil rights of seven people. Please do not resist."

The police officers had drawn their weapons and pointed them at the three team members. Out of the side of his eye Mark saw Raisa being released from her restraints and taken out of the interrogation cell.

Mark realized that the Omicron Cartel had a much bigger hold on the Spanish government than they had expected. He looked at the law official and said in a low voice, "Mr. Pennatas, you are interfering in an international investigation of terrorism. There was only one person killed and that was in self-defense. The only rights we interfered with were those of a terroristic murderer that your police have evidence against."

Mr. Pennatas bridled at the counter charge and pointed his finger at Mark, "I beg to differ with your account. There were seven dead men at the airport, each one with their throat cut!"

At this point Mark knew that the fix was in and they would be in Spanish jails until they were too old to care, or they would be killed in the next few hours. Looking at Charlie and Linda he tipped his head slightly. In a lightning move he grabbed Pennatas' hand at the wrist and yanked the man to him. Spinning him around with his right hand he pulled his Paraordance 10-45 out left handedly and placed it to the man's head. "Put down your guns or he will die first!"

The police looked to the tall man that was the defacto leader for direction. The man smirked and said, "Kill them!"

The words hadn't even left his mouth when Charlie and Linda Wu moved like they were in fast forward while everyone else was doing normal time. Each one targeted two of the police officials and disarmed them before they could fire a shot. Mark pushed Mr. Pennatas away from him and ducked under the arm of the leader. Coming up behind him Mark clubbed the man over the head with his handgun. The fact that there was a lot of adrenal in flowing because it was life or death may have added to his zeal, but the man was knocked unconscious from the blow.

Mark tipped his head to the left and the Wus moved the police officials to that side of the room and used their own handcuffs to secure them to each other and the bench in the room. A quick shakedown produced six keys for the handcuffs which were removed. Mr. Pennatas stood there stunned looking at the man on the floor with blood running from his head and back to Mark standing there with a gun pointed at him.

Mark knew how serious the situation was but had to struggle to stop from laughing at the expression on the man's face. "What's the matter Mr. Pennatas? The callous dismissal of your worth by your friend here bothers you? Tell me his name and what he does, now!"

Mr. Pennatas shook his head to clear it. "That is Mr. Psi" The way he pronounce it was "Sighe"

Mark nodded, "And he works for?"

The Spanish official wrinkled his brow, "Mr. Psi is the department head of the Spanish Anti-Terrorism Administration."

Charlie laughed, "Put the fox in charge of investigating raids on the chicken coop!"

Mark asked, "That's what he does, who does he represent?"

Mr. Pennatas looked at Mark, "The Matrix Construction Union, why?"

Linda answered the man, "Because the Matrix Construction Union is a front for the Compas' company which is a front for the Omicron Group. This man here is probably Mr. Psi, another Greek character name which they use to mask their real names. Maybe you have run a DNA on him?"

Mr. Pennatas was mad, confused, and now terribly unsure that he hadn't compromised his government's role on terrorism. "What are you going to do?" Like in America, when you are officially placed under arrest the only way to be released from that arrest is by a judge.

Mark had been thinking strategically while Linda was explaining the facts of terroristic life to the man. "Our collection of Ms. Delta, or Raisa Ivanova, was with the permission of your King and the President of the United States. Since we are operating under your King's protection that makes your arrest of us null and void. What is this about murders?"

Mr. Pennatas blinked, "There were five bodyguards and two pilots who were killed at the airport, apparently by you three."

Linda pulled out a small computer and set it on the table. Selecting a video file she let the official watch as their capture of Raisa took place. Mark noted for the man, "The only death was that of the driver because he attempted to bushwhack me and Charlie took him out with a 40mm grenade. Even that was unintentional."

Linda smiled. "Now let's see what happened after we left. I left the webcam in place in the hanger." She fast forwarded until there was motion. Backing up the file she played it at normal speed.

Two cars came up to the aircraft. Some of the bodyguards were starting to move about. Five men exited the two cars and one looked in the luxury car. He then motioned to the others who cold-bloodedly slashed the throats of each of the four bodyguards. One man went into the plane and came out a few minutes later wiping blood off of his knife. Linda manipulated the view and enlarged the portion of the screen showing the leader's face. It was a full face view, not even very grainy. It was Mr. Psi.

Mark looked at the National Police leader. "Now you know the truth. Either you have been duped and now understand the situation, in which case you will help us; or you are a part of the problem and won't help us. Which is it going to be?"

Mr. Pennatas frowned and reached into his pocket and produced a cell phone. Hitting a speed dial button he waited until the call was answered. He spoke in Spanish which Mark understood. "This is National Police Commander Pennatas. With complete secrecy I want all of Mr. Psi's people arrested and held without notice or bail on terrorism charges. I will deal with them when I return. Mr. Psi is in custody and I am remanding him to the American team for interrogation. Do not let anyone know what is being done and do it immediately! Am I understood?" He listened for a minute. "No, that was false information and I have the proof of that. The Crossfire Team is legitimate and as of this moment they have the full backing of the National Police and of the King. If they need anything, and I mean anything, see that they get it or answer to me. Understood?" He listened and hung up. "I have a lot of cleaning up to do."

Mark put his gun away and told the Wus to release the police officials and to tie up Mr. Psi. He shook Mr. Pennatas' hand and warned him. "This is not over. This man is only one cog of a big machine and I'll bet you that they have more fingers in both of our governments than we can imagine. You need to speak to the King himself about this and warn him that Omicron is moving on all governments through their own procedures and processes so that they can control the government eventually. You might want to assign a top, trustworthy, person to Mr. Psi's Anti-Terrorism position and have him review what has been done. I'm sure that the Omicron Cartel has been given many positions of power by Mr. Psi and it could go deeper than that."

Mr. Pennatas nodded. He shook Mark's hand again. "I apologize for our earlier confusion and look forward to working with you again. Assuming I can stop whatever this slime has done to our government first."

CHAPTER THIRTY-EIGHT

Jack, Laura, Sarah, and William Codson watched the Dassault Falcon 2000 sitting in the private hanger at Heathrow airport. They had carefully filtered into the hanger and gotten within fifty feet of the aircraft as they waited for Mr. Alpha to arrive. About ten minutes later a car pulled into the hanger and a man got out of the back of the vehicle. The aircraft started its engines. Jack stared at the man through mini binoculars and said, "Something's not right. That's not our man."

Sarah was watching a small handheld monitor that was being fed by a miniature camera affixed to the outside of the hanger near the door. "There's another vehicle, a minivan, waiting outside. This guy is just a ruse to see if there are any problems."

They held their positions as the man walked to the landing steps of the jet aircraft. He paused there and looked around. He then took a position facing outward at the bottom of the steps. He looked around again and spoke into a small transmitter in his left hand.

Sarah said, "The minivan is moving this way."

The minivan pulled into the hanger and stopped behind the car. Jack whispered, "Remember, there's still at least the driver in that car."

He watched as two large men got out of the van and it backed up and turned and left the hanger. The two men talked and walked towards the boarding stairs. William IDed the man in the tan coat as Mr. Alpha aka Manfred Pendragon. Jack said, "Now!"

Having a clean field of fire Sarah fired a capture net at Mr. Alpha, Jack fired a flash-bang grenade at the car's windshield, and Laura fired a tranquilizer dart at the man with Mr. Alpha. As the three men near the stairs turned to see what the noise was, the capture net reached Mr. Alpha and wrapped him up with the weighted bolas balls flying around him twice. The other man whipped up his black coat and deflected the dart. It caromed off of the coat and flew into the chest of the smaller man at the base of the stairs.

The smaller man and Mr. Alpha went down just as the flash-bang detonated at the windshield of the car. Jack stood up and sprinted towards the aircraft with Sarah hot on his heels. The man with the black coat looked at Mr. Alpha and the on-rushing warriors and turned on his heel and ran toward the stairs to the plane.

Jack told Sarah, "You get our target; I'll take care of the other one."

The man ran up the stairs into the plane with Jack closing rapidly. He was yelling at the pilot to get them out of there. As Jack entered the body of the plane it started to roll. The door came up automatically and the man fleeing stopped and spun towards Jack. Jack saw the gun in his hand and dropped to the floor behind the seats next to the closing door.

The man fired four rounds at Jack which hit the seats and tore through them. One of them hit Jack in his upper trauma plate over his chest and knocked him back against the cockpit wall next to the door.

Hearing the shots the pilot realized the urgency of his boss' demand and gunned the aircraft onto a long taxiway and slammed the throttles against the bulkhead. The plane leaped forward and went airborne in less than six hundred feet. The man with a gun was thrown back down the aisle to the rear of the plane. The plane had a 3100 foot per minute climb rate fully loaded. It was fully fueled but had only two people on board. It screamed into the sky from the taxiway with the tower screaming almost as loud at the pilot. Realizing they could easily be killed by incoming aircraft the pilot pushed the wheel forward and the aircraft went into a slight dive. This would keep the plane out of the normal flight paths until they could escape the area around the airport. The plane was already going 280 miles per hour and quickly accelerating. The aircraft was flying level at an altitude of three hundred feet above the ground.

As Jack struggled to get his breath back, the gun in the man's hand jammed. Throwing it down the big man ran back up the aisle toward Jack and literally jumped on him. Jack turned to his left and deflected most of the man's energy against the floor. Jack then used an upward thrust of his right elbow and hit the man on the chin. The strike was hard enough to glaze the guy's eyes and make him stop attacking. Jack followed that up with a knuckle strike to the side of the man's head which drove him to the floor of the plane.

Jack's back was against the door as the man gathered his strength and lunged at Jack again. Jack was ready for him and was about to deliver a hammer fist to the back of the man's head. Just then the enemy of all mankind weighed into the fight. A demonic hand caused the explosive bolts holding the door on to ignite and the door was blown off of the plane. Both Jack and the man tumbled out of the plane as the door cart wheeled backwards and slammed into the right engine of the jet. As Jack and the other man flew out of the aircraft they were blown away from each other by the wind. Jack was falling quickly towards the ground at close to three hundred miles per hour and was upright and traveling to his right as the ground rushed at him. His lateral speed was carrying him directly towards a building with woods beyond it. Jack knew he wouldn't clear the house. As it rushed at him he thought of Laura and said, "Father. "

On the plane, the impact of the door caused the engine to explode and impeller blades sliced through the aircraft body and cut the hydraulic lines controlling the flight surfaces at the back of the craft. Unable to shut down the wide open engine on the left or to control the direction of flight the pilot screamed as the business jet rolled to its left and screamed directly down into a bog in Heath just west of Iver at over three hundred miles per hour.

In the last seconds of his life Jack could see the grain pattern on the wood that made up the house and the dull gleam of the sun behind a cloud off of several windows. The wind noise was the only thing he could hear. He found he was at peace and not worried about dying.

There was a rustling noise and a flutter in front of him and the angel Rose appeared and put her arms around him. He felt the peace of Yahveh settle around him as he sensed more than saw fields of force that could have been wings circling around him as they reached the unoccupied building. At better than two hundred miles per hour they smashed into the building wall and through it. Jack didn't feel anything from the collisions as they continued to smash through the two story building's walls and out a large window at the back of the building. They then smashed through a half a dozen trees until they stopped at ground level. The wings or forces surrounding him faded away. Rose's face was close to Jack's and she kissed him softly on the cheek. "It was not your time. The enemy of man got involved even after he had been told his time to help them was over. Keep up the fight." And she faded away.

Jack turned to look at the perfectly circular seven foot holes he could see as a descending line through the uninhabited house. They had been travelling so fast they'd just punched holes in walls rather than bring down the whole house. A crackling noise made him look up and then run for his life. The trees that had lost their trunks were collapsing to the ground. Jack cleared the area and came to a road. He got down on his knees and with tears of gratitude running down his face thanked Yahveh for saving him. Then he got up, rubbed his eyes, put his sunglasses back on, and started walking back towards Heathrow.

He took out his cell phone and called Laura. She was so choked up to hear his voice she handed the phone to Sarah and just cried. Sarah said, "I saw you leave on your flight and I see where it ended by the smoke. How did you manage to get out of that?"

Jack smiled, "I'll tell you later. Did you get Mr. Alpha?"

Sarah said, "Trussed up like a little baby in the back of our helicopter. I gave him something to sleep so he wouldn't worry. By the way, while you were off having fun, Mark called. It seems that Omicron is much better connected and professional than we thought. We need to avoid our government until we can tell the good guys and girls from the bad ones, Capiche?"

Jack said he understood. "Listen, I'm at the edge of a big field here, see if you can lock onto my GPS coordinates and pick me up."

Sarah smiled, "Already on the way. We should be there in less than three minutes."

She was as good as her word. As the helicopter landed Jack climbed in and directed Sarah to fly towards the house he had recently had such an impact on. From the helicopter they could look completely through the house by the holes.

Laura stared at it wide-eyed and asked, "Okay, how did you do that?"

Jack smiled at his beautiful wife. "Rose and she kissed me too."

Laura smiled at her husband and patted his hand, "Good."

As they flew away from the house Sarah cut the power and went to hover over a culvert a short distance from the house. "Look, down there. That is where the other guy came down. From their height it looked like a large watermelon had hit the ground going very fast. It left a red smear for dozens of feet across the road and ended down in the ditch.

Jack shook his head, "Let's get out of here. Where's William anyway?"

Sarah glanced at him, "He stayed behind to clean up things at the hanger. About ten more of his MI-5 guys showed up as we lifted off."

Jack asked, "Where exactly did you get this helicopter from anyway?"

Sarah smiled and looked away. "Let's just say we "borrowed" it for an efficient means of transportation. The guy warming it up for us generously loaned it to us when he saw the guns and the hostage. MI-5 is taking care of that right now. But, we have to give it back to him without damage and a full set of tanks."

Jack laughed, "With our activity level that may be a hard order to fulfill."

CHAPTER THIRTY-NINE

Mark and Jack talked over an encrypted phone connection while they were both in the air. Mark cautioned his friend, "This Omicron Cartel is much bigger, better connected, and dangerous than anybody thought. It seems that they have targeted us for extermination probably because of what we did in the Philippines and Saudi Arabia to their truck bomb scheme. Now that we have captured or killed three of their top people I'll bet they'll pull out all the stops to eliminate us as a group or as individuals. I'll get the word to the others to batten down the hatches and to keep a weather eye out for enemy attacks."

Jack thought about that, "Mark, if what you're saying is true, then we need to pray and see if we shouldn't go on the offensive rather than hunker down. We've hit them five times now and come out on top. That won't last unless the Father wants it to. In the world, we're just as much the hunted as the hunters and the odds are against constant success like we've seen in our collisions with this group. Let's warn the others and meet back at the fortress with our packages. I'll be interested in what we learn from that red-haired mistress of the dark!"

Mark sighed, "We lost her to a Spanish botch-up. They tried to hold us and let her walk. I have a better idea than heading back to Colorado." He suggested that Jack and his team take a different route. "I think we need to vacuum these two characters and I only know of one place that is safe enough to do it." Mark explained his plan and both aircraft changed headings.

Six hours later the two aircraft sat side-by-side at Ben Gurion Airport in Israel.

David Zahavy was very glad to help the team debrief the Omicron agents. He had a crew of specialists work with both subjects for the next two days. At the end of that time he met with the team to discuss their findings.

David relaxed in the conference room setting and keyed up the big screen above the circle of connected workstations. He brought up a picture of Manfred

Pendragon. David stared at the picture with a sour look on his face while he drummed his fingers on the desk surface. Looking over at the team he smiled a small smile. "You never fail to bring me major headaches you know."

Sarah looked at her old boss and asked, "We try. Tell us."

David checked his creases in his Seville Row suit pants. "First, let me tell you what we have here. Manfred Pendragon is an extremely complex and intelligent man who is totally sold out to Satan. His entire theology is based on the superiority of Satan over Yahveh. He works in the world on that basis and has, as much as possible, become as evil as his deity."

David thought for a few seconds. "Manfred Pendragon is an exceptionally formidable opponent with contacts, moles, spies, and collaborators in most of the Western governments. His task, as he perceives it, is to bring each of those governments under the control of Omicron. This man has several hundred strike troops available at his every whim. Your capturing him was very fortunate for all of us and incredibly good fortune because he normally knows everything the police and military units are about to do. The Crossfire Team slipped in through the cracks because you weren't directly tasked by any government to go after him and, at that time they weren't aware of your capabilities."

David looked at each one of the people in the room with him, one by one. "Understand this. Your team and each of you individually are now probably their number one targets due to your acquisition of this man and his partner in crime." Seeing the looks on their faces David held up his right hand. "We'll get to him in a few minutes."

David stood up and started pacing. "We were able to pry a great deal of information out of Mr. Alpha. Things such as contacts, schedules, upcoming events, general operational tactics, and his own goals. Then we got a real surprise. Mr. Alpha is not the top man in Omicron. In fact, this extremely dangerous and dedicated agent is only on the third rung of the ladder of supremacy in Omicron. There are twelve levels ladies and gentlemen. That means that there are nine levels of more sophisticated and powerful people above our Mr. Alpha!"

"Unfortunately, Mr. Pendragon does not have any information concerning the levels above his or who is in at those levels. The Omicron Cartel works on the Communist cell principle which restricts damage to that cell only if it is compromised. The method of communication and control is the ubiquitous cell phone and a rapidly changing series of codes. When a call, which is encrypted, comes to him with the proper daily code, then Mr. Pendragon knows it is from a superior. He deals with whatever his superior tells him to do, period."

David sat down, "I know that God instructed you to go after the upper people in this group. You are most likely unaware that you have opened up one of the biggest nests of vipers and destructive potential for all civilization since the U.S.S.R. in the days of the cold war. It is obvious that this group has wormed itself into the governments of all western as well as European countries. How deep their penetration and control is at this point is unknown but now we have some clues to look for and root out this enemy."

Mark asked David, "You say that this man is a minor functionary of a much more powerful organization. How do we tackle the bigger guys?"

David shook his head, "I don't know at this point. I'm not sure who I can trust in my own organization let alone the Israeli government. I'm open to any suggestions."

Laura said, "This is going to take some serious fasting and praying to determine what Yahveh wants us to do."

CHAPTER FORTY

David continued his summary of the findings. "That brings us to subject number two. Dieter Koch or Mr. Tau as an Omicron alias."

David leaned back in his chair and pointed at the picture of the second man on the screen. "This serpent in a human body is very deadly. He is used by Omicron to eliminate those that bother the "Group", such as you. It seems that Dieter has been a bad boy. He was the force behind the attack on your jet by the stolen Russian fighters not to mention a host of murders. One of his "eliminations" that he is very proud of caused the death of over ninety innocent and uninvolved citizens of Israel. A bus bombing that one of the Palestine terrorist groups took credit for last year. His target was the bus driver. He has a motto, "Bettered dead than alive" which is how he solves all of his problems."

"He's a creative enforcer on the way up the ladder at Omicron. He's not as smart but still one level above our other visitor, Mr. Alpha. Mr. Tau is, or was, being groomed as the next level four leader. He was even granted authority to complete the infiltration of the Spanish government on his own terms which meant retirement by death for many of the existing leaders. The one good thing about his capture is that he has information on the next two levels up. Organizational details and, especially pleasing for us, names behind the Greek character titles. It seems Dieter was already planning to eliminate some on his own so he could assume power."

Sarah looked at the second set of printed data they had received. "Is this the information he gave up?" David nodded.

Jack asked what the Mossad was going to do with their "guests".

David frowned, "Well, they both confessed to crimes against Israel so they will remain guests for the foreseeable future. That future will not be long for Dieter Koch though. Despite the fact that he lost a considerable number of brain cells during his debriefing which would handicap his ability to function in the future he will be tried by a military tribunal and executed for his murder spree last year. Mr. Pendragon has elected to stay here knowing that Omicron will eliminate him if they find him."

David looked at his friends and fellow warriors with a caring glance. "I would also recommend that your team work out of Israel for the near future. I can ensure your protection even against my own government if necessary. I can't see that President Bollen can do that in your country."

Mark looked at the others, "We need to seek guidance and we'll let you know."

Charlie had set up his own link out of Mossad headquarters and was updating his darling computers back at the Fortress. He was taken aback when his computer told him that his situation was not secure, data wise. He ran two programs he had written while still in Colorado and stared at the results. He took a piece of paper and wrote a quick note on it. He passed it to Jack who looked at it and gave it to David.

David read the note and set it aside. He sat up without a word and typed on his workstation keyboard. Studying the results he motioned for Sarah to join him.

Sarah got up and stood behind David's chair. On his screen she saw a split view of a man's face and a remote camera view of that man working on his computer. David had her bend down and he whispered to her. She nodded and turned back to the team. David made an announcement. "Let's go get some lunch and talk about what to do when we return." David got up and pointed at Jack, Laura, and Linda Wu. He then tipped his head and headed out of the room with them on his heels.

Sarah pointed at Mark and Charlie and headed the other direction. The two men were right behind her. After they left the conference room she spoke quietly to them. "Charlie told David that he located a Mossad agent that has been eavesdropping on our conference room. They're going to collect him now. We will be the backup team."

She said all this while moving quickly through the headquarters complex.

As they passed one of the security guards Charlie stopped and made a request. He ran to catch up and handed Mark a new Model 44001 advanced TASER M18-L.

The M18-L has an Integrated Laser Sight, and has almost 100% effectiveness using the new Electro-Muscular Disruption (EMD) technology. In police studies, the new Advanced Tazer has a higher instant incapacitation rate than a 9mm hand gun. The Advanced Tazer police version shoots out 2 darts attached to 27 feet of wire. 50,000 volts travels over the wires and over-rides the central nervous system providing incredible take down power. EMD weapons are specifically designed to stop the most elite, aggressive, focused combatants.

Mark took the weapon and ran hard to keep up with his wife. They reached the area of the suspect agent and saw David walk over to the man's cubicle. There was a shout and a struggle and the man burst out of the cubicle and ran away from Jack who was coming down the aisle towards him. He reached the aisle that Mark and Sarah were on and dodged to his left to avoid them. Mark put the TAZER's laser mark on the man's back and pulled the trigger. The two wires flew to their mark and the air exploded out of the man's lungs. He fell to the floor and assumed a fetal position.

The entire crew rushed up to him and quickly frisked him for weapons. David put a pencil sideward across his mouth and secured it with a rubber band so he couldn't close his teeth and activate any suicide capsules. They used riot cuffs to secure his hands and feet and lifted him off the ground.

A large number of employees had stopped to see the action and David shooed them off. Mark gave the TAZER back to the officer and told him it was impressive. Three officers took the inert man's body and headed back to the interrogation ward.

David frowned and looked around to see if anyone was listening, "If I find out that he was working for the Omicron Cartel I will start such a violent housecleaning that a Russian Pogrom will seem like a company picnic! I promise you it will be something that hasn't been seen here in twenty years!"

Sarah knew he meant it too.

After returning to their room, Jack felt the burden to pray. While he was praying he felt the need to sit and listen. He sat quietly and was given a vision that disturbed him. He got up and went out to where Mark and Laura were discussing their next steps. Sitting down he explained the vision and what he thought it meant. They came to a consensus and Jack made a phone call to Washington.

CHAPTER FORTY-ONE

The furor in the U.S. and Britain had continued to grow primarily out of fear and frustration. The Congress listened to the people and pressured the Executive Branch to respond as a unified voice of the American government.

President Bollen had listened to so many people on this issue he was ready to thrown a chair through a window in the Oval Office into the Rose Garden. He hung up the phone and slammed his hand down on the desk. "This is unreal! I can't believe that the Zultarians are stonewalling us on this issue!" He looked at his staff of advisors. "Everyone knows that all the people involved in this plot to blow up our country and that of England are Zultarian extremists. All the people caught were Zultarian extremists. If it quacks like a duck, walks like a duck, and looks like a duck, then it dang well is a duck! All right, I will do something to stop this growing discontent in my country." He looked at the assembled group who were each remembering what this man had done after the poisoning of the U.S. and Israel not so long ago.

The President sent a quick prayer heavenward. "Set up an urgent press conference for tomorrow night at six p.m. Eastern time. Get world-wide coverage, especially the Middle East and stress the importance of recording this one. I'm going set some time lines and some guidelines. End of story!"

Dismissing the staff the President called for the Chairman of the JCS. When General Miles arrived at the Oval Office he found himself alone with the President. "Yes Sir. I came as quickly as I could."

The President nodded, "Thanks Howard, I know you did. I need some advice from you and I think we need to get on our knees on this one."

There was a knock on the door. The President knew his secretary would not bother him during this session unless it was urgent. When she came in she handed him a piece of paper. He looked at it and picked up the phone. "Yes Jack, what is it?"

Jack replied, "Sir, I have had a revelation from Yahveh that the team has confirmed, discussed, and we feel is urgent for you to know about. Primarily, Yahveh has given us an understanding of the multiple levels this Omicron Cartel is working on. The vision showed an America in turmoil and a new President taking over and running the country for the Omicron Group. We think that your taking the Zultarians to task for the truck bomb situation will allow the moles the Omicron Cartel has planted in the various world governments to shut off the supplies of oil to the U.S. This will lead to riots, famine, and eventually your impeachment. This effort will be led by the U.S. government moles of their group. They will then get their man into office and have complete control. At least, that is what the vision showed us. We thought you'd want to consider that before the Congress forces you to do something about the situation."

The President said, "Thank you Jack that is something to think and pray about. I appreciate it and I think we can both thank the Father for the timing of your call."

After the President hung up he looked at the General. "As I said before we really need to seek His guidance for this one."

The next evening at six p.m. Washington, D.C. time the press conference began. The President sat flanked by General Miles and the two leaders of the Congress. Behind the men was a huge video screen. Looking relaxed and firm President Bollen opened the conference with pleasantries and a simple prayer for understanding. He then got down to business. "After the attempted mass bombings of the United States of America and England the need to find a resolution to these types of attacks has become critical. Since the last century the U.S. and Britain have always held to the concept of religious freedom. We have never pointed fingers at one religion or another. Until now. Every one of the terrorists arrested and identified in both countries, with a few exceptions which we will deal with later, have been Zultarian extremists."

The President took a sip of water. "These people are decried and rejected by the mass of Zultarians. But, the fact remains that they espouse a twisted expectation of world domination through violence in the name of their religion. For the last fifty years these violent men, women, and yes, even children, have dealt death and injury in the name of Zultar. They strike, and if they don't kill themselves, they melt into the general Zultarian population and disappear."

The President took on a very serious look. "Enough is enough! It is time for the Zultarian people to take a stand. Your population is not only the breeding ground for these terrorists, but it is also their fortress. I would say that the average Zultarian is a peace-seeking, honest contributor to society. But many of you know who the terrorists are and protect them by not saying anything and even contribute to their cause and in some cases work with them. We, the free world, cannot attempt to root these violent people out of your population without a great deal of collateral damage to uninvolved Zultarians. But, you can show the world where you stand by how you react to this request. Cleanse your faith of the unfaithful that are killing others in the name of Zultar."

"We, the free world are waiting and watching to see what you, as a faith, will do. This is not an American request alone. I have conferred with the leaders of other countries in the world and they also feel that it is time to ask you to clean house."

The President pushed a switch on his podium and the screen behind him lit up with the leaders of thirty-six countries including Russia and China.

"We are confident that we can peacefully assist you in any way your countries desire to remove this poison from your societies. Thank you."

The reactions to the President's speech were from one end of the spectrum to the other. The terrorist groups tried, mostly in vain, to convince the world that the President of the United States was declaring war on Zultar and his followers. The leaders of Zultarianism came out supporting the President's position and actually were gratified by the conciliatory nature of the speech especially since it lacked any aggressive attitude or "do it or die" elements.

The majority of the world applauded the speech as a reasonable approach to the Zultarian guerilla warfare problem.

The Omicron Cartel Executive Council was coldly furious. They didn't have anything to hang an impeachment trial on and their scheming, planning, and expenses for the last three years was wasted.

A highly encrypted phone call came to Mr. Beta in Spain early the next morning. Seeing the ID on the phone he answered it, "Beta here."

"Mr. Beta, you are to assume Mr. Alpha's operations immediately. I will give you the passwords and IDs. I will assume that you monitored the President's speech last night. Something derailed history and one of our agents informed us that the President took a call from Jack Malone just as he was on the brink of declaring war on the Zultarians. Therefore we must assume that call was the factor that changed the President's mind, and therefore, his speech. The executive committee has declared the total elimination of the Crossfire Team our only objective until it is accomplished. You are being elevated to level 4 and you are being tasked to locate and eliminate the four core personnel of that team. That is Jack and Laura Malone and Mark and Sarah Connelly. Use whatever Omicron assets and funds necessary to accomplish this mission. Do you understand that you must eliminate them or we will eliminate you and give the job to someone else?"

Mr. Beta knew his rear end was on the line on this one. "Yes Sir!"

The connection was broken and Mr. Beta began to plan and sweat.

CHAPTER FORTY-TWO

David, Mark, Sarah, Jack, Laura, Charlie, Linda, and Su Li sat in the conference room at Mossad headquarters and after some serious prayer made some conclusions on their own. David said, "I don't see that there can be any other reaction."

Jack agreed and the others nodded acceptance. Jack summarized their decision. "We're agreed that the Omicron Cartel will probably figure out that we messed up their deal and will make a maximum effort to eliminate us individually and corporately. We've also prayed and feel that Yahveh wants us to go on the offensive rather than wait around and try to defeat their attacks. Lastly, Yahveh has told most of us separately and we've agreed that we need to pull out all the stops on this one and take down the entire Omicron organization. Right?"

Laura said, "That is what Yahveh is urging us to do because it is literally them or us this time. It is for times such as these that He has anointed us to do battle with His enemies. They've lost the insight and services of Satan and his demons because Yahveh allowed Satan's relationship with this group for a certain amount of time on this earth to bring death and destruction. That time is past and they are to receive the wrath of Elohim. Expect them to react to the loss of their supernatural help with random and unintelligent death and destruction to prove to themselves that they are still powerful."

David looked at the others. "Contact the President and the CJCS and get their "written" permission allowing us to "pursue, arrest, and if necessary, eliminate" any and all members of that organization. Let them know that could be leaders in Congress or even on their own staffs. I will get a similar agreement from the leader of my country. We should ask our leaders to secure the same authority from the other countries. Leader to leader would be the proper way to ensure such authority."

Phone calls were made and faxes sent and within twelve hours the Crossfire Team had the authorization of the entire free world and some of the not-so-free world to hunt down, arrest, and/or remove any and all members of the organization called the Omicron Cartel as a terroristic organization. The members of the Crossfire Team would be held liable to prove that the people they arrested or eliminated were part of the group, but after the fact. No warrants would be issued, no warnings given, and anyone providing information to the Omicron Cartel would be considered a member of that group and face the same judgment.

The Executive Committee of the Omicron Cartel met the next morning to discuss this event. They had dozens of confirmations of the authority being given and the goal of the Crossfire Team. The top man in the group looked at the rest of the committee and pursed his lips. Then with a scowl he said, "Get them first."

David had been given authority by the Israeli government to join the team for the duration of this effort. He brought with him two agents that he could rely on, Judah Maritz and Aaron Jacobson. Both Judah and Aaron were Jewish and not believers. When Mark raised an eyebrow at David concerning the selections, David just smiled and said, "They need to see how God, His Son, and the enemy operate."

The entire team flew in secret to Victor Chamberlain's island and he rejoined the team, both as a financier and as one of the hunter group. They were also joined there by Stan and Debbie Hargrove.

Victor Chamberlain was one of the world's wealthiest men. He had been ousted from his control of his wealth by a group of men bent on destroying Israel. In their quest to gain control of the crucifixion nail held by Jack they had involved the Crossfire Team and were eventually destroyed by Yahveh working directly against them or through the team. Victor had been led into the kingdom by Jack and Laura and had evidenced a major change of direction in his life. He now used his brilliant mind and creative energies for the Father.

The entire group of Jack and Laura, Mark and Sarah, Su Li, Charlie and Linda Wu, David, Judah, Aaron, plus Stan and Debbie Hargrove climbed out of the van in front of Victor's island home.

He greeted the twelve person team with joy and love. "I can honestly tell you that my life has much more excitement when you are around. Tell me what I can do to help you."

Jack introduced Victor to Charlie and Linda Wu, Su Li, and to the Hargroves. Stan Hargrove had been a Captain on the police force in Salt Lake City when Yahveh had drawn him into combat alongside the Crossfire Team. His wife and he joined the team and worked for Mark's company as investigators. Stan was a good-looking man in his late thirties and continued his healthy ways of living so that he was in great physical shape. Debbie Hargrove was a refined beauty of a woman also in her early forties. Brown hair, cut short, framed a cute face and a set of pretty blue eyes. The fact that she was also a contract sniper for the CIA with many missions was hidden so well, her police department husband didn't find out about it until the President of the United States told her to tell him. Theirs was an interesting marriage.

Victor and David were friends from earlier missions. David introduced his two companions and warmly shook Victor's hand.

Jack hugged the tall black man and stepped back. "You're looking very fit Victor. The last few months have been good to you." Laura also gave him a hug. "We're glad to see you again Victor, how is your walk with the Father going?"

Victor smiled. "I've redirected my food empire from a straight profit motive to one of kingdom service. I've made sure that the workers are well taken care of and that there is enough profit to build more plants, but, I'm listening to the Father and giving food to those who need it but can't afford it. That has entailed a host of major efforts in the third world and especially in Africa where there is so much hate and suffering. But, since I'm now working for the right reasons the food seems to multiply when it gets distributed. Also, the more money I pour into His efforts the more seems to come back. The gross worth of the companies is now three times what it was before."

Mark asked him, "How's your net worth these days? Weren't you one of the wealthiest people on Earth?"

Victor shook his head. "Today I literally have no net worth. I put my money into the kingdom and His efforts. I control billions of dollars but own none of it. I don't want it because it becomes an idol before Yahveh. I can't tell you how much freedom there is in being a person of no means. I haven't even had a credit card offer in months!"

The entire crew sat down to a healthy but hearty lunch. After lunch Victor inquired as to the other members of the team such as Sensei Grady and possible attacks against them and the team's house in the U.S. Mark took that one. "The other members of the team that could be identified have been warned and are staying at the Fortress for the duration. Yahveh has promised us that He will protect the Fortress and that is good enough for me. Jack's dad and his uncle have moved their operations from Texas to the Fortress as well to prevent Omicron from using them as levers or striking against them. Other, part-time, members are taking precautions on their own.

After lunch they started praying about what efforts they should mount against the Omicron Group.

CHAPTER FORTY-THREE

As the team joined in corporate prayer the heaviness that Jack associated with the presence of the Holy Spirit didn't just become evident, it rolled over him like a breaker in the surf. For some time he rested in what he called the "river of life", the essence of the Father flowing out of heaven. He felt a need to express the reason for the prayer and made a petition. "Heavenly Father, you are awesome beyond words and your name is exalted on high and esteemed by all who know you. In our war against the enemies of righteousness we have come to this time of combat and need your leadership and guidance so that we don't go astray in our pride in our eagerness to do your will." Then he sat back to wait on the Father.

The response was instantaneous and very clear. *"Your enemies are aware of your mission and seek to destroy you before you can destroy them. Know that the enemy of mankind is rebellious in these last days and even though I have ended his evil association with these people, he is seeking ways to circumvent my commands. I will walk with all of you and because of the enemy's disobedience I will have my messengers fight for you. But in the end it will be each of you that decide the outcome of this battle. There is far more at stake than you realize. Millions of innocent souls will be lost to the enemy if you and your team fail to destroy the Omicron Cartel and their plans. Seek Me as you decide what to do."*

Jack prayed his thankfulness and obedience to the Father of the universe. He was about to address the others when a light shown in his mind and it quickly formed into the angel Caleb. Caleb was in his youthful, formidable personage and looked very strong and powerful. He smiled at Jack in the vision and said, "I would use the information David Zahavy got from Dieter Koch to advance two levels up the enemy's hierarchy." Caleb looked at Jack for a moment. He then moved closer and spoke quietly. "I am awed beyond words because this mission may well have ramifications and echoes throughout the rest of mankind's history on Earth. "

The angel was terribly serious. "While Yahveh knows all things he cannot tell you how to battle these forces because it would mean that he is not just. You see, He made the rules of spiritual and mortal combat and it governs everyone, including Elohim Himself. If He were to violate His own rules then the enemy could also violate them with impunity. The training from your earlier combats should allow you to make the right choices. Stand in His esteem, stay in the spirit, and fight the good fight. My input on this matter is simply this, "Under no circumstances underestimate these enemies." The angel faded out and Jack opened his eyes to find everyone else still in prayer. He sat quietly until they all stirred and sat up.

After repeating what Yahveh and Caleb had spoken to him Jack asked for confirmations.

Laura laughed a quiet laugh. "Rose told me very much the same thing."

Mark smiled, "I heard the part Yahveh told you through Caleb Jack. I believe it is a true revelation."

Several of the others were nodding their heads. Jack then sighed, "Alright, David, let's go over the information that Dieter Koch gave you."

David pulled out his notes and started reading. "There are nine people on the second level above Dieter which would be the fifth level; seven men and two women. The men are the directors of some of the largest businesses in the world while both women are in government service. One is in the U.S. government while the other is in the British government at a cabinet level. None of these people are without security and government or corporate protection."

David looked at the list and pointed at one name. "This is the woman we want to focus on." He looked at the others, "She is the lynch-pin that holds the fifth level together. Her name is Sandra Thornton-Angleton, or as she likes to be called, Lady TA. As the current Leader of the Lords, Lady TA is the Secretary of State for International Development. A pivotal role that allows her to influence the

Prime Minister and just about everything else. How do you suggest we remove her from office?"

Mark asked Yahveh for direction and got some. "We need to "interview" Lady TA and see if we can get information on the levels above her. Hopefully each level will have less people in it and we can move quickly to reduce their effectivity." Mark looked at David. "Can you do a deep debrief on her like you did the two level-three thugs?"

David smiled, "That's what I brought the boys along for." He looked at Judah. "How long to debrief the British Secretary of State for International Development?"

Judah shrugged, "That depends on her conditioning, her will-power, and several other factors, but twenty-four hours is a good estimate regardless."

Jack asked, "Okay, Mark how do we acquire the personage for the interview?"

Mark smiled, "Easy, we kill her and interview her while they are making funeral arrangements."

Laura lifted an eyebrow at Mark, "I'm not sure that will work."

Sarah nodded, "Oh yes it will work. I've done it several times and it hasn't failed yet." She rolled her eyes at Laura's innocence in some things. "Laura, sweetie, we don't really kill her, we switch her for an existing corpse that is close to her size, weight, and features which we mangle to the extent that they can't positively identify the body. In the meantime, we spirit her away and get her to sing. Either way she is out of the government running business for good and everyone gets over her death at the hands of terrorists and moves on without her."

Laura realized that she had forgotten about Sarah's Mossad past again. "Oh, okay." Sarah patted Laura on the knee and smiled at her "You'll get used to these little quirks of the business.

Sarah looked at Mark, "I suggest we make the grab and switch and use a car bomb to reduce the possibility of the forensic scientists to make an ID. We can make it look like revenge for foiling the truck bomb scheme."

Jack's mind recalled television programs such as NCIS and that drove him to ask, "What about DNA and forensic science proving that the Lady TA's body they find isn't the real thing?"

David smiled, "There are some things the Mossad does that most people don't know about. We will destroy the body so thoroughly that they won't be able to get any DNA from it and we will leave some things that contain her traces. They will test the obvious and determine that it is her."

Mark nodded, "Okay folks, let's get cracking on determining where and when we will accomplish this feat of legerdemain

CHAPTER FORTY-FOUR

Enlisting the aid of Scotland Yard to help "protect" the members of Parliament, the Crossfire Team was able to set up their "grab and cover-up" in only a few hours. Mark and Jack played two straight men actually improving and strengthening the operations to protect the politicians while Sarah with Laura and Su Li set up the sting operation. Enlisting the aid of Stan and Debbie Hargrove and David Zahavy they acquired a very close match to Lady TA's body type that had passed away two days ago. She was a known criminal without family ties which could mess things up.

Conferring with Charlie Wu who was back at the Fortress in Denver on techniques to obliterate the majority of DNA leads they prepared the corpse with clothing and jewelry they stole out of Lady TA's home. Sarah and Laura had acquired the needed items the first night. Laura thought back to that night. She remembered admitting that she was nervous committing a criminal act to steal stuff but had prayed about it and felt it was what Yahveh wanted in the war with Omicron.

-----------------------******-----------------------

The night was overcast and occasional rain fell in heavy drops splattering on the early autumn leaves on the ground. The exclusive neighborhood was quiet except for a barking dog two doors away. Laura and Sarah were dressed in what Sarah called "clandestine fashion" in all black body suits with a minimum of equipment to keep the possibility of noise down. Their faces were covered with combat cosmetics and they wore soft shoes and gloves. Soft caps covered their heads and hid their hair. They were just outside the residence near the basement entrance they needed.

Studying the plans before they had tackled the house Sarah had shown Laura the basics for penetrating a quasi-military defense establishment. "Actually it's easier than an owner built defense." Sarah explained. There are standards and routine methods of building your defense that can be exploited. An owner system tends to be unconventional and full of surprises that we don't want. The plans we got from Scotland Yard gives us the times and locations of the guards and security systems."

Laura looked at the triple-redundant, overlapping alarm systems and shook her head. "How do you get past all of this?"

Sarah smiled, "We throw some curves into the game." She pointed to two locations on the plans. "We bypass select systems here and here and then we give them something else to investigate while we slip in and get what we need. One word of caution. I think the Omicron Cartel will have added some defenses of their own to her study and computer facilities. We won't go near them. I doubt that they have seen any reason to add security to the bedroom which is where we want to go."

Sarah watched and timed the video camera that scanned the entire back and side yard. Right after it passed, she ran to the portal and passed a small monitor over the edges of the door. Quickly retreating to the bushes where Laura was she showed her the monitor. It showed a magnetic sensor at the top of the door.

Watching the camera they waited while it passed their location again. Rushing over to the door Sarah inserted a magnetized plate and watched the monitor. She quickly picked the lock and then ran back to the bushes. The next time the camera passed they both ran to the door, opened it and slid into the dark inside. Closing the door before the camera returned they waited for five minutes to see if they had set off any unexpected alarms.

Turning on an LED flashlight Sarah looked around at their position. She made a small noise and moved out. Laura followed her by two steps as she had been instructed to do. They passed unused furniture and cabinets until they reached an innocuous looking electrical panel. Laura used a multitool to unscrew the six screws holding the panel to the wall.

Sarah waited patiently until the panel was removed. Then she inspected the video cables and electrical connections inside the box. None of them were labelled and there was no way to determine which video line or electrical connection went to what. Shaking her head she was about to start guessing when Laura bumped her slightly. Looking in the dark over at the dimly seen blonde woman Sarah saw that she was still holding the cover panel. "What?" Sarah whispered.

Laura said quietly, "Shine your light over here." Sarah did and discovered the layout diagram for all the circuits in the box. Knowing that she was supposed to be teaching Laura the ins and outs of spydom Sarah felt embarrassed at overlooking the cover. She whispered, "Good thing it's dark down here so my red face doesn't show!"

Laura giggled quietly and held the cover while Sarah determined which two leads she needed. Locating the video feeds for the bedroom and the hall outside of it she carefully slid a coupler over each of the lines. She brought out a 5" LCD screen which she hooked to the couplers. Each one showed the area of interest. Using a miniDVD recorder she taped each of the two video streams for two minutes. Carefully mounting the player in the box and pushing two switches she watched her screens as she unscrewed the leads from their normal connections. The pictures held and looked reasonable. She put an anti-stat bag over the two leads so they wouldn't short out to anything and then she disconnected two electrical leads and did the same with them. Taking the panel from Laura she put it back in place and replaced the screws.

Leading Laura up a small stairway to the second level Sarah carefully opened the door to the hallway. Seeing no one she boldly stepped out into the hall with Laura right behind her. Going to the second door on the left she opened it and stepped in. Laura came in and carefully shut the door. Using their flashlights each one of the women went to different places and selected the clothing and jewelry they needed. Finishing up they quickly gathered by the door. Sarah checked the time on her watch. Quickly opening the door the two women retraced their steps to the basement and the electrical panel.

Sarah watched her LCD screen as she rushed quickly to unscrew the panel, remove it and reconnect the video leads and the electrical connections. She finished just as she saw one of the security personnel enter the hall and walk down checking the rooms. Sarah grinned and pulled the recorder and the couplers as well as the anti-stat bags and stuffed them into her pockets. Replacing the panel they made their way back to the outer door.

Sarah stopped suddenly when she heard a voice on the outside near the door. Peering carefully out the window she saw a security man who had a small radio in his hand. He was talking to his control room in the house. "No, I don't see anything. Tell Mrs. Gulliver that there are no Ninjas running around down here. Old bat sees things."

Laura asked quietly, "Can we wait until he leaves?"

Sarah shook her head, "No, they'll do their sweep of this room in the next ten minutes." She continued to watch the man outside. Apparently he had decided to stay for a while. He reached inside his coat for a cigarette and Sarah saw the Mac-11 hanging on his shoulder. Quickly looking around the basement she couldn't find anywhere the two of them could hide during the sweep unless the guard would be asleep. The whole purpose of this raid was not to be detected.

There was the sound of a door being opened at the top of the stairs at the far end of the basement. Sarah was deciding if it would be better to mug the guy outside or the one inside when she heard another voice outside. Peering through the window she saw a cute blonde stepping carefully across the grass with her white high heels. She had on an attractive if somewhat low-cut blouse and matching skirt. She came over to the outside guard and asked him if he could help her with her car which seemed to have stopped just outside the house. The guard told her that he could look at it when all he was looking at was her figure. As they walked off Sarah heard the woman say, "Thank you, my name is Alexis." As they walked out of sight Sarah opened the door and she and Laura slipped out and shut the door. Sarah pulled her magnetic plate out and the two of them slipped into the bushes just as the lights came on in the basement. Checking that the blonde was keeping the outside guard busy she scanned the surrounding windows in the houses nearby. She spotted an older woman staring in their direction with a big set of binoculars. Pulling a small package out of another pocket in her combat suit Sarah created a small cardboard cone with a tiny device at the small end of the cone. She watched until the old lady looked directly at them and she pushed a tiny button. There was an extremely bright flash but of very short duration at the big end of the cone that lit up the window where Mrs. Gulliver was looking out. It would be a while before Mrs. Gulliver would be able to stare around the neighborhood.

Collapsing the cone Sarah led the way across another yard and down to the street to their car. Slipping inside they watched as the blonde got her car started and drove off. The guard straightened his collar and went back to the side yard. Sarah and Laura cleaned the cosmetics off of their faces and then pulled out into the street. Laura was still amazed that Sarah could drive on the "wrong" side of the street with such ease.

Sarah shook her head, "I've really got to find out who this "Alexis" woman is. She shows up at the critical times to save our bacon and doesn't even stay around so we can thank her. To me that spells someone who is very well connected, highly trained, and capable. I'm concerned that our operations are so easy for her to figure out. She seems to know where we are and probably what we are doing all the time and that's just not right."

Laura, who had been practicing the spy craft that Sarah had been teaching her, was watching their backtrack in her mirrors. "Well, if it concerns you so much, why don't you ask her? She's two cars behind us right now."

Sarah checked the car and agreed with Laura. It was the blonde woman. She looked at Laura, "Either you're a lot better than you let on, or I'm going brain-dead when we're together. I should have spotted her before you did."

Laura laughed, "Don't let it bother you, we're a team, remember? You probably saw me checking and unconsciously figured you didn't have to do it too."

CHAPTER FORTY-FIVE

Sarah drove slowly through the expensive suburb of London until she spotted what she wanted. She pulled down a quiet side street and pulled to the curb in an open space. She saw the other car also pull over even though its lights were off. "Stay here with the engine running" She told Laura.

Sarah got out and walked up to the house. Her walk was shielded by trees for the last half of the walk. Slipping off the walk she carefully but quickly made her way around two buildings until she was behind the blonde's car. Kneeling behind a bush in the dark she watched the woman's silhouette and thought to herself. "Hah! Thought you were better at this than me." The smugness that came with the thought jarred her spirit. Realizing she was being proud and arrogant Sarah stopped to pray and ask Yahveh's forgiveness for her pride.

Feeling a lot more professional and a lot less personal she prayed to see if what she was doing was what Yahveh wanted her to do. She didn't feel any urging to avoid the situation so she quickly crept out and attempted to stay out of the mirror range of the American Ford Mustang. Having spent a great deal of time practicing stealth she managed to get next to the driver's side where the window was down. Standing up silently she saw the woman was intensely watching the house she had gone up to with night vision glasses. Sarah put her hand on the fake walnut window trim and asked quietly, "See anything interesting?"

The blonde lowered the night glasses and casually turned to look out the window. "Not really." She shook the night glasses, "I think these things are defective or something."

Sarah didn't feel any catch in her spirit or feel any hostile sensations from the woman. "Would you like to tell me who you are, who you represent, how you can be wherever we need you, when we need you, and why you're following us now?"

Alexis looked at the black haired woman standing outside her car. She had read the impressive record this lady had amassed in a relatively short time. She knew that Sarah was capable of dealing death if it was warranted and that she was very intelligent. So she went with her own strength. She smiled, "No." Still smiling at the ex-Mossad agent Alexis started her car and pulled out knowing that Sarah wouldn't stand in her way.

As the Mustang drove down the street and made a quick right turn to disappear, Sarah walked back to her car and opened the door left handedly. Grabbing her bag, again with her left hand, she pulled out a white cardboard strip and lifted the plastic cover. Taking the piece of tape she had carefully placed on the blonde's window trim she carefully transferred the three prints she'd pulled off the trim strip to the cardboard strip. Putting the strip back in her purse she undid her belt buckle and removed the miniature camera and voice recorder miniDVD that she'd used to take a dozen pictures of the blonde woman and record her voice. Putting them both in her purse she got in and Laura drove them back to their flat.

Charlie Wu carefully uploaded the pictures, voice recordings, and fingerprints to his laptop and transmitted the entire set to the Fortress with the inquiry to Crayton, "Find out who this is!"

Both Sarah and Laura took showers and cleaned up after their little espionage outing. They showed their purloined goods to Mark and Jack. Jack smiled at them, "Good work girls. I think that should help identify Ms. TA to the investigators."

Sarah checked with Charlie but he didn't have a reply as yet. As it was after midnight local time most of the team retired for the night.

The next morning around eight a.m. Sarah wandered over to Charlie who was working at his computer accompanied by a large cup of American coffee. He had a reply from Crayton. He brought up the message and she read, "Thanks Sarah, you give me all the challenging ones. I had to go through three false identities before the truth came out. It even took Crayton a while to work out this identity." There was a file attached which Charlie had printed out for her.

Reading the file woke Sarah up completely. She took the six sheets and went to find the others. They were having a conversation in the Malone's bedroom. Mark was sitting on the dresser while they discussed the various details needed to make this kidnapping work seamlessly.

Mark looked up as Sarah came into the room and his face brightened and he smiled on seeing her. That gave her a warm feeling. She smiled and handed the file to him, "Your mystery blonde."

She watched Mark's face as he read the file. Bemused curiosity and a keen interest in anyone involved in their affairs was all she saw until he hit the last page. She thought that would be an eye-opener for him.

Mark finished the file and passed it to Jack and then looked up at his wife. "I had no idea."

Sarah smiled a small smile, "I didn't expect that you would."

Jack and Laura read the file and looked at their friends.

Mark shook his head, "I should have expected that the NCS would be interested but not involved in our operations, it makes sense." Seeing the blank looks on the faces of the Malones, Mark called the others in from their suites and explained that they had apparently been given a high level baby-sitter in the form of an agent from the National Clandestine Service or NCS.

Mark decided to give them some education on a little known American intelligence operation. "The National Clandestine Service is the American national authority for coordinating U.S. human intelligence or HUMINT services. The organization absorbed the entirety of the CIA's Directorate of Operations, and also coordinates HUMINT between the CIA and other agencies, including, but not limited to, the Federal Bureau of Investigation, Defense Intelligence Agency, Air Intelligence Agency, Army Intelligence and Security Command which is known as INSCOM, Marine Corps Intelligence Activity, and Office of Naval Intelligence. The Director of the NCS reports to the Director of the Central Intelligence Agency."

Mark saw that the group was absorbing the information with no problem so he continued. "The NCS was created by a bill from U.S. Senator C. Patrick Roberts, in the wake of the September 11, 2001 attacks. The investigation by the

9/11 Commission reported that HUMINT had been severely degraded in the past two decades, principally because of the end of the Cold War and because of investigations by U.S. Senator Frank Church."

"The NCS has an analogue in the National Security Agency that handles signals intelligence, the National Geospatial-Intelligence Agency, imagery intelligence, and the Defense Intelligence Agency taking care of measurement and signature intelligence".

Sarah picked it up at that point with some background. "The Directorate of Operations was the branch of the CIA that ran covert operations and recruited foreign agents. Today, its successor, the NCS, reportedly employs one to two thousand people and is headed by a deputy director for operations. This directorate consists of, among other subdivisions, a unit for political and economic covert action which is called the Covert Action Staff, or CAS, for paramilitary covert action, the Special Operations unit, for counterintelligence, and for several geographic desks responsible for the collection of foreign intelligence."

"The Directorate of Operations also houses special groups for conducting counterterrorism and counter narcotics, for tracking nuclear proliferation, and other tasks. Administrated by the Directorate, the Special Operations group maintains an elite cadre called the Special Activities Division, that are highly skilled in weaponry; covert transport of personnel and material by air, sea, and land; guerrilla warfare; the use of explosives; and escape and evasion techniques. They are prepared to respond quickly to a myriad of possible needs, from parachute drops and communications support to assistance with counter narcotics operations and defector infiltration. Special Activities maintains a symbiotic relationship with the Special Forces, and is run and manned largely by ex-Special Forces soldiers."

"For special operations missions and its other responsibilities, the Special Operations staff attempts to recruit assets with the appropriate specialized skills, though the geographic desks remain the principal units involved in the recruitment of personnel in so-called denied areas, you know, Libya, North Korea, Iran, etc. Special operations also provide special air, ground, maritime and training support for the Agency's intelligence gathering operations."

Mark smiled, "It seems "Alexis Taggert"is one of NCS' assets and has been assigned to keep tabs on us and apparently is authorized to help us succeed. Be aware that she will most likely be around where we are operating, so please don't shoot her by accident." He handed out the photographs of the young woman to each of the team.

CHAPTER FORTY-SIX

David Zahavy was a master at clandestine operations. Not only was it his job at the Mossad, he actually enjoyed designing and executing a perfect caper. This one was trickier than most due to the Omicron's participation on top of the regular security provided by the British government for their Ministers.

David had carefully used his men, the Hargroves, the Wus, and Victor Chamberlain in a rotating watch on the activities of Ms.TA. He had Linda Wu call and attempt to arrange a meeting with the Minister to no avail. But that wasn't his intent. He wanted to find out if there were any trips planned for her in the very near future. There weren't any scheduled for the next week.

Bringing everything together they moved the pieces into place and decided that the next day would be the most opportune to "borrow" the woman from her carefully controlled life.

It had taken a considerable amount of careful spy work to locate the Omicron security without giving them warning. But Judah and Aaron were very good at what they did. On the morning of the next day there were three watchers from Omicron that the government security wasn't aware of around Ms.TA. Two would be in a car that usually sat across the street from where Ms.TA's car picked her up after her day at the office. The other one was on a third-floor flat half a block down from the same location.

The routine of the days had dulled the alertness of the government security and police officers surrounding the Minister as she left the office on that warm Tuesday afternoon. Surrounded by three police officers she made her way across the sidewalk to her car. One of the officers opened the back door and checked the interior. Seeing nothing he stood back as she entered and he closed the door. Taking his position outside the car and looking away he presented a barrier to anyone rushing at the car from the sidewalk area.

As the officer turned away, a large lorry pulled up next to the car, stopped for a period and then pulled away. The Omicron security was very familiar with the truck traffic in London. Heck, they had helped plan the truck bombings for Britain. It was not at all unusual to have this kind of traffic.

While the truck blocked the Omicron men's view and that of the watcher on the third floor of a building a half of a block away, a fine spray had immobilized the Minister. The other side of the back seat folded down. Mark's strong arms had quickly pulled the comatose woman into the large trunk of the Bentley. He and Jack then moved the corpse, dressed in similar clothing from Ms.TA's closet, into the sitting up position where the real thing had been seconds before. They had previously drugged and removed the driver. A well-constructed dummy sat behind the wheel but, it was Charlie Wu who was driving the car from a remote location.

As soon as the switch was made. Mark brought the other side of the back rest up and into position. Jack had already dropped through a hole in the bottom of the trunk and stepped down into an open manhole. Reaching back up he took the unconscious form of the Minister from Mark and lowered her down to David below him. He climbed down to clear the way for Mark who carefully put the hole cover in place in the trunk, climbed down and put the manhole cover back in place just as the truck left and Charlie smoothly pulled the car away from the curb and past the truck.

The Police and government security agents headed back into the Commons building as the Omicron car pulled out to follow the Minister's car back to her place. As the car drove through the major intersection of Sanctuary and St. Margaret's Street a shattering explosion occurred inside the car which opened it up like a ripe melon. There was no collateral damage because the force of the explosion was straight up and not sideward. The venerable Bentley had contained the force of the explosion quite well. The only car that had gotten past the truck except for the Minister's was the Omicron car. It had slammed on its brakes and the occupants had gotten out and rushed to the fiercely burning car. The interior was burning with such a white-hot heat that they couldn't approach it.

The fire department responded quickly and put out the fire after twelve minutes. By then there was no sign of the driver and only a partial skeleton in the ashes of the back seat. The news media was on the scene before the fire brigade. The nation would be shocked at the violent death of the woman Minister.

Moving quickly away from the scene of the devastation, Sarah, Mark, and Jack drove their captive to a safe house that belonged to the Mossad in London. They left Ms.TA in the capable hands of Judah and Aaron and returned to their flat.

Sarah was quiet and then she said, "You know that was an excellent Op. I think we fooled everybody. But, I for one will be very suspect of the information we get from her. I'm sure the Omicron Cartel will have prepared her for the event of her being taken."

Mark nodded, "We'll check everything we can but we have to assume that they aren't any better at planting information than we are at detecting the false input."

Laura sat at the flat and watched the developments on the telly. She was praying for the team and the successful conclusion to their audacious raid. She was concerned about the reaction they would get from the enemy on this one.

CHAPTER FORTY-SEVEN

The media headlines trumpeted the terribly cruel murder of Ms.TA. Scotland Yard promised to capture the killers. The telly and radio talk shows made it the centerpiece of their formats. The world was outraged. By the second day the latest increase in oil prices and Iranian politics captured the headlines and the story on the Minister's demise moved to page three and an "on-going" investigation with the arrest of several probable terrorists.

Jack called the group together when Judah and Aaron returned. David discussed their findings and briefed the group.

Attired in a new Seville Row suit of impeccable taste and hue the dapper man was in his element discussing the fine points of espionage with a group of knowledgeable people. "Our subject, Ms.TA turns out to be a curious blend of knowledge and false leads, as we suspected."

He turned to his two agents, "Judah and Aaron are to be congratulated for their excellent work and the tireless efforts needed to extract the few gems without shattering the clay jar they came in."

He glanced at each person present. "There is a real possibility that we have been out-smarted this time. The Omicron Cartel is very intelligent and has some excellent street smarts in these types of operations. For those of us that have performed interrogations of pre-programmed subjects we know that sometimes you have to penetrate several levels of false information, which the subject believes to be true, before you reach the level of actually true data. Judah says that this woman had seven levels of disinformation. Each level a complete and almost believable world that offered tantalizing morsels of information. The fact that these data would prove to be untrue or misleading is very dangerous.

After working their way to the seventh level Judah believes that we may have gotten to the real woman that is the Omicron entity called Ms. Mu. There are a lot of operational kinds of things which are passé since she is no longer in her position."

David smiled at the assembled cast. "The one salient fact that we can really use in our campaign against them is an upcoming meeting, next week, of her level and the one above hers which will be the fifth and sixth levels I believe. One of the reasons we believe this fact to be true is that she was slated to take two days off next week and be out of town. This fact is known to her as a regional meeting of her peers on the top levels of her mind, not recognized at all on the middle levels and only on the seventh level as an Omicron meeting. So, she has set up subterfuges for her office personnel and her working staff. Now the question is; do we believe it?"

Mark asked, "Is this the only thing she can give us concerning the next levels or the functions of Omicron?"

Judah answered him, "The process of wringing information from her has been pretty hard on her. This piece of information was pretty much one of the last things we could get from her without throwing her into a complete mind wipe or catatonic shutdown. If we give her time to rest, say a week or so, we could go back in and possibly get more when she is strong enough."

Mark nodded, "In cases where there has been extensive pre-programming of a subject there is a limit to their mental and physical stamina and there are usually traps included in the programming that will destroy a person's mind if the wrong technique is used or if the interrogation is too intense."

David said, "Well, all the planning and all the work leave us with this gathering of the enemy. Do we take advantage of it or do we look elsewhere?"

Laura had been praying and felt that Yahveh wanted them to tackle this upcoming meeting.

Mark knew the decision was his alone to make. He smiled as he recalled a truism he had gotten from his first military instructor. "The burden of leadership is that one has to lead."

"All right, we don't have time to wait for them to strike us so let us plan this one as if it may be a trap and that it may be productive. When and where is the meeting?"

Judah consulted his notes. "The meeting is going to be in a chalet in Switzerland on Wednesday. We have the location."

Su Li and Victor had been talking quietly and Su Li raised a question that was on all of their minds. "Do you think that Omicron bought the death of their agent or will this alert them to prepare for us at the meeting?"

Sarah answered that one. "Conventional wisdom says that it was, or will be, a trap to capture or kill some or all of us. But Laura feels that the Father wants us to go for it and I believe that we should attempt to outsmart these people by using their trap against them."

So it was agreed that they would take the bait and see if they couldn't slant the odds in their favor in the hopes of getting more out of it than they would lose.

In Spain, Mr. Beta was on his knees with his head on the floor. In his case it wasn't adoration he was evidencing it was fear. He was listening to the demon Oray. A particularly ugly specimen of the type. He hissed and growled and told Beta how to set the trap for the Crossfire Team. He promised he and many of his kind would be there to help destroy the pests. After the demon had gone back to wherever it had come from, Beta got to his feet and felt like he needed a bath. The sliminess that he felt whenever he was in the presence of Oray always disturbed him. He shook it off and took the information he had gotten from the demon and finalized his plans to eliminate the Crossfire team. He knew he would be right there to do it himself because if it didn't work there was no hope for a long life for him anyway.

The man checked all the angles and made sure they were covered. The location was remote. It was a large chalet in the Swiss Alps. There was only one way in and out. He had three levels of coverage on the area and the chalet. Video cameras were everywhere and they all had nighttime capability. He would know exactly where the Crossfire Team was when he was ready to strike. To allay their suspicions he had ten members of the third level actually holding a meeting there. They had no idea they were bait and that was the way it should be. Beta was fairly certain that they would be in no danger. Then he reviewed his chosen method of eliminating the enemy team. He laughed when he saw how complete his plan was and how easy it would be to destroy the Crossfire Team. He stopped laughing when he realized his laugh sounded a lot like Oray's.

CHAPTER FORTY-EIGHT

The moon would be rising over the Swiss Alps and illuminating the chalet in three hours. The target building sat on a plateau at 4265 feet altitude. It was undoubtedly one of the best, and it was accessible only through a private drive. It served as a dual season ski resort. The chalet was only a ninety minute drive from the Geneva airport. Strict building controls had retained its traditional Alpine charm while it had all the modern conveniences. The rented resort was an up-scale, well-kept secret, perfect for a clandestine meeting in the mountains of Switzerland.

Sarah and David had been in position outside the chalet for over two hours and had located and identified over thirty cameras watching over the area. Their white, winter combat suits allowed them to blend into the snow surrounding the chalet and kept them reasonably warm. As the rest of the team moved into their positions David used his combat radio to warn them of the video coverage. "Be very wary. This place is covered better than the Emmys."

David assigned three cameras to each of the team while he was going to take the hard ones himself. When everybody was ready he counted down from five to zero. At zero he used a silenced Amalite.22 caliber rifle with a ten-power sight to systematically destroy all four of his selected cameras. He heard ten "done" statements which meant that all the known cameras were taken out. He said, "Teams 1 and 2, Go!"

He watched as the two four man teams raced to the building and prepared to enter it from both the front and the back at the same time. He heard Mark say, "Now!" and both teams blew the doors off the chalet with Primacord and tossed in four flash-stun grenades. The bright flashes and loud bangs lit up the inside of the large A-frame building like angry flash bulbs. David and his troops continued to watch the area surrounding the chalet for reinforcements or traps. He had assigned Victor, Linda Wu, and Aaron Jacobson each a quadrant while he watched everything. He had a bad feeling about this raid so he was especially vigilant.

As Mark entered the building with his night vision gear in place he led the way with his M-8 carbine. Right behind him was Sarah, Su Li, and Judah. Coming in the other side of the building was Jack, Laura, and Stan Hargrove, and Charlie Wu all dressed in combat white with their M-8s.

The scene in the chalet was utter chaos. The lights had been blown out and papers and furniture were strewn wherever the exploding flash-bangs had thrown them. There were at least a dozen people in various stages of consciousness all toward one side of the room. Most were on the floor unconscious. Several were staggering around holding either their eyes or their ears or trying to do both at the same time. The two servants had been in the main room when the grenades went off and were out of action.

Mark pointed to the other floor and the bedrooms. He had Sarah and Su Li bind the standing people with riot cuffs and put them on the floor and tie their ankles too. Then they turned to the unconscious ones and did the same thing. While they were at it, Mark, Judah, and Jack's team checked all the other rooms in the house. They were empty of people although there were the belongings for the ten people staying there. Charlie got some lights working in the main room so they could work without their night goggles.

Mark came out of the last room and met Jack as he exited his last search area. Raising his NVG he said, "There are no guards, no security. "He pressed his combat comm switch and spoke into the microphone next to his cheek. "David, we've got a dozen people and some servants but no security at all. This is not like the Omicron Cartel. Do you see anything?"

David's reply was short and not too sweet. "Yes, I and the others are coming into the chalet right now." He'd hardly finished speaking when they come busting through the open doorway and slid to a halt inside the room.

David looked at Mark and Jack on the balcony above the floor. "There's got to be over two hundred fully armed troops surrounding the chalet. Some of them have RPGs too."

"That's not all they're bringing", said a sweet voice from the back door. All heads swiveled to see Alexis stepping into the room in a white military combat suit similar to their own. She looked at the captives and the rest of the team. "I was going to help you escape but the OC has pulled a fast one and brought in an unknown battle group to eliminate you all."

Jack noted, "Well, that will now include you too."

Alexis smiled and pulled her H&K G36C Commando version assault rifle off of her back by the sling. "Then I suggest we make them pay dearly."

Everyone headed for a window or door to defend when a noxious smell invaded the chalet and Alexis shrieked. Turning around Laura saw a demon with one hand on Alexis's rifle and one holding her immobile by the neck from behind. Laura felt the pure white anger against the unholy creature. She dropped her rifle and started walking toward the ugly being. The demon smiled, which was not a pretty sight. The demon twisted Alexis's head around to look at Laura and what he was about to do to her. Alexis's bright, intelligent mind was in turmoil. What had her couldn't possibly exist. It couldn't be real. But it was real and it was dangerous. She couldn't even move a muscle. She wanted help but she didn't want to see Laura killed and those emotions washed over her face as Laura came toward them.

Laura started running at the demon and praying Psalm 23- 4 *"When I walk through the valley of the shadow of death, I fear no evil. For You are with me; Your rod and Your staff, they comfort me."* With an almost explosive force her golden armor, shield, and the sword of Elohim burst into sight. The power of creation was flowing off of the blade and Oray quailed at the sight. With one swing of her sword Laura beheaded the demon and turned around to go get her rifle, her armor fading from sight.

The demon turned to greasy smoke and disappeared. Released, Alexis fell to the floor and just stared at Laura with her mouth hanging open.

Jack realized that the demon had violated Elohim's commands not to help the Omicron Cartel and that gave them some hope. He started praying,

"Father, as Elisha prayed, Do not fear, for those who are with us are more than those who are with them. I pray that the heavenly host will surround those helped by the evil one to your esteem. I also ask that you open the eyes of everyone here and let them see.

And Yahveh opened the eyes of those in the house, and they looked and saw the mountains covered with horses and chariots of fire all around the chalet.

Jack said, "Father, strike these evil warriors with blindness and mental confusion, I pray in the Holy Name of Yahshua." And Elohim struck them with blindness and fogged the minds of the two hundred Omicron mercenaries so that they couldn't act. There were random fire fights between groups and many fled the area in their confusion.

Mark was about to order the troops to gather up the attendees when six more demons appeared in the room and attacked Laura. Laura's armor flared up and she started defending herself from the onslaught,since they had obviously stepped over the boundary between the human and spiritual dimensions they were vulnerable to gunfire. Jack shot one in the head and it disappeared as red smoke. Mark and the others caught on and as more and more demons appeared they shot them down. It was a repeat of an earlier action they had been in outside Denver.

Suddenly there were dozens of angels in the room and all demons stopped appearing. It was so sudden that Victor fired off a shot at one of the angels before he saw what it was he was shooting.

The angel casually deflected the bullet into the ceiling with his sword and stood there impassive. All of these angels were at least eight foot tall and powerful. Everyone in the room heard *"The enemy of mankind has been rebuked and will not bother you again today."* The angels faded out of sight. As they faded the one Victor fired at winked at him.

As their heart rates started dropping back toward normal the team relaxed. Then David said, "Look at the captives." Everyone looked and saw that they had all been killed by the sword. Mark slammed his rifle onto the floor. "The demons were a diversion to keep us busy while they eliminated the source of information. We're back to square one!"

Alexis was still trying to get her breath. "Not true! If someone will help me up and go with me outside I have a little package the demons may have missed."

Mark and Jack helped her up and supported her as she led them out the back door. A few seconds later they came back in dragging a man bound hand and foot and gagged efficiently. This one was still breathing. Jack pulled his gag off and had Mark help carry him over to the other Omicron people lying in their blood on the floor. The man looked horrified and said, "How could you kill them with their hands and feet bound like that!"

Jack said quietly in his ear, "We didn't kill them. We wanted to interrogate them. The demons killed them so they couldn't talk. Who are you?"

Staring at the slaughtered people he had known and had personally selected as the bait for his trap, the fifth level director saw how the enemy behind the Omicron Cartel would treat him. He was also aware that he had no future at all with OC after this failure. He realized his only chance would be to cooperate. "I'm Milton Warrow, previously known as Mr. Beta."

CHAPTER FORTY-NINE

The team extracted from the chalet with their captive. After calling her superiors Alexis asked if she could accompany them. The team had to avoid the bands of mercenaries wandering around blind and confused. Then they had to avoid the police responding to the attack on the chalet. They called in the report to the Swiss police citing their authority from the Federal President and returned to their plane at the Geneva airport. They flew from Switzerland to Tel Aviv arriving just before noon.

Judah and Aaron said their good-byes and headed to an interrogation room at the Mossad with Mr. Beta in tow.

The rest of the team went to a secret safe house in Haifa that David had arranged for before they left. Everyone wanted to clean up and sleep even though it was still early afternoon. That evening around ten p.m. local time the ten warriors reconvened in the large living room.

Mark summed up the entire effort from the planning for Ms.TA's kidnapping until they left the chalet earlier that day. When he was done he asked for opinions.

Jack sighed, "Well, it seems we may have moved up a level but all we really did was to defeat an extremely well designed trap that they had set up to catch us."

Alexis shook her head, "No, you dealt them a serious blow. I know a little more about this group than apparently you do and I know how your surviving and capturing Mr. Beta is going to shake their confidence."

Mark tipped his head to one side as he stared at the NCS agent. "Would you like to share what you know that we don't?"

Alexis thought about saying, "No" but she'd already used that line. "The NCS has been watching some of the activities of the Omicron Cartel for the last year. They have their tentacles into every government in the world. Their goal is world domination through absolute control of services and governmental agencies. They have an administrative council called the Executive Council that decides all matters and metes out punishments and rewards. There are ten people on that council but we still don't know who they are. They have vast resources in the form of capital and troops yet don't try to take over anything. They are very intelligent and focused on their goal."

She stopped to take a drink of tea. "Mr. Beta was probably in charge of the trap at the chalet and it was probably do-or-die for him. That is probably why he is so willing to cooperate. But, even then, he was able to set up his forces such that I didn't see them when I decided that you needed some help to escape the chalet. But, I did see him and was able to sand bag him for later conversation. Still, when the trap was sprung, I was caught in it just like you were."

Jack asked, "Why are you hanging around us?"

Alexis smiled, "Why, because I like you guys."

Sarah laughed, "Fine, but I think Mr. Caufman might have given you a different set of orders than just liking us."

Hearing her direct boss' name made Alexis realize that these people are also well informed and connected. "True, he did insist that I keep an eye on your group because we're working at the same end result and we don't want to trip over each other. In fact, if you're willing I would like to work with you as a part of your team rather than have to figure out everything you're going to do. Sometimes you throw me an unexpected curve and I have to really scramble to make up for it."

Mark smiled, "We will have to pray about that, okay?" Alexis nodded her head. "These people certainly do things differently." She thought.

Victor spoke up, "Okay, what's our next move? These guys aren't going to stop trying to kill us because we won at the chalet, right?"

Everyone knew the answer to that one. Mark tipped his chair back on two legs and smiled, "We need to turn up the heat and get these arch-criminals off balance so we can take them down. How we do that I don't know yet. I think some prayer and some information from Mr. Beta should suggest a new path."

Laura added, "Don't forget that Yahveh said that Satan and his crew couldn't bother us today. That doesn't mean they won't get after us one minute after midnight tonight."

The session broke up with everyone deciding to do what they needed to stay in the field for quite a bit longer.

There was a phone call for Laura. She listened for a few seconds and said, "Okay, about an hour from now." and hung up. She went to Jack and told him that he and David might want to accompany her to the Mossad headquarters to talk to Aaron Jacobson about the spiritual activity that had taken place at the chalet.

David laughed softly. "I told you that they would get a chance to see Yahveh, Yahshua, and the enemy in action and it would change their paradigm."

Jack agreed to go along and they let David drive them over to the building. They were so used to the unique garage facilities and the six direction elevator it seemed normal to them.

When they were seated with Aaron in a conference room David asked him how the interrogation of Mr. Beta was going. Aaron shrugged, "He's so cooperative we haven't had to drug him as yet. Everything he's telling us is checking out so we will continue to chat for a while."

Laura watched the Jewish man as he talked to his boss. He seemed relaxed but there was an underlying tension that she could pick up. She prayed that Yahshua would give her the words for this child of Elohim.

Aaron reached over and respectfully ran his fingers over Laura's arm and shoulder. Laura looked at his action and grinned at him. "Careful now, I'm armed and my husband teaches martial arts."

Aaron pulled his hand back and turned red in embarrassment. "I'm so sorry; I was just remembering the golden armor you wore during the fight."

Laura nodded, still smiling at the young Jewish man to take the sting out of her statement. "What do you want to talk about?"

Aaron took a big breath and jumped in with both feet. "I have never seen a demon before. I've also never seen a demon dispatched either. While I think about it I've never seen an angel before and there were so many in the room." He looked at Laura with big eyes, "I don't understand what happened or why it happened. I think you have some answers that I need. And I hope you'll tell me what all that was about. It seems to be critical for me to understand."

Laura prayed again for the words she needed. "What about your faith Aaron? Tell me what is like so I can tell where to start explaining what happened."

Aaron slightly hung his head. "I am not a good Jew. I don't go to temple often and I really don't think about God all that much. My work is my life and I'm good at what I do. I think that should count for something with God, don't you?"

Laura frowned a little. She thought to herself, "This is going to be harder than I expected. Father strengthen me and grant me the words this child needs to find you."

Laura looked in Aaron's eyes. "No, I don't think it counts for anything Aaron." Seeing the irritation start up in his eyes she plowed on. "And let me tell you why I don't think it counts. You are doing a great job but it's for you and it's your decision as to what you want to do with your life. You're not doing it for God. Understand this; God loves you more than anything in the world. He wants the absolute best that you can have for yourself. But you have to want to do it His way because it is His way. "

Laura studied Aaron's reactions. "I know you've been taught individual ethical behavior is what is most important in this life and it will determine your path after this life. Unfortunately, that is a false teaching. I know Yahveh is love but he has spelled out each person's options clearly. You know that many Jewish people of the Old Testament walked with and were obedient to Yahveh and God took some of them to Heaven. There was a new covenant with God spelled out when Yahshua walked the Earth. Today, If you truly love and seek God and put Him before all idols or man's reasoning, I believe you will be led to accept His Son, Yahshua."

"Like I said, He loves you but if you don't love God enough to ask Him how you will live with Him in Heaven, regardless of the works you do, Yahveh will have to judge you and you will go to Gehenna."

Aaron's anger subsided and he listened intently.

Laura continued, "This is only my viewpoint and you will need to ask Him yourself. I believe that you're put on this Earth for two things. The first is to choose God's way or your way. If you choose your way you might get the things you want on this Earth but it is only for a handful of years. Your soul doesn't die when your body does. Where it goes is totally dependent on the choices you make down here. You can't save yourself or attain Heaven by being good at doing things, even doing good things. You need his Son to provide a path to God and the only way to Heaven for you. That's the first choice, your way or God's way. Understanding that God's way isn't a path you walk alone. When you give yourself and everything you have in this world to Him he will save you from going to a place of eternal damnation."

Laura gauged his response so far. "That brings you to the second choice you have to make on this Earth. You need to learn to draw close to him through repentance and getting the sin out of your life. Getting your ancestor's sins out of your life. Then learn to walk in the spirit every day and every way. You need to understand that God wants love and obedience from you so that he can live through you and give others love and eternity. He wants you to become His light to others so that he can draw them to Himself."

Aaron thought about all she had said. "Could you please tell me about demons, angels, and that armor of yours and how they fit into a walk with God?"

Laura laughed. "I don't have time to explain all of that in detail but I will tell you this. Demons are thought to have been the one-third of the angels that took Satan's side in his rebellion against God. When Satan was thrown out of Heaven to the Earth they were thrown out with him. Over time his evil has warped them into the dark creatures they are today. Satan uses them for his need and doesn't care a wit if they continue to exist or not. Normally demons don't come into our dimension but remain in their spiritual dimension. Since time is short before the end of the age before the return of Yahshua they are now crossing over to accomplish Satan's plans. If you walk closely with Yahveh you normally don't need to worry about demons bothering you. His light is too bright for them to come near."

Aaron looked confused. "You are apparently walking closely with Yahveh but the demons are certainly trying to kill you!"

Laura laughed. "That is true, but then I, and the others with me, have been given the role of warriors for Yahveh and we are expected to do battle for the Kingdom regardless of the enemy's efforts."

Laura continued, "Angels are God's messengers and sometimes his warriors. They have the job of protecting God's people from the enemy and anything else. They are there to do God's will in all things. My armor is a special gift from God to use in our combat with the forces of evil. I got it because I submitted my will and agenda to His completely and continue to walk that way every day. My having this special gift is dependent on my obedience. He wants us to act as sort of policemen in protecting the innocent of the Earth."

Aaron thought for a few minutes. "I have this huge pressure inside me that wants to know more about this and learn to live for God. Will you teach me?"

Laura smiled, "I probably will not have the time in the near future but I know somebody who can teach you everything you want to know. Someone who is close to you and someone you'll trust."

Aaron looked introspective as he thought of everyone he knew. "Who?"

David spoke up, "I'll teach you, Aaron." His quiet authority and honesty made the statement friendly.

Aaron smiled. "Yes, you I'll trust."

Laura got up and hugged Aaron, "You won't ever be sorry you made this choice."

CHAPTER FIFTY

The next morning Laura and Jack were sitting alone at the breakfast table, lingering over a cup of coffee.

Jack looked at his beautiful wife and realized that she had grown in vitality and strength on their adventurous walk with God. "You know you're becoming more beautiful every day."

Laura felt a warm glow listening to her husband compliment her. "You're not doing so bad yourself, sailor."

As they sat there contemplating their lives and futures Laura said, "I'm concerned that this on-going war with the Omicron Cartel will wear out some of our members. It's a high stress environment that doesn't let up."

Jack nodded, "You seem to be doing all right."

Laura smiled, "I have my Elohim and you to keep me from worry. I really love you, you know?"

Jack smiled, "Yeah, I know. I am hoping that we can find a way to destroy the Omicron Cartel and get back to ....."

Laura laughed, "Get back to what? Our quiet little everyday home life with you working at the plant and me working at my company? Please! Give us both a break. We would not be doing His will and face it, you'd miss this new and somewhat normal harrowing life of nuclear weapons, bombs, guns, and death around every corner."

Jack laughed. He was no longer worried about his wife and their way of life. It was their way of life and he couldn't be happier. He knew that they were directly in the Father's will. "I still think we need to move on Omicron soon. I have a sense that they have something major in the works that has been brewing for quite a while and it's about to come to fruition."

Laura sat there quietly agreeing with him.

The Crossfire Team will return in "*Jagged Crossfire*"

If this story has awakened your spirit or moved you to seek the love of Christ and His power for your life, whether you've never accepted Jesus as your savior or you've fallen away, repeat the following prayer and begin a most wonderful journey into eternal life with Him today.

Father God in heaven, As You said in Your Holy Word, (Romans 10:9) that if we confess the Lord our God and believe in our hearts that God raised Jesus from the dead, we shall be saved.

(The prayer on the next page is a sample prayer when asking Jesus into your heart as your Savior. You can also pray this in your own words.)

Salvation Prayer

Dear God in heaven, I come to you in the name of Jesus. I confess to You that I am a sinner, and I am sorry for my sins and the life that I have lived; I need your forgiveness. I believe that your only begotten Son Jesus Christ shed His precious blood on the cross at Calvary and died for my sins, and I am now willing to turn from my sin.

Right now I confess Jesus as the Lord of my life and my soul. With all my heart, I truly believe that your Holy Spirit raised Jesus from the dead. Today I accept Jesus Christ as my personal Savior and according to Your Word, right now I am saved.

I thank you Jesus, for your unlimited grace which has saved me from my sins. I thank you Jesus that your grace that never leads to license, but rather it always leads to repentance. Therefore Lord Jesus, transform my life so that I may bring glory and honor to you alone and not to myself.

I thank you Lord Jesus, for dying for me at Calvary and giving me eternal life.

Amen.

If you just said this prayer and you meant it with all your heart, believe that you are now saved and have been born again.

You may ask, "Now that I am saved, what do I do next?" First of all you need to get into a spirit-filled, bible-based church that teaches the Scriptures, and you need to study God's Word.

Once you have found a church home, you will want to become water-baptized. By accepting Christ you are baptized in the spirit, but it is through water-baptism that you publically announce your obedience to the Lord Jesus. Water baptism is a symbol of your salvation from the dead. You were dead but now you live, for Jesus Christ has redeemed you for a price! The price was His atoning death on the cross. May God Bless You!

www.ingramcontent.com/pod-product-compliance
Lightning Source LLC
Chambersburg PA
CBHW071307250626
47159CB00004B/1338